The Pupil

Titles by this author

SLEEPERS OF THE CAVE SERIES

To Kill One

By The Waters of Tasnim

The Zaqqum Tree

The Garden of Lost Remembering

The Owned

The Murder Club

AS KINGSLEY CROSS

And Nothing But The Night

At The Counting Of The Dead

VISIT THE AUTHOR'S WEBSITE AT:

billy-conn.net

The Pupil

Billy Conn

ISBN: 9798695030624

*This book is dedicated to
the Music that haunts us all
And the tunes that will not leave us alone*

Chapter 1

Antique Ugly

Another man might have thought, if only he hadn't met John Barrowman, things would have been so different but he'd never been able to think like that. Things happen. Events occur. Chance is chance. There's nothing complicated about it. There couldn't be. He'd said it before, 'fate only takes a hand when the idea has already taken your brain'.

Everyone has their own way of thinking about themselves. The very people who are in the worst position to judge. He saw himself as a man who could look at the stars and see an opportunity to expand his mind, to dream, to hear the music of the spheres. He knew why he'd chosen to live in a corner of the world where those who'd never had an idea of their own could feel superior. Thinking about corners of the world nearly said it all. So not fate, obviously. No, this surrender to the art of the ordinary had suited him for some time now. Most people would complain about the repetitive, mechanical sameness of their days, not work for it. Who would plan a week of seven Mondays? It was true though, that his life would have gone on in an unnoticed and uninterrupted way for an unpredictably greater length of time, if that meeting had never taken place. Demons would have remained locked in their lead boxes.

However the meeting had taken place. It was in the Mitre, the village pub where he was a regular but not frequent visitor, reliably arriving only once a week. Thursday was his day without a pupil. A day of rest. His routine was to indulge himself with a small steak. He knew that a man can acquire invisibility through routines. If he could help it, that's the way it would stay. Eating alone at home most other days his meal would often be no more complicated than pasta. He, who had once hypocritically possessed gourmet appetites in all things in life. After a while the pasta diet stopped being boring and simply became his lotus plant, the very sameness, his narcotic.

It wasn't that he couldn't cook other things. Indeed, the village shop run by Fiona Bellow, still sold Fray Bentos Steak and Kidney pies – oh how are the mighty fallen. Occasionally one of these became his evening fare both because they reminded him of his distant student days and because of the long shelf life. Her name and selling these pies amused him. No one else seemed to get the joke, if there was one. Not that he'd much opportunity to share jests with another adult these days. His situation didn't allow for conversation apart from when they dropped their children off for lessons or picked them up. Then they usually just wanted to know how their child was getting on, or if they were behaving themselves. Sometimes, like a perfumed fart, the weather opportunistically eclipsed all other topics.

Of course on Mondays and Wednesdays he had his adult lessons. He wasn't complaining. It had been his choice to live this way, in so far as things we end up doing can ever be regarded as a result of true choices when he believed that almost every facet of our make-up limits our options in some way. Accepting this is important for survival. In the past when he said such things he'd been accused of both fatalism and intellectual arrogance, as though thinking for oneself was voluntary, even perhaps a lifestyle choice. It was just who he was. Being oneself should be a good thing but he knew that was only up to the point of being no longer the same as the others. Then one became different.

Adrian sat in his usual seat by the window. From here he could not only see the small, kidney shaped car park but the main entrance. This opened from what those locals with a sense of the absurd, still called the High Street. When he allowed himself to be honest he recognized occupying this seat was also a matter of habit and that such habits reduced the need for anyone to think about him. Allowing oneself to be honest was difficult enough over trivial things, for the rest people avoided the need for reflection by keeping themselves busy or distracted. Or worse, buying into the prepacked solutions marketed by the world's churches which had perfected the art of selling new coats to chameleons.

To Adrian the cobweb quiet that often settled on the pub was welcome. It was disturbed only by the occasional distant laugh or the sound of glasses clinking, all close enough for security but far enough away for privacy.

Four years ago the Mitre was in danger of closing. Villages are no better than people at surviving without their hearts or for that matter, livers. Rescue came in the shape of a group of locals who bought it and opened it to a silent fanfare, as a co-operative. There had been some talk that it would become a post office as well but nothing had come of that. The natural fate of plans and dreams. The food had changed from crisps and sandwiches to actual meals with knives and forks with the predictable jocularity about trusting some named locals with these or of needing an instruction manual. There was even a wine list limited as much by the tastes of the owners as the disposable income of the customers. He didn't really know the ins and outs of the workings of the whole arrangement apart from that there were three main shareholders and a few others who put in much lesser amounts. He had been invited to participate as had everyone who lived in the village but they probably knew he didn't have the money. He wasn't even the owner of the cottage he lived in. That the lack of intellectual companionship had affected him was reflected in the fact that, none the less, it amused him to have ended up having a steak in the pub.

Whatever the invitingly humdrum details of the ownership, he was sure that if it failed the major shareholders would probably recoup their losses by selling the site. Business as usual. Planning permission was unlikely to be too much of an issue with one of the three being Derek Holmes who chaired the parish council and was the Master of the local Lodge and much else besides. He was said to be a convivial man till crossed. If it wasn't that Derek Holmes's niece was having violin lessons with him he wouldn't have felt a need to remember even that much.

"Mr. Grayling" said a quiet voice, "I'm John Barrowman. Sorry to interrupt your evening. I waited till it looked as though you'd finished eating".

Adrian Grayling looked up. He hadn't been aware of the other man who must have been watching him. He recognized a Scottish accent. In this village, that had a certain rarity value. John Barrowman was probably a bit over average height and of robust, even possibly muscular build, an effect distracted from by the fact that he had the appearance of a guilty schoolboy standing nervously in front of the headmaster. Despite this he managed to look rather older than his voice would have placed him.

"Yes" he said, "I'm Adrian Grayling. What can I do for you?"

"You're the piano teacher" he said.

"Yes" replied Adrian, "I teach piano and violin".

"We're new here" he said, "I work at Franklins servicing lawnmowers and the like".

"I don't have a lawnmower" said Adrian, not meaning to sound quite so much as though he didn't want to continue the conversation. Giving this more brusque impression had been happening more recently. That was unhelpful.

"No, sorry. That's just where I work. I have a son Gabriel. We call him Gabe. Everyone does. His mum didn't like it. She had wanted Gabriel after her father. He was a suffragan bishop. I don't think he really approved of the marriage. Maybe he was right. Who was I to marry a bishop's daughter?"

"Do I take it you want Gabe or Gabriel to have music lessons?" asked Adrian privately noting the shift from 'I' to 'we' and the intermittent use of the past tense.

"Sorry. Was I going on about Celia? Everyone says I never get to the point. Sometimes I wonder what the point is. Maybe that's the problem. Everyone's got some irritating habits don't you think? I'm not saying you have. You might have but I don't know about them. You're right. I do want Gabe to have piano lessons. At his last school they said he had talent".

"Do you want to sit down?" asked Adrian who had never liked people standing when he was sitting. Perhaps he had taken the phrase 'standing in judgement' too literally. Usually he would be the one to get up but the table made this impossible.

"Thank you" replied John, "can I get you a drink first?"

"Are you having another one?" he asked looking at the almost empty pint glass in John Barrowman's left hand.

"Yea" John replied, "so what're you having?"

"What was that you were having?" he asked.

"That's Antique Ugly" he replied and seeing the look on Adrian's face added, "no I'd never heard of it before either.

Apparently they're getting a lot of different stuff from a boutique brewery one of the owners here has an interest in. It's good, at least I think so. Others must too. It's in for some sort of award".

"I'll try it" said Adrian, "just a half though".

It seemed to Adrian that it took a very long time for John to get served. It wasn't that the bar was yet that busy. Still busier than when he came in and a lot more so than it used to be on a Thursday. When he did finally come back he had two pint glasses.

"I just wanted a half" said Adrian reflexively.

"I know. Sorry. I got talking to Gwyneth at the bar. Before I knew it she'd poured two pints. She's nice that Gwyneth".

"Thanks anyway" said Adrian still looking rather warily at the large glass as John sat down.

"You lived here long?" John asked, "sorry that's none of my business. Celia used to say I asked too many questions but didn't really want answers. It's just the way I am. Sorry".

"Don't worry about it" said Adrian hoping that if Gabriel came to him for lessons, he would be both less prolix and less apologetic. Ever since Dorothea Adams had run out crying and refused to come back when he told her off for not practising, he really needed another pupil to make ends meet. Six a week with his small other income was enough to get by. "I've been here seven years" he said, "I like the quiet". Then, to get off the subject of his own life, asked "where were you before?"

"Me" said John as though surprised anyone would be interested in him, "we lived in Scotland. Near St. Andrews. That's where I met Celia".

"At the university?" asked Adrian.

"Not me" replied John smiling as though it was an amusing idea, "Celia went there though. I worked at it on the maintenance side. It gets some right posh people there, even royals".

Adrian wondered how a bishop's daughter at St Andrews got together with a maintenance man but was afraid, if he asked, John would tell him at some length. Anyway John Barrowman was by most standards a handsome, somewhat rugged man, if it was possible to be both rugged and anxious. Maybe that was it, just his physical looks had attracted Celia. He asked, "how old is Gabriel?"

"Gabe's coming up fourteen years. They say he's a good-looking boy. Even got teased about it at school. Can you believe that? I suppose other boys got jealous. I'd got picked on at school too so I knew how he felt. With me it wasn't for being good-looking. He's not what you'd call very pushy. Doesn't really like to stand up for himself much. Anyway he's doing better here. It's a mixed school. Nothing like the same problems and the girls all seem to like him, well some of them. The only problem is that he has to get the bus, the school bus. The ordinary bus service is hopeless. Two a week and it might get cut. But you'll know that. It's not too bad for me, I've a little car, a Ford Ka, one of the first ones they made but that's ok because I do my own repairs and maintenance. Don't you think they really need a proper bus shelter here? It's ok in summer but what's it going to be like on a wet cold winter's day with the kids waiting for it that time of the morning. Mind you it's nothing like the Scottish winters. We're one of the first pick-ups you know. Of course you wouldn't. We've only just met. The school bus goes round all the villages so takes forever".

Like your conversation, thought Adrian but instead asked "has he had many piano lessons before?"

"None" replied John, "you'd be the first proper lesson. His last school had a music department. They'd singled him out as one with talent".

"Specifically for the piano?" queried Adrian.

"I'm not sure but they definitely said musical talent".

"It's just that most lads of his age want to play the guitar" said Adrian, "if you choose piano he couldn't practise between lessons. That's a very important part of learning to play".

"We have a piano. It might need to get tuned up a bit. Celia used to play. Gabe still messes around on it and he can play tunes she taught him and that he picked up himself".

Adrian felt a little embarrassed that he had made an assumption about the family, a classist assumption based on his impression of John Barrowman.

"Excellent" he said, "not many people have pianos nowadays. At best electronic key boards. There's the cost but also having enough space for one. What make's yours?"

"It's called a Bechstein, if I've got that right" replied John, "Celia said she preferred it to the Steinway. I'd heard of the Steinway".

"Good piano the Bechstein" said Adrian, "very good. Celia's serious about her music then".

"It was her mother's. She inherited it, not that her mother was dead. She did play. They said she was very good".

"You said 'was'. I don't mean to pry but is Celia no longer with us?"

"She's no longer with me. She left us" responded John, "Gabe really missed her. I think he still misses her but he doesn't say much about it anymore, well about anything really. I know he still has a photograph of her".

"When did she go?" asked Adrian.

"About three years ago" said John "he was coming up for eleven".

"Are you in touch with her?"

"We were during the first year. Now she doesn't make any contact apart from sending Gabe birthday and Christmas cards and me money. She always said she wanted him to have piano lessons. That's what the money's for. She had a thing about teachers and teaching. I never got round to trying to sort it out. I haven't spent a penny, not in the whole three years. Then someone at work mentioned that there was a good music teacher in the village. I made enquiries and found it was you. I was told you come here on a Thursday evening".

Adrian was keen to know who it was had recommended him. He didn't want to ask directly. Instead he said, "I didn't know I was that predictable. So who is it who knows my movements so precisely?"

"Benny, Benny Thorne" said John.

Adrian had no idea who Benny Thorne was.

"If I ever meet him I should thank him for the introduction and the compliment" he said.

"Oh he didn't say the bit about a good music teacher. That was Gwyneth at the bar when I asked her if she knew you. Benny just said music teacher. I got them mixed up. Sometimes I get things the wrong way round. Never at work though, you can check it out with anyone. People have started coming into the shop and asking for me".

"How did you end up in this village? It's a long way from Scotland" asked Adrian.

"Oh I haven't lived in Scotland since Celia finished her degree. I've been among the Sassenachs since then. I've got used to it and I think Gabe likes this country. A bloke I knew at my last place told me there was work going. I'd wanted to get away from the city for Gabe's sake, then my landlord wanted the place back because some new regulations were going to make continuing to let it difficult for him so we came up here one weekend. I had heard of it before. Celia knew something about it or maybe had lived here as a child. There was definitely some connection. She never said much about her childhood. I think something happened. Anyway I liked this place. It is quiet. Gabe liked it straight off and Franklin's still had the job going. My six month probation period is just over. The only thing is I've a short lease on the place we are. Still, I'm sure we'll find something. So what do you say? Would you take on another pupil?"

"What we can do" said Adrian "is you can bring Gabriel round and I can see what he's like and if he really wants to do it. If he's up for in and I think I can do anything for him I have space for another one at present. Would you be looking for after school or the weekends?"

"I don't know" replied John, "what do you think would be best?"

"Why not bring him on Saturday morning. About 10. Once we've had that first session I'll be in a better position to advise you. And if you need a piano tuner the woman who does mine is very good. I have her number at the cottage".

"Thank you" said John "your cottage is the one with the funny name isn't it?"

"Magus, if that's what you mean?" said Adrian noting that John Barrowman already seemed to know a lot about him. Still, it was a small village and he'd been trying to find him. There was nothing sinister there. He mustn't start thinking that his past was catching up with him. He really should work up more of a back story; an illness, being a widower, a depression, the more commonplace, mundane and monotonous the better. Merely being a recluse can attract speculation.

"Will you have another?" asked John apparently unaware how little Adrian had drunk. For his part Adrian had noted the thirsty way in which John Barrowman had consumed his pint.

"No thanks" he said, "I have to go. Paula Byrnes comes before school on a Friday morning. I always like to plan what I'm going to do with my pupils. Anyway I'm not much of a drinker as you can see".

"That's good. I like that. Preparing for the pupils, I mean. I hope you do take Gabe on. See you on Saturday then" said John.

Adrian slid along the seat and got up. There was an awkward moment when he reached forward to shake hands with John who was not expecting this. He had to wait with his hand hovering midair while the other put his glass down. John Barrowman had a firm handshake, not squeezingly firm but still noticeable. They also had the roughness of someone who made a living with them.

"Saturday Mr. Grayling".

"Saturday it is" replied Adrian.

He had been about to say 'call me Adrian' but thought the better of it. After all, though he needed the money, he might not be taking Gabriel on. He knew from experience that taking on hopeless cases was a very self-defeating tactic. It usually ended up with aggrieved parents doing your reputation no good at all. Still he was hopeful given that a previous school had apparently said the child had some talent. He went to the bar to pay Gwyneth for his meal.

"You going to take Gabe on?" she asked.

"We'll see" he replied wondering what privacy a village ever really had to offer.

Adrian always left a small tip which Gwyneth routinely acknowledged. When he had first done this he hadn't been at all sure that she wasn't mocking the smallness of the amount but, having heard her saying much the same thing to other customers who were in a position to be more generous, he decided that he was wrong about this as about so much else. As Adrian turned to leave John Barrowman came back to the bar and, putting his empty glass down firmly, smiled at her and said, "refill my good lady".

Gwyneth chose a smile from her collection that she kept for male customers. Adrian could see that it was serving its purpose well.

Chapter 2

Twenty Pence

Though Adrian had drunk only the beer he had paid for himself and not all of the pint of Antique Ugly John Barrowman had bought for him, a headache as abusive as any from his quondam days of excess, lay on the floor behind his eyes, screaming and kicking at his skull like an overgrown, tantrumous child demanding to be allowed out to play. It followed him to bed where the fact that he had fallen into an unwelcome state of not being conscious rather than asleep on the settee, was further punished by the sort of periodic wakefulness that functioned like a cat walk for all the anxieties in his life. Self-reproach had never helped him. His father would have said it had never helped anyone. Adrian should have known better about a lot of things in his life. He just hoped that Gabriel proved to have some talent.

The pastoral work that was an aspect of his previous incarnation had provided him with some satisfactions even when it sometimes felt as though it was being delivered through a catheter. When an uncle had required one, Adrian's attempted pun on the word catholic had disproportionately enraged his mother. He had known of many men who had walked out and left their wives and children but hadn't come across a tale quite like that of John Barrowman and Gabriel in which the wife had left, making only feast day contact with her only child. But Celia Barrowman, daughter of a bishop, had provided for music lessons. Surely every thoughtful person knows people are complicated, neither all good nor all bad. He wasn't in a position to condemn someone for giving up on a long term commitment. The moral high ground is always booby trapped. Hopefully a future session would tell him more. It was unlikely that Gabriel himself could cast much light on it but if his father came to the pub on a regular basis perhaps there was a chance. He wouldn't be having Antique Ugly though, however good it had tasted at the time. At the last it biteth like a serpent, and stingeth like an adder. He'd probably have to reciprocate and buy John Barrowman a drink. There wasn't going to be much point in taking Gabriel on if he was going to squander the extra money.

Adrian felt a need for something more filling, much stodgier, for breakfast but it was an almost empty larder that taunted him with the inescapably disapproving tones of his mother's voice. A steak and kidney pie would not have seemed right. Extra bread was all that was available. He had rather got into the practice of rationing himself. Now that, his mother would have approved of. Though not obsessive he knew precisely how long a loaf would last and was additionally in the habit of cutting it into smaller portions so that it would look more on the plate. As he finished Sunday's toast having already devoured Saturday's allocation, he knew he would have to visit Fiona Bellow. His life really had achieved the ordinariness and simplicity he sought when that was an event.

The middle part of Adrian Grayling's days were usually quieter though twice a week he did have his two adults who came while their children were at school. They were what passed for the social punctuation of his week occupying Monday and Wednesday mornings and allowed for a semblance of adult conversation. Andrea Linkleader wanted to learn the piano and was making progress however painstaking it might be, while aspiring violinist Julie Moyer caused him to substitute the Cremona SV175 for the SV600 he normally used with adults, as he could not bear to hear what she did to the 600.

It would be fair to say that Julie caused Adrian much, what his mother would have called, soul searching. He didn't want to dwell on why his mother was more frequently in his mind these days or on the coming anniversary. In any case as one gets older there are naturally more milestones. And tombstones. Some you don't need to try to remember, they stalk you as though across a bridge of poisoned thorns. Julie Moyer had recently been proposing to give a private recital and had sought his advice as to what she should play. The word 'truant' came to his mind. He managed to resist the temptation. She had been having lessons for some time.

Adrian knew better than most that pupils often develop a crush on their teachers. The signs had been there early on and, though she was a very attractive woman in her early forties, he was careful not to give any encouragement. The tactic of suggesting perhaps delaying the recital had failed. She had clearly taken this to mean that he wished for her to have more lessons and had volunteered to pay for another session. Adrian's sense that her real aim was to spend more time with him was something he knew his mother would have regarded as male arrogance. She wasn't always wrong.

Much though he had needed the money he had told Julie that, unfortunately at present he was fully booked. Then the gifts had started, most recently an expensive violin. She liked him to play it for her at the end of their session and would sit as though transfixed, just listening. Sometimes she would cry and, in those moments, assumed a hard to resist vulnerability. At least one that he found difficult to resist. Not that many years ago his surrender would have been guaranteed. He would have offered comfort, so often the gateway to his favourite sin. To him, there had always been a cruel poignancy that sometimes achieved tragic proportions, in the inherent gap between aspiration and talent and, with additional irony, all this in the 500th anniversary year of Leonardo da Vinci's death. Da Vinci had done to the succeeding 500 years what he was reputed to have done to Verrocchio the master painter, to whom he was apprenticed. In the way of the times the best apprentices did some of the work. Da Vinci was said to have contributed the youthful angel lightly holding the robe of Jesus in The Baptism of Christ. Verrocchio it seems had recognized this portion of the work as so superior that he never painted again. To Adrian, some apocryphal stories deserved to be true. Beauty and perfection had always mattered in his life. Perhaps that was why a drink called Antique Ugly seemed to have such a negative effect on him.

That day, for once, the rotund figure of Paula Byrnes rolled in early for her lesson. As always she brought her own violin, a gift from her uncle Derek Holmes. He had often wondered what it was about small worlds that causes them to make themselves smaller still. Adrian had not prepared what they were going to do. Some teachers simply coasted through sessions but that was not his way. Music was too important to him not to want everyone to share in the experience, but today, when he asked

Paula what she thought she would like to do, she looked at him blankly for a few moments then said, "I want to be a violinist or a hairdresser".

Though she was not, in his view, without talent she was unlikely to reach the level required even by a second tier professional. Despite the earliness of the hour she was groomed beyond the ordinary requirements of a school day. Her mother was a hairdresser who visited people in their own homes.

"That's not what I meant Paula" he smiled at her, "I meant what would you like us to do in today's lesson? Sometimes I like to give my special pupils a choice".

"Am I special?" she asked.

"Of course you are" he replied, "so, you can choose between preparing your piece for the show in the village hall or learning something totally new".

"Something new" she said.

As he had asked the question Adrian knew he had worded it badly. Now he was stuck with the 'something new' option. He remembered a recording of various not very difficult pieces for children he had made for one of his sessions with Dorothea Adams, "I'm going to play some music and then I want you to try to play exactly the same thing without any help from me".

Though Paula did not look especially enthusiastic he played a snatch from the recording. What she produced in response bore as much resemblance to the material as this session did to a proper music lesson.

"Let me show you" he said, picking up his own instrument, "I'll play it a few times then you try again".

He mechanically did exactly this. Paula tried again though her attempt was little improved over the first time. Some days are like that even without the Antique Ugly.

"Can I do it on your violin?" she asked.

"Not really" he said, "your hands are still a bit small. It would be harder for you".

Paula looked glumly at him. He was well aware what an unnatural instrument the violin was in terms of playing position for beginners. Neither of them said anything for a few moments then he said, "ok, just for today mind. You can have a go".

She put down her own instrument on the table and took his from him, a smile that was both sweetly scented and vaguely victorious seeming to dance across her face. He helped her position the violin. As he did so his face brushed against hers, "you've got whiskers" she said, "my dad has and so does uncle Derek".

He knew she wouldn't be able to manage but he let her effort squander some minutes. He then took the violin back, "you've done very well" he said, not even convincing himself, "very well indeed but why don't you have another go on yours. Your uncle bought you one that cost more than a grown-up one and has a lovely tone. Why don't you play something for me?"

"Uncle Derek likes me to play for him too" she said as she began to play a simple tune he had taught her months before.

When she stopped Adrian applauded and said "encore, encore" so she played the same piece twice more. He remembered teaching her about encores. It amused him that she had taken him so literally. An almost furtive glance at the mahogany clock on the mantelpiece. Time was nearly up. He would normally have prepared what he would ask her to practise before the next session, something that would capitalize on what they had done in the lesson. He was about to make a suggestion when Paula suddenly said, "I forgot. I can't come next week. I'm going to be a bridesmaid".

Adrian's immediate thought was that this would mean a drop in income for next week. These things always seemed to happen at the wrong time.

"That's nice" he said, "whose wedding is it?"

"Mummy's friend Clara. She's going to marry Ivan. Nobody likes Ivan. My mum thinks she's making a terrible mistake".

As the old-fashioned pull-cord bell sounded in the hallway, Paula's comment was a reminder to Adrian that it is hard to keep secrets with children around. They are likely to tell someone, "I've got a secret". He knew that one of the things about secrets is that they are always a bit heavier than you have the strength to carry them. That makes them tiring. And some experiences don't so much teach as brand you.

"Sorry I'm a bit late Mr. Grayling" began Mrs Byrnes though she appeared to him to be exactly on time, "come Paula" she said reaching for her daughter's hand before adding, "I didn't get to the bank Mr. Grayling. I'll sort you out next week if that's all right? Derek's still trying to get a post office for the Mitre. That'll make things a lot easier for everyone, don't you think? If that doesn't work he's said at least he'll get a cash machine".

Adrian wanted to say, 'but don't you have Clara's wedding to go to and by the way I don't think Ivan's as bad as some people say. No one's ever as bad as the mob makes out' but he didn't know either Clara or Ivan. Instead he said "that'll be fine Mrs Byrnes, Paula's a good girl. Doing well".

"Bye Mr Grayling" said Paula, still holding her mother's hand but raising her violin case slightly in her other hand as a surrogate wave.

Adrian went into the kitchen and put the dented whistling kettle on the range then sat down more out of habit than tiredness. He picked up and put down the empty bread wrapper before beginning to push his loose change around the table top, arranging it by denomination. Pathetic that it should have come to this. The repetitive minutiae of the days he had created seemed not so much to be invading his thinking as appropriating it. He began to wonder if even invited boredom isn't a way people have of punishing themselves for not doing something worthwhile. Beauty and boredom must surely be incompatible since boredom is always ugly.

Adrian did have money put by for rent but he would never touch that. That would be a step closer to homelessness. His previous life had taught him how unexpectedly easy it is for that to happen and how getting out of it is like trying to climb a rope with your arms tied behind your back.

The whistling from the kettle interrupted his thought. The teabag already in the mug, he picked up the milk carton and shook it in a pointless act of confirmation but it still felt empty. Somewhere were some of those little plastic tubs of long life milk from a café he couldn't remember visiting but had no idea where they were. So black tea it was then.

Adrian knew not to get to the shop before ten o'clock. By then the morning busyness of parents who had dropped their children off for school would have gone. He had no more pupils today. Nothing else was going to happen till tomorrow morning when, with any luck, John Barrowman would arrive with Gabriel in tow. He now knew that Gabriel would have to be so utterly without talent that Julie Moyer would look gifted for him not to take him on, at least for a few trial weeks. Hadn't John Barrowman told me that he had saved all the money Gabriel's mother had sent for music lessons. That to him was her saving grace. He could understand how a woman would leave her husband but to abandon her child when she might still have some direct contact he found harder to take. Maybe it was just his upbringing. The worship of the ideal. The sanctity of mother and child. Then there was reality. He knew too well that for some children, to have been abandoned, would have been a blessing to them. Maybe all things that come to be worshipped are really warnings.

There was only one other person in The Handy Stores when Adrian arrived. She was busily engaged in conversation with Fiona Bellows. Fiona called out, "hello Mr Grayling". The woman looked round. He vaguely thought that he had seen her before somewhere but couldn't quite place her. He heard Fiona Bellows say in a quiet voice as though it was something disreputable, "the piano teacher".

The idea of Bellows and a quiet voice again disproportionately amused him. Perhaps he had been teaching children so long that his sensibilities had been stained by their sense of humour, he who had once been considered witty. His child pupils often delighted in telling him jokes. He had always meant to write them down including the various misconceptions they had about so many things. Recently while trying to get a lesson started, he had been explaining something to the very earnestly religious Timothy Paulson, whose grandfather had been the vicar here many years before. In giving the boy answers to his questions, he had already used the stock response of 'that's God's mysterious ways' when Timothy had asked another question. He had merely said 'that's God too'. Timothy had said in all his seriousness, 'I haven't seen God 1". He had been tempted to say 'nor have I'. The exchange had amused him.

Now he went to the counter with his wrapped sliced loaf and carton of milk. Fiona asked if he knew Miss Walsh. Close up he could see how pretty she was despite having a small port wine stain just visible above her left eye. "I haven't had the pleasure" he said shaking her hand.

"And you won't" responded Miss Walsh, then she and Fiona Bellow both laughed.

"Sorry Mr. Grayling" said Fiona, "Siobhan Walsh, you are a wicked woman".

Siobhan responded "he didn't look as though he minded".

Why she couldn't have addressed her comment directly to him he had no idea. He began to count out his change to pay for the milk and bread.

"You don't mind if I get rid of this change?" he asked.

"Change is always helpful" responded Fiona.

Adrian had miscalculated. He was twenty pence short. "Sorry" he said, "I don't have my wallet with me".

"Don't worry" she replied.

With a magician's flourish, Siobhan Walsh then put a twenty pence piece on the counter, "you owe me a cup of tea" she said, this time addressing her comment directly to him.

"Siobhan" said Fiona, "you playing hard to get didn't last long. Well no surprises there".

"Fiona Bellows" laughed Siobhan, "if I knew what incorrigible meant I'd say you were it".

Adrian had never been comfortable with women. It was the plural that did it for him. Individually he could be charmed by them and, he knew, charm them. In his former life his role was a barrier to some and a lure to others but it was another, forbidden pheromone, that haunted him.

Directing his "thank you" to neither of them in particular, Adrian left the shop clutching the loaf and the milk carton to him as though someone might try to snatch them. His assumption was that Fiona Bellows and the very attractive Siobhan Walsh would have continued to talk about him.

Not long after he got back to the cottage the phone rang. It was John Barrowman. Adrian experienced a momentary sense of dread that he was going to cancel tomorrow's appointment. Instead he was merely confirming it. Occasionally a cancellation had come as a relief to him. But now, well he needed Gabriel Barrowman. He hadn't thought to ask how John Barrowman had his landline number. He was not in the phone book. His card gave his mobile number. That reminded him he would have to get more printed. He'd have to wait for a while till he was better sorted out financially. The call however had one other timely effect. He wondered if it was possible to suspend the line rental on the landline.

Adrian passed the rest of the morning by again tidying the cottage and hoovering using the old Panasonic that was already in the cupboard under the stairs when he rented the place. It was not much younger than the house and noisily of industrial strength. He had turned off the radio as he worked. Generally it was tuned to radio three but he hated the thought that there was fine music that he couldn't hear properly. Now he switched it on again. Bach Piano Concertos were among his transporting favourites. He recognized the piece being performed. It had to be the EMI recording under Neville Marriner though he had a more personal reason for his fondness of the Murray Perahia at the Academy of St Martin's in the Fields. He sat down to listen.

Adrian wasn't sure what woke him but then he had no idea he had fallen asleep. Someone was playing Britten's Suite No 1 for Cello not very well but, to Adrian, Rostropovich had made it impossible for anyone else. Indeed hadn't Britten dedicated the piece to Rostropovich? His more immediate concern however was that perhaps he had fallen asleep in company. He looked anxiously around. Several times recently he had been concerned that he was turning out to be a lot like his mother who, albeit at a considerably older age, had taken just to going asleep at apparently random times. She had still been alive when he had made the decision that had changed everything. He knew she was disappointed, no, more than that, angry and unrelentingly upset. How could he? After all their sacrifices. Adrian had just taken it. You can't explain love like that, least of all when it happens, then it's too late. It's all consuming till the vengeance of God falls on it or it stops. It seems that perhaps God cannot cope with someone or something being loved more than him. Love itself, he thought, is surely always pure, but when the heart is the epicentre, the perfect pearl dropped into earthly waters can create an earthquake. He knew the ripples could grow to a tsunami that is heedless of consequences however much anyone might try to minimize it.

It was now two twenty. So a late lunch it was. He had a tin of tomato soup six months past its recommended date and a piece of toast. He had never really trusted best-before dates or even use-by dates. They were too much caught up in marketing, really too much self-interest involved, substituting the actuarial for the actual a friend had said. He did have friends once. Some of them very able, all of them capable of generating humour, like the suggestion that ideas should have use-by dates. Uncommon sense was what was needed about food dates apart from in the case of Antique Ugly. Mind you the man who introduced him to it could be his financial saviour. Perhaps he owed it another go. He was aware that he was allowing himself to invest too heavily in the prospect of this new student.

Adrian felt a need to get out of the cottage, to be reminded that there was a bigger world out there. He hadn't been for a walk in a while. The village had woodland nearby open to the public on marked paths and other long walks with sometimes inspiring views when a delinquent mist had not descended on them. Today the conditions were fine. That's what he would do. A walk then something to eat and an early night in readiness for the following morning. Killing time. So often he had told others, life is for living not for preparing for the next thing. The next thing might be death then there would not be anything else. Carpe diem. It had taken him rather too long to reach that conclusion.

Before going out Adrian looked again at his food cupboard. He shook his head as he checked the date on the Fray Bentos Steak and Kidney pie but determined he would have it later anyway. He glanced at the ornate hook with the keys to the cottage hanging on it but did not pick them up. As he left someone on a bicycle seemed slowly to materialize like a cinematic special effect. It was Siobhan Walsh. In the early afternoon sunshine she looked even younger. The effect of the neon lighting in the shop was ageing. She was definitely attractive, perched as she was on an old bike that was a little too big for her and causing her legs to have to stretch out. She grinned at him like a child might and said, "so this is where you live. I'll know where to come for my twenty pence worth".

"Hello Siobhan" he said, "thank you for that. That was kind. Do you live locally?"

"I do for the moment" she said. I'm staying with a friend while works being done on my house following a flood".

"A flood" he said, "how terrible. How did that happen?"

"Nothing biblical" she said, "just a burst pipe in the loft, nothing to write home about, just to the insurance company".

She almost sounded indifferent about what would be to many a calamity but then he knew better than most that it was hard enough to know what was going on in your own life let alone in someone else's.

"Well your misfortune is my good luck because we have met" he said.

Siobhan smiled knowingly, "must be on my way" she said leaning back a little and stretching out her leg to place her right foot on the pedal. He could see the outline of her leg under the dress.

"Well do call in anytime" he said.

"Oh I will" she responded, "I could do with a lesson", then, raising her left hand in the air, pedalled off, initially a little wobbily but then at speed, as though in need to get away from him. She had flirted with him. Definitely. He had been known to get that sort of thing wrong but now as he walked toward the woods he was sure of it. She must be what, fifteen, maybe more years younger than him, but that didn't matter. Age, they say, is a number, it's just that not all parts of his body always seemed to know that. There was of course, by the grace of a beneficent God and the accidental assistance of Pfizer, suddenly a solution for those in need. Out of the blue pill comes salvation. It's just that there wasn't always someone to share his joy with.

Meeting Siobhan Walsh had changed the whole tenor of his day from the inauspicious twenty pence shortfall to the 'I could do with a lesson' finale. He thought of the developing crescendo that bridges the third and fourth movements of Beethoven's Fifth then immediately wondered if Ziggy Stardust might not appeal more to her. In any event it was on such little evidence that he stepped nimbly through the woods in which the sunlight, glimmering through the canopy above seemed to him to construct musical notes out of light.

Back home he had eaten his steak and kidney pie which he felt had matured with age unlike the glass of Burgundy he had with it. It was the remnants of the bottle that had possibly been open a little too long. Perhaps, he thought, that should be taken by him as a symbol of the timeliness of what might be a new beginning. He went to bed early, full of an almost boyish anticipation. But if it was a symbol he was looking for, perhaps the fact that he had severe indigestion in the night should have been considered for the post of diminuendo.

Chapter 3

The Metronome

The easy light of the Saturday morning saturated as it was with early bird song, found him already shaved, showered and still oddly expectant. He followed his usual routine starting, with all the unoriginality of a pop song, with breakfast. No further sign of the affliction that had made his night an unmelodious and discordant thing. The dishes from the previous evening were quickly washed up together with his breakfast mug and plate and stowed neatly away. The degree to which his life before had become embalmed in an inner commentary on its immediate trivia was reflected in his thought that normally he would have left them to dry by themselves. This was reinforced as he checked the living room and again dusted the piano then slightly repositioned one of the violins on its stand. Now the duster was back in the piano stool. Standing back a little he surveyed the scene. Everything seemed to be in special readiness.

Adrian sat on the settee and looked towards the clock. Next to it was one of his six metronomes. This was a treasured possession. Dating from the late nineteenth century it was in a rosewood case in close to perfect condition and stood on three brass feet. It was much admired by visitors even by those who did not know what it was. The oval brass plate on the door he knew amused some of the older boys he had taught over the years. It read R. Cocks & Co. This sometimes allowed Adrian the private jest of telling them it was in full working order. Some of them would try to suppress a further snigger thinking that he did not understand what he had just said.

Despite his anticipation Adrian seemed startled when the doorbell rang. He felt unusually anxious as he put his hand to the handle. He hesitated before opening the door to avoid seeming too eager. There in front of him stood John Barrowman looking as though he was dressed for an interview in a suit, shirt and tie. A figure he took to be Gabriel was standing behind him so that at first Adrian could only see that the top of his head which came up to his father's shoulder.

"Hello Mr. Grayling" said the over dressed John Barrowman as he reached his hand out. Adrian shook it.

"And I take it that is Gabriel behind you" he said with a lightness of tone more suited to someone younger who might be hiding behind a parent.

"Sorry, yes", responded John stepping to one side. Adrian looked at the boy suffused in what seemed like deferential sunlight. His own demeanour was of such a level of astonishment that he could but hope would not be too obvious. Here before him was the most strikingly beautiful child he had ever seen. There are children everyone would agree were cute, some who could be described as pretty and others handsome, but here in this moment this boy was quite simply exquisite. His hair, shimmering in raven blackness, hung in natural ringlets down to his delicate shoulders, his skin diaphanous was palely flawless, his lips wine red and poetry ready and his eyes had a sadly wistful blueness that seemed to intensify as they were looked into.

For a moment Adrian hesitated to take the proffered hand, seeing in its long fingers a delicacy that he feared he might fracture. He gently shook hands. The boy said, "hello Mr. Grayling".

"Adrian" he said, "call me Adrian. I like my students to feel relaxed with me". He immediately turned back to John Barrowman fearing that the lingering of his gaze would betray how wholly captivated he was. "Come in. Please. You go first. It's the door on the left".

He followed them in noting how firmly slim the figure of the boy was, rather like Donatello's David but without the effeminacy. That figure was of course naked but for a bonnet-like hat and boots. Gabriel Barrowman was not far off the height of David in that work which had for many, during the six hundred years of its existence, represented the embodiment of male beauty. For others it was impeccably executed homoerotic soft porn.

Once they were seated Adrian had to work hard to keep his eyes off the child. He tried to focus on John Barrowman as he explained how he liked to work. Lessons in his experience were best individual rather than group. He liked to negotiate with the pupil the nature and duration of any practice he was asking them to do. He preferred to teach simple tunes from the start rather than endless scales and finger exercises. He would spend some time teaching his pupils to listen to music without which progress was unlikely. He then found himself adding something he had seldom said before, namely that while a parent or guardian was welcome to be present, from his experience he had learned that this could slow down his pupil's progress. There was something about this boy that was not for sharing.

John Barrowman appeared to listen intently to everything his son's potential piano teacher was saying. Then Adrian turned to Gabriel and asked him if he understood. He merely nodded. "Ok" said Adrian "next thing for today Gabriel is for you to come and sit at the piano".

Gabriel got up and walked across the room to the piano. He pulled out the stool and sat down. When his father had first mentioned to Adrian that he had messed around on the piano before, his heart had sunk. Normally that meant a slouched posture, poor finger positioning and wholly misguided expectations, all things that could be hard to correct. But Gabriel adopted a good upright posture and positioned his hands appropriately on the keys then silently waited. From behind it would not have been possible to say if it was a male or female pupil.

For a moment the scene seemed to Adrian like a professional pianist about to begin a recital. Having already noted that Gabriel seemed to be right handed, Adrian went and stood to his left side. He touched him lightly on his shoulder. Gabriel looked around and up at him. The eyes, alive with questing allure, drew him unstoppably in. Adrian took his hand from his shoulder as though that was the conduit for some of the effect.

"Your father tells me you can already play a little. It would help me to hear what you sound like at this stage. Please play a little for me. Anything. You choose".

Gabriel turned back to the piano, seemed to hesitate for a moment then began. It took but seconds for Adrian to recognize Bowie's Stardust though he had never heard it arranged for piano before. While the fact that he had been thinking of Ziggy Stardust the afternoon before with Siobhan Walsh registered with him, what hit him most was the sensitive movement of Gabriel's fingers, their effortless glide across the keys, their ability to depress a note with vigour without appearing to apply visible force and, crowning it all, the uncomplicated look of joy on the face of the boy. There was no movement of the lips as he played. It was the music that he allowed to escape from the instrument that inspired him. Whatever the words, which Adrian felt he undoubtedly knew, might have meant to him, primarily he surfed the sounds. He let him play. He would have let him play it again if he hadn't stopped at the end and looked round.

Immediately Adrian wanted to applaud, to shout 'bravo, bravo', but the voice of John Barrowman interrupted, "so what do you think? Would you take him on?"

Adrian turned to him, "you hadn't told me he was so good, so advanced" he said, "it would be my great pleasure to nurture a talent like that. You wouldn't believe how much piano teachers dream of a moment like this". He had also wanted to say how beautiful his new pupil was, how he would teach him for nothing just to have him coming for lessons but he needed the money and the self-respect. He refocused on Gabriel. He again put his hands on the boy's shoulders and asked, "would you like to come for lessons? I think you have a rare gift that should be cherished and fostered".

"I think I may like to come" said the boy, his voice in the way of his father, sounding even younger than he looked. Adrian wondered if it had even broken. Then he added, "but first I would like to hear you play".

"I often play for my students, the adults as well as the young people" he said, "I hope I will have many opportunities to play for you".

"I want you to play today, now" said the boy, "then I will decide".

It had never happened to Adrian before that a child student wanted in effect to audition him. All teachers knew the importance of establishing who was in charge with their students otherwise much authority could melt away but he knew he had lost that fight on the doorstep when his father had stepped aside and Adrian had first laid eyes on Gabriel Barrowman.

Reinforcing his request Gabriel got up and stood by the stool. Adrian obediently sat down. "Anything in particular?" he asked.

"No. You choose. Just play".

To Adrian at that moment it had to be the Bach. Music indeed hath charms to soothe a savage breast and the breast at this moment in need of soothing was his. So he began to play at first a little anxiously then with abandon, he played as though no one else was there but Gabriel Barrowman, as though what mattered most to him in all the world was to please this child who was more than a child, who had a knowingness about him. When in due course he thought he should stop he looked round. There was a faraway look of unredeemed sadness on the enchanted face of the boy. It looked as though he might weep. "I will never be able to play like that. My mother did. I do not know where she is. I do not truly know if she knows where I am so that she could find me? I do not know if there is a meaning to it but I know she plays for me".

Though lost in the strangeness of what the boy had just said and the language he had used that was both archaic and adult, Adrian stood up and put his arm around his shoulders, "you already play better than me without tuition. You just haven't been taught how to play what I just did. Gabriel, agree to be my student and I will show you the greatness that is in you, then you will see you won't just play music, you will live it".

The eyes of Gabriel Barrowman again looked into his, this time with ageless knowing, "I will come" he said "for twenty-one lessons". The boy again fell silent.

"Twenty-one" said Adrian, "why twenty-one?"

Gabriel did not answer him but turned to his father and said, "twenty-one. Did she send enough for that?"

John Barrowman now got up and walked across the room. He got out a wad of cash from the pocket of his suit and began to count. When he had reached the required amount for twenty-one lessons he stopped. There was none left. Everything about this encounter was bewildering Adrian. He said, "you do not have to pay in advance. After each lesson is normal".

"Please" said John, "take it now. I'd prefer it that way so if something happened to me he could still come. Don't worry, he will be here when you say. He will come for twenty-one lessons because he has said twenty-one and because you have been paid you will do it".

Adrian did not want there to be time limits on being able to see Gabriel, certainly not to consider a time when he might not be there. To him a life without beauty was loneliness for the soul. And the money was not just welcome but vital at this time. But just twenty one sessions. He hoped that there would be room for negotiation later though there was something in the way 'twenty-one' was said, something that had the finality of all breathing things about it. Then there was the unexplained manner in which John Barrowman had exactly the money required though he could not remember discussing his charge per lesson.

"When can he start?" asked John.

"Tomorrow" said Adrian immediately, though he really wanted to stagger the sessions so that he could anticipate seeing the boy for longer. He was used to having inner conflicts. He was used to losing them.

"I will be here at twenty-one minutes past ten" said Gabriel not giving his father time to respond.

They left in the business like way of the last part of their encounter, though as he walked down the pathway of Magus Cottage, Gabriel Barrowman half turned and smiled sadly at Adrian. The smile which came towards him had the delicacy of the slow flapping of wings. It seemed also to carry some other message or a hint of consequence.

Chapter 4

The Bicycle Bell

Adrian returned to the living room and sat on the settee looking towards the piano upon which rested everything that was in him and the payment for precisely twenty-one lessons. He wasn't at all sure what he could possibly teach this beautiful boy but he had a sense there was something this pupil could teach him. It wouldn't be good dwell on that thought. It was important to get a grip on things. There was shopping to do. Taking a random amount of money from the piano he put the rest behind some books on the shelf to the left of the cabinet in which was the TV set he seldom watched.

The shop was busy. Adrian had with him a straw basket with wooden handles. His mother had given him this for a birthday before his betrayal of her dreams had caused her no longer to acknowledge birthdays. There were other things too she had done to punish him. Though the shop had blue plastic baskets stacked at the front by the door, he put his shopping directly into his basket, something he had seen other shoppers do. The plan was to replenish his larder including his emergency supplies. He added to the list of inconsistencies in his life by carefully checking the use-by dates on everything before making his final choices.

Adrian waited in the short queue made up entirely of women. Fiona Bellows looked at the goods as he got them out, "you expecting snow or something" she said then without waiting for a response asked, "have you got your wallet with you today?"

Looking past him to the women behind, she announced "he forgot his wallet yesterday but fortunately Siobhan Walsh was here to bail him out". Having shared that information she redirected her attention to Adrian, "you want to watch that one" she added, "you know what they say about Irish women?" Laughter in the queue behind.

For a moment of terrible coldness Adrian wondered what they knew or had somehow guessed. He'd never heard anything particularly said about Irish women but from her tone he knew Fiona Bellow had something salacious in mind. When he paid with the money John Barrowman had given him, Fiona picked up two notes and held them up to the light, "new twenties" she said, "look fresh printed this morning. So that's what you get up to when we think you're giving lessons".

"Damn" he said in attempted humour, "I thought since music is about notes I'd get away with it".

A tinkle of laughter then one of the other women said, "well, if you have any spare you can let me have them, even ones that didn't come out right".

"That's you all over Thelma Burke" rejoined Fiona, "I've been in your tea shop, you'd know very well about things that didn't come out right". More laughter.

"Talking about that" said Thelma, "did you hear about Christine Sharp's baby. It was born yesterday but there's something not right with it".

"I heard nothing about that" said Fiona handing Adrian his change with the words 'thank you' said with about as much feeling as a McDonald's 'have a nice day', her attention now belonging elsewhere.

Adrian was grateful that the focus was no longer on him. He left the women still speculating with the sort of idle insensitivity that passes for concern, about Christine Sharp's imperfect baby. He wanted to stop and say we are all imperfect in some way, that we sometimes do things or make decisions that aren't for the greater good or that simply don't work out as planned, but he knew it would just sound strange and preachy and be unlikely to change anything they thought.

He had hardly got to within ten paces of the little wooden gate that led up to his cottage when he heard the dull metallic tinkle of a bicycle bell. He looked around to find Siobhan Walsh astride her steed, the sandy red of her unruly hair enlisting the aid of the breeze that appeared somehow to have just been summoned, to show it off. She was, he noted, wearing the same floral dress as yesterday.

"I've come to claim my prize" she said "and don't tell me you have a pupil because I saw them leave before you went to Fiona's shop".

"Have you been watching me?" he asked.

"Someone has to" she replied, "I know all about that cottage. What's always gone on there. It'd send shivers down your back. Why do you think the rents so cheap? Only someone desperate would live there. Are you desperate? I am but for a cup of tea".

Siobhan, clearly considering her own words an invitation, got off her bike, leaned it against the wall and turning to him said, "you've got the key". He did not resist as she took the basket from him anymore than he had when Gabriel Barrowman told him to play.

"It's not locked" he said, "I hardly ever lock it".

Siobhan looked at him as though he was trying to tell her something else and opened the low oak front door. Once inside she led the way to the kitchen where she put the basket on the table. "Have you been here before?" asked Adrian.

"Everyone has" she said, "at some stage in their life everyone has passed through this house".

Seeing the look on his face and grinning widely she said, "just joshing. Why does everyone fall for that? You can say it wherever you are and you nearly always get the same reaction. Even if it's a new house you can tell them there was a dwelling on the site before. It's important to say dwelling. It's old-fashioned. Then they wonder what was it that dwelt there?"

She began to unpack his shopping looking at each item as she did so. He hadn't realized before how intrusive it was to have a stranger examine your shopping. It felt to him like being stripped.

"You'd best put them where you want them otherwise I'd have to keep coming round to find things for you".

"Not a bad idea" he said, slipping into her flirtatious style. None the less he began to put the various things in the places habit had allowed to become theirs.

Siobhan picked up the kettle, held up the part of the spout that whistled and, with the words "just whistle and I'll come" put some water in. She got out two mugs and looked in the empty tea caddy. She went to the cupboard in the corner and got a box of teabags out. For a moment he looked startled. "Don't worry" she said, "I've just seen you put them away. That's not what I know about the house".

As she put a teabag in each mug she said, "my grandma in Ireland used to read the teabags".

"Don't you mean tea leaves" he responded.

"No" she insisted, "teabags. It used to be the tea leaves but then teabags came in. She'd get her visitors to tear open a teabag then sprinkle the leaves into the cup, add a little water, swill them round, then start".

"I never know when to believe you" he said.

"Good" she replied with an intensity implying a story behind it, "believing people is never a good idea".

Adrian was about to say something in reply when the shrillness of the kettle whistling interrupted in seeming chastisement of Siobhan for giving away a secret. She poured water into each mug. Reflexively he said, "I like my milk in first".

"There, there babykins" she said without looking towards him, "don't worry. It'll be all right. You'll be all grown up one day and do the things big people do". He had the ridiculous but strong feeling the words were not meant for him.

When she had finished preparing the mugs she picked up both, then turning towards him said, "biscuits?" in such a way that it could either have been an expletive or a request.

Adrian went to the cupboard and got out a packet. She walked towards the living room. She put both mugs on the small glass topped coffee table which already had two coasters, then sat on the settee patting the place beside her byway of invitation for him to sit down. Someone outside the situation would have assumed it was her house. He sat where suggested as she cradled the mug of tea.

"I like the way you have it here" she said looking towards the piano, "no matter what they say about this cottage, I like it here".

"What do they say?" he asked.

"Nothing" she replied, "well only that things seem to happen. They say no one ever stays long. It was empty quite a long time before you moved in. I don't know. There are people who have lives that move around a lot, maybe they're the ones who moved in and it has nothing to do with the old stories. How long were you wherever you were before?"

"I moved around quite a lot so you'd be right about me. Do you know the old stories or is that another thing you're just making up?"

"Which would you like?" she asked "it's all the same to me".

"I don't believe that" he replied as she took a biscuit from the packet.

"These are soft" she said taking a bite, then picking up the packet went on, "goodness they're nearly a year beyond their best-before date".

"Sorry" he said "I don't really pay much attention to those"

"Then you should store them better, in an airtight box. Fionna Bellows has some at the back of the shop and Ashley Fenton does tupperware parties. No, forget that. I can't see you at a tupperware party. I could do it for you. Do you want me to get a couple of boxes for you just to show you?"

Adrian surprised himself by saying what was for him a relatively firm "no" then almost immediately adding in a more placatory tone, "I can't expect you to do that".

They drank their tea with no more talk of tupperware. If Adrian had been asked what they had actually talked about he wouldn't have been able to contribute anything. When they had finished Siobhan put the biscuit with the bite out of it in her mug and carried both of them to the kitchen. Adrian followed her.

"I don't care what they say about this place. It feels homely, I mean it feels right." said Siobhan, "I like it. Would you mind if I saw round?"

Though he momentarily wondered what state his bedroom and the upstairs bathroom were in, if Adrian hesitated for a second it was not apparently something that registered with Siobhan.

"Ok" he said, "if you really want to but remember I haven't prepared for visitors".

"Don't worry about that Adrian" said Siobhan softly, using his name for the first time since she arrived, "the kitchen I know and the piano room. What else is down here? Where do these doors lead to?" she asked gesturing toward two doors one on either side at the back of the kitchen.

"That one goes out to the garden and this one is locked" replied Adrian, "it used to be a pantry but now it's a downstairs toilet. There's another door from the hallway. This one really should be bricked up. Regulations apparently don't allow a toilet to open from a kitchen".

Siobhan led the way out of the kitchen and immediately went to the stairs at the end of the hallway. That the wooden treads were well trodden from years of use was highlighted by the dip in the middle.

"Shall I go first?" she asked and proceeded to do so without any further word from Adrian. "I like these" she said as she went up, "they're not just a way up. They have a different belonging. My grandmother had some like this. She used to say the problem with them is they're too narrow to get a coffin down".

"Was she always a gloomy person?" asked Adrian.

"No" she said as she reached the top, "she didn't need to be. She had my granddad for that".

The top of the stairs opened onto a narrow corridor that was lit by a single bulb. He saw Siobhan glance up at the ragged frame of the lightshade that had once hung there, then at the door immediately at the top of the stairs.

"That's the way up to the attic room" he said, "but let's look at this floor first. The room on the left" he said noting that her gaze had lingered briefly on the door to the attic stairs, "is what I call the garden bedroom".

Siobhan entered. This clearly was not a bedroom in current use. There was a window at one end and a bed covered by a green dustsheet. The space to the right of the bed was occupied by a tiny chest of drawers. This would have meant that the bed could only easily be accessed from the left hand side. There was also an old wooden chair with a straight back at the bottom of the bed with a dusty suitcase on it. Siobhan walked to the window and looked out.

"I can see you're not much of a gardener" she commented, "unless you like the wild overgrown look. You've even got a shed down there. I bet in all these years you've never even been in it".

Adrian did not respond. She turned towards him and said, "I like this room. I think if I lived here this would be the bedroom I'd choose".

Next door to this bedroom was the bathroom with an old-fashioned metal bath to which had been attached some plastic shower fixtures. A towel lay on the floor by the bath. He noted that Siobhan instinctively picked it up and draped it over the side of the bath. For a moment he almost felt a need to apologize but managed to resist it.

Opposite the bathroom and a little further along was the other bedroom on this floor. A window provided a view over the tiny front garden to the main street through the village. Unlike the garden bedroom, this one had curtains. At the opposite end from the window was a large old-fashioned double bed that had not been made. A wooden chair that looked like the twin of the one in the other bedroom was positioned to one side of this. There was also a chest of drawers with a wooden framed mirror which, from the small number of toiletries on it, doubled as a dressing table.

Siobhan stood by the bed looking towards the window. He tried to imagine her naked in the bed. As though able to read his mind she looked back towards him and smiled.

"I like this room too" she said, "but I still think I'd prefer the smaller one".

"I'll keep that in mind" he said, "so that's about it".

"The attic" she said, "you haven't shown me that or have you someone imprisoned up there?"

He was going to say "not yet" but thought the better of it. He led the way to the door of the attic stairs. This time he went first. He had been shown it when he first rented the place but not ventured up there since apart from storing some cases. The stairs creaked a bit. At the top was another door which was ajar. Adrian pushed it. It made a very human groan of protest but then gave way to his pressure. He moved away from the entrance to allow Siobhan to join him and stood looking around. His cases and an old trunk were to the left. There was a simple upended table with a broken leg. The triangular window looked as though it had accidently spilled the light that was in the room. It fell on an ornate but abandoned piano stool long surrendered to dust.

Perhaps someone had once carefully positioned it there to view the outside world from this vantage point. Just to the left of the window was an old coat stand with one of the ornate arms broken. Hanging from this was what appeared to be a vintage set of keys. The layers of dust illuminated by the struggling light had long remained undisturbed and in themselves bore testimony to the lack of use. It had the sort of fusty smell that seemed to have the ability to get inside you. He coughed.

"You alright?" asked Siobhan.

"Sure" he replied, "it's just the dust up here. I don't use this much".

"Really" she said, "I am surprised". Seeing the look on his face she smiled, "of course I can see that it's not in use. What surprises me is that you don't. I'd make a great place to sit and read. It could be cosy. You don't otherwise have somewhere to sit that's not a work room. Your living room is obviously your teaching room so you don't get away from it".

"I never feel I need to get away from music" he said.

"I'm sure you don't, not from real music but I imagine the sounds some of your pupils make probably isn't always musical".

"Of course that's true. I just never thought about sorting this attic out".

"Or the other bedroom" she commented.

"Or that" he agreed, "don't forget it's not my place, but of course you already know that as you mentioned that the rent is cheap. It doesn't always feel like that".

"I can let you have twenty pence anytime" she laughed.

They made their way downstairs. Siobhan went into the living room which she felt would be too much like a work room for her and stood looking around then went back to the kitchen.

"You look as though you're trying to find something" he said.

"Yes" she replied, "the cellar".

"There isn't a cellar" he responded.

"No cellar" she said, "are you sure?"

"I'd know if I had a cellar" he said.

Siobhan looked at him as though trying to assess if he was joking. "Perhaps you really don't know" she said "but there is a cellar here. I just don't know where the entrance is".

"I don't know what you're on about" said Adrian, "but what is obvious is that something's going on here. Why are you so certain there is a cellar? Who are you really?"

"Easy on Adrian" smiled Siobhan, "goodness. It's not as if I'm accusing you of anything. It's just that I keep hearing stories about this house. In some of them there's a cellar. I've never been in here before. I love old places. I'm Irish for Christ's sake, we can make a story out of the fact that there's no story to tell".

"What are these stories you've heard. I thought you were just visiting a friend while your house was flooded? You seem well in with the shop and appear to know more about the village than I do".

"I never said it's my first time here" said Siobhan "I've been here loads. This time it really is because my house is flooded but I leap at any chance to come here. Beckie Miller is my oldest friend. We go way back to our university days".

"So how can you afford just to come here when you want to? What about family, work?"

"I can work anywhere" said Siobhan, "I'm a freelance writer so it doesn't matter where I am as long as I've a broadband connection and, as for family, they're all in Ireland or at least the ones I know about are. My dad used to travel a bit if you get my meaning".

"Is what you're working on anything to do with me or this house?" asked Adrian.

"Not a bit of it" grinned Siobhan "but you've now made me curious. Is there something about you that people might want to read about apart from you're a good-looking bloke living by himself and giving piano lessons and the sound of haunting violin music that reaches into the despairing loneliness of the night? Maybe I should be asking what's the story behind this? Where is Mrs Handsome stranger? Why is he keeping the cellar a closely guarded secret? For more read the next exciting instalment of Siobhan Walsh's gripping best selling thriller.

"If only there was something to write about but I'm afraid what you see is what you get with me, but you didn't actually say what you're writing about".

"Oh well" responded Siobhan, "you'd have found out anyway when your teenage girl magazine arrives. I'm doing a commission for a magazine. A teen thing on the growth of superstition among the young, especially girls, you know werewolves, vampires and the like. When I've done the groundwork I might also try my hand at a story about that. I've never written fiction, written about it but never got going on the real thing if that makes sense about fiction. I could use this cottage as the place where whatever it is happens".

"As long as you don't identify it" said Adrian, "the last thing I want is bus loads of teenagers besieging the place".

"You could write some scary music to go with my story" she said, "every story now has to have a utube video to go with it".

"Not me" said Adrian "but I'd be interested to read whatever you do write. So what's wrong with all the men you meet that a beautiful girl like you is unattached?"

"Attached" she said looking at him disdainfully, "is that how you see it?" Her face then broadening into a smile of second thoughts she said, "now you tell me that just as I'm about to leave and after I've been in your boudoir".

"I'm not going anywhere" said Adrian, "come back and see me another time".

Siobhan stepped forward and kissed him. In that moment he felt the full warmth of her lips, moistly fervent they were, promise rich in passion and seeming to bridge their worlds with a tender connectedness that resurrected the first forbidden kiss with another in a yesterday he had chosen to forget but that seemed to remember him too well to let go. The kiss that had changed everything, reincarnated. A sin reborn as itself. Then she stopped with the abruptness with which she had begun. She simply let go of his head, turned and left. He stood and watched her pedal down the road till the distance between them was great enough for him to feel able to move.

Adrian made his way back in. He picked up and shook the kettle to see if there was enough water in it, topped it up and put it on the range. At that moment the need to do something was strong. The routines that had held his life together, that had served him well by keeping him so occupied that he didn't know he had nothing of importance to do, suddenly seemed as empty as the kettle had been when he shook it.

Sitting caressing the mug of tea Adrian's head filled briefly with the melodic romanticism of a Schumann symphony but the tea he had hoped would medicate his mind had instead grown cold. He didn't know how long he had sat there. A lot had happened, nothing had happened. But something seemed to have changed. As so often before he found it was the small things that appeared to make the greatest difference. Perhaps because they seem manageable they allow us to be deflected into a new set of unplanned possibilities. He got up and brought his undrunk tea back to the kitchen. He stood looking around. Cellar, he thought, there can't be a cellar. No one before today had ever mentioned it.

Chapter 5

The Piano Stool

Gabriel Barrowman arrived by himself for the first of the planned twenty-one lessons. Since the first moment when his father had stepped aside and Adrian had set eyes on him that image of the boy had returned repeatedly to his head. It had not quite haunted him but it had persistently come back to him with a frequency that was gently intrusive and which had concerned him. Now once again the beckoning beauty of this palely fragile child stood before him.

Adrian invited him in and watched as he moved gracefully back into the room where they had met the previous day. He seemed to centre himself and turned back towards his teacher as though waiting for instruction about what to do next.

"Would you like to sit at the piano?" asked Adrian.

Gabriel did not speak but quietly went and positioned himself, assuming the same upright pose as before. Adrian moved closer and again stood by his left side. He looked at the reflection in the polished maple of the Steinway which created a more distant image like a sepia photo of someone trapped, perhaps lost forever, unable to emerge from the surface of the piano.

"The primary purpose of today" said Adrian looking into the reflection, "is for me to get to know you a little. To me all real teaching is a marriage of what the teacher has, whether that's knowledge or skill, with the precious uniqueness of the pupil". Christ, he thought, what a way to explain something to a child.

"My mother" said Gabriel, his interruption as effortless as his fingers resting on the keys were graceful, "… told me that there is no teaching only learning from another".

"Yet she sends money for music lessons".

"Yes" he replied, his tone still carrying resignation, even melancholy, "she sends the money that buys the time of the other. She said it is for the pupil to absorb and for the teacher to learn".

From their first meeting on the morning of his enchantment, just twenty-four hours ago, Adrian had been aware of how disturbingly un-child-like his pupil was. This was more than being adultified as too many of the others appeared to him to be, ensnared as they were in an empty parading of self-congratulatory, insufferable utterances they could little understand. His own mother would say to him variously that he had an old soul or an old head on young shoulders. He had not understood it but knew it was meant to make him special. And for a long time it worked. But it was against all nature. And in the end it failed him when the age of his shoulders surpassed that of his soul. Then it seemed like a betrayal. But what was it in this boy that made it different? Maybe it was the intolerable conjunction of beauty and sadness, yet this explanation did not fully persuade him. It now seemed to him more the endlessness of mourning for what can never be. That was certainly a pain he knew too well ever to be free of it.

Having said what he wanted to, Gabriel had gone back to silently looking towards him from the open lid of the piano, without any hint of impatience.

"Your mother must have been a very special person" he said. Gabriel absorbed his words.

"One day though not, I think, today I would like to know more about her" went on Adrian, "but for now it is time for music".

"She said music is what happens when the best of what words can mean is translated so that everyone can feel them".

"And I agree" said Adrian, "that is a good way of putting it. So let's see if we can begin to share feelings with each other".

He turned and picked up some music from the little table by the piano. He had chosen this in preparation for today. Now suddenly he realized he had not checked if his pupil could yet read music.

"Gabriel, he said, "this is sheet music. Reading it can give you access to all the feeling music has and that is all the emotional meaning in the world. Do you yet know how?"

"No" replied the boy, "my mother could. She was going to help me but then she wasn't there".

"Ok" said Adrian, "now we are going to set out together on an adventure like when you first learned to read words. Like all true adventures it will make your world bigger. When you first learned to read you were really learning to convert, translate was the word your mother used, the symbols on the paper into meaning. She was so right. Music is a language. The symbols we are going to look at tell you everything you need in order to play, even how fast or loud to make it. The notes are like the letters. They can be put together to make words that in music get called measures, which can be built into the phrases that are really like sentences. With the ear you have and your sensitivity this is not going to be too difficult for you because it is something you already know but just didn't know what it was called".

"I want to play today" said Gabriel. It was a tone Adrian recognized. He had heard him use it with his father.

"Good" he replied, "I think it will always give me pleasure to listen to you. I will play something for you then you can perform it. On other days I will point out on the music what you are doing".

Gabriel began to stand up to surrender the music stool to him, "no" said Adrian, "stay. I will get another one".

This was not something planned for today. But there was another piano stool. Moving across the room Adrian was unexpectedly conscious of lacking his pupil's grace. He went immediately upstairs to the attic. The door opened noiselessly to him where before it had groaned. He picked up the piano stool only seen the previous afternoon when Siobhan was having her tour but could not otherwise remember it. It must have been already there when the cottage rented. He vaguely tried to dust it as it was carried downstairs.

Gabriel had remained not just seated but with exactly the same posture he had when Adrian had left. He looked at the stool as Adrian brought it to the piano.

"I like that" he said, "my mother had one like that. Can I have that one?"

"It's dusty" said Adrian, "I will get it ready for you for next week".

Gabriel stood up and pushed the other stool into the position that Adrian would occupy at the piano. Adrian could not determine if he was being challenged or ignored. Whichever it was he would not have accepted it from any other pupil, at least not without comment. There would have been a felt need for some re-establishment of the natural order of things. Instead, with one last attempt to dust the seat with his hand, Adrian placed the stool for Gabriel to sit on. He then sat by him and, after a brief pause, began to play.

As he sat down and repositioned the piano stool a little, it had been in Adrian's mind that he would play from Chopin's Nocturne in E Flat Major. It was a passionate and energetic piece that he enjoyed both performing and listening to but instead found himself playing the Clara Schumann Piano Concerto. He had played only a few bars of this when Gabriel joined in. Adrian had seldom played a duet with a pupil, given the level of student he more usually had, apart from an occasional set piece that they had carefully planned and much rehearsed. He would normally have to be the primo and the student the secondo. Despite this he would need to have charge of the pedals. Now, without even having been told what was going to be played, this boy, more than coordinated, fused perfectly with him. It was as though it was a much prepared and practised performance. Though he had the pedals he did not feel he had charge of his legs. They moved when and as the boy needed them. He vaguely remembered when he had first driven a car with cruise control, that feeling that your will was lost to another as the car accelerates to its set speed. Though Clara's Concerto was not a long piece when they had finished an utterly drained and exhausted Adrian was drenched in a feverish sweat. He looked towards his pupil who had a calmly ecstatic, other worldly, almost sublime smile. He held this for some moments before turning to Adrian,

"My mother used to sit on a piano stool like this and play that. She liked it. Sometimes when I was alone at home I played it. I have not heard it or played it since. She told me that Clara gave up composing because she thought that women could not do it as well as men".

"Did she tell you that Clara was about your age when she composed it, at least most of it?" he asked.

The boy did not respond. Adrian did not ask him if he knew that Clara's mother had left her when she was five years old, leaving her in the care of her father.

"I think for Clara the problem might have been because she was married to Robert Schumann" he said, "and she was much younger. It was an age in which women had different roles. They could dabble in things but were not taken seriously, more seen as an unnatural curiosity when they could do things. I think Clara was the first female pianist on the circuit".

Still facing the piano Gabriel said, "thank you for playing with me".

"I am your teacher Gabriel but that was my pleasure, and it was a truly humbling pleasure. I don't know what just happened there. Have you played a duet before? You must have surely".

"Only with my mother" he replied, "we played that piece".

"Would you mind if one day we talked more about your mother, at least a little?" asked Adrian.

"She left" responded Gabriel, "what is there to say?"

"I know" responded Adrian, "your father told me. You were just about eleven years old. You must have been sad".

"I was sad before she left".

"Why? What made a beautiful, talented boy like you, sad?"

He hadn't wanted to say the word 'beautiful' aloud. That had just slipped out. Escaped from the cellar of his mind. He was old-fashioned enough to believe that most boys would not feel comfortable with it. Handsome, yes, possibly. Good-looking would have been ok. But withdrawing the word beauty, apologizing. That would make it worse. And in any case he couldn't take that word from his pupil. He was rescued from his dilemma by the boy.

"My mother said men will always find me beautiful and women strange" he said, "she told me it was a curse that can only be lifted by music. You are my teacher. Do you think she was right?"

"I don't accept such things as curses" he replied, "but if there were any powers like that, I would find it easy to believe that they could be defeated by music. I've always loved music. No one else in my family did but somehow it was part of me from the start. I suppose in a way all gifts can be seen as having a cursed side. My family couldn't understand why I wanted to learn music. My mother swanted me to be a priest".

"So why did you not do as you're mother wanted?"

"I always tried to" he replied, "so did you always do what your mother wanted? And what about your father?"

"My father always said my mother did not know what she wanted. She said he was only a good man, nothing more. She told me she knew how Pontius Pilate felt when he said 'I can find no fault in this man'. Then she left".

Adrian listened as attentively as though he were the pupil. Generally he was so good at compartmentalizing his life. 'The past is the past'. The words of his passively subversive father unearthed as though from a disturbed time capsule. Adrian hadn't talked about his own parents in such a long time. He didn't believe in unburdening and certainly not in the curative power of the confessional, particularly not to a boy. But Gabriel Barrowman was not just any boy. Even his mother thought he carried a curse. Though the choice of the word 'beautiful' could be seen as misguided, there was no denying that he was exquisitely pleasing to look at. Adrian simply couldn't believe that women wouldn't find that so. He did however know what she might have meant by 'strange'.

For seven years Adrian had lived in this village. He had chosen it almost at random from those he could see from the map were more remote. He was grateful to the geography teacher who taught him to read maps. He remembered that tall laconic figure standing by his desk and helping him. Using a physical map rather than an online search would leave no trace. That didn't always assuage the anxiety.

When an early pupil had achieved some minor success he had resisted having his photo taken with her, "it's her moment" he had insisted. He had grown more confident that the furore surrounding him was likely to have died down but it was the sort of story that could get rekindled. Human interest they called it. A 'where are they now' story. Not a who-done-it. They already thought that they knew that.

"I think it is time for me to go" said Gabriel.

For a moment Adrian experienced a new panic, a profound fear that the boy was bored or offended. What is it that makes losing the beautiful so egregious? What if this child no longer wished to be his pupil? It wasn't giving the rest of the money back. He could continue to make do. It was, he felt, the anticipation of the immortality of loneliness. That's what he had come to believe the absence of beauty in a life to be.

Sometimes Adrian felt that there was an unbreakable pact between fear and certainty that led to the belief that the worst you can imagine is bound to happen. For him blessedly this anxiety was dissipated when his pupil reprieved him by asking, "when can I come again?"

Tomorrow was Monday which meant Andrea Linkleader in the morning. For the first time in a long time it felt to him as thought his timetable was too full. Adrian knew that he wanted to see Gabriel again. As soon as possible. Ideally this would be on a day he had nothing else on. That meant Thursday, three whole days away. "Can you come on Thursday?" he found himself asking.

"Yes" replied Gabriel, "it is a school day but I do not like school. I like music. I think you…you understand me".

"School is important Gabriel" said Adrian half-heartedly, "do you want to ask your father?"

"He will agree with me" replied Gabriel.

"Why don't you like school?" he asked.

"Too many people" he replied, "there are always too many people, everywhere. All just faces. And the noise. It is not possible to see what needs to be seen. But now I must go. I will see you at ten twenty on Thursday".

"I'm not sure I understand all this or your way of choosing times" said Adrian.

"But you will be here?" said the boy.

"I will" he replied.

As he left, once again Gabriel shook hands and looked deeply into Adrian's eyes as though he could see something there that no one else could. It was a probing look, penetrating, unsettling. This was a truly unnerving pupil. Adrian returned to the living room and sat down looking towards the piano now with the two stools. It had to be more than the physical appearance, he thought, however sublimely beautiful. There was an effect here that was hard to pinpoint, that seemed to position itself always to be just out of grasp. But it was there, a vague uneerieness to what was happening, something perplexing. He was struggling not to think of his pupil as somehow other worldly, and all of this as some form of warning. That was his mother's way of thinking and one he thought he had long relinquished.

He didn't stay seated there long but got up and went to the piano stool that Gabriel had insisted on sitting on. He looked at it properly for the first time as an antique dealer might at a fare. It was still very dusty. It was a little time before he actually touched it. To his inexpert eye it was mahogany and probably 19th century. It had an upholstered seat that had once been patterned but he could no longer make this out. It had curved carrying handles and shaped legs. There were the remnants of gold paint in the frieze. What made it unlike any other he had seen was not that it had a storage area under the seat but that this one was lockable and indeed locked. He didn't want to force it but was intrigued. When he shook it something seemed to move inside.

Adrian carried the stool into the kitchen and brushed it with short sharp sweeps using the small green brush from the dust pan. The movements reminded him of his own father brushing dandruff from the shoulder of his suit jacket. He made no effort to get the dust into the pan instead coughing as it hit his lungs, bringing back to him that period as a child when he was thought to have asthma. The worried look on his mother's face as the family doctor had said this, became an unwelcome visitor to his mind.

Putting this from his mind Adrian got a knife from the drawer and tried to prise the seat open. It was quickly clear that it would require the sort of force he didn't want to use. The next plan was using a bent length of wire which was randomly wriggled in the small lock, though he had never achieved success with this approach with anything beyond a suitcase lock. But this one stubbornly resisted his efforts.

As he carried the piano stool back towards the teaching room there was a sound from outside. An old farm vehicle was clattering by. In an unasked for moment that sound catapulted him back to his schooldays and the headmaster walking along the corridors rattling his keys as he went. Even at the time this had seemed to him like biblical lepers having to call 'unclean, unclean' as they went about their lives. He didn't know where the bit about ringing a bell came from or if it had ever been so, but this schooldays flashback had reminded him of where he had seen keys. It was in the attic hanging from the broken coat stand.

Putting the stool down Adrian made his way up to the attic. The stairs still seemed to moan a little under his tread but the door that had opened smoothly the last time now offered more resistance and creaked dissent. Why had it started to do that again? Making his way directly to the window confirmed that the keys were exactly where he had remembered them. There was one very large ornate key, another about half that size, then three smaller ones and two very small ones either of which could possibly be the right size. It looked as though none had been in use in a long time. He re-examined the smaller ones. Yes, it could be. It was certainly worth trying.

Back down in the piano room he sat down and pulled the stool closer to him. Adrian selected the larger of the two smallest keys. It fitted. It was hard to get it to turn. He got some oil from the kitchen. As he brought it into the room he could hear his mother's voice saying his name disapprovingly. She would never have permitted such a thing in the drawing room of his childhood. He paused only fractionally then squirted some into the lock and put a little on the key itself. After some moments of jiggling, the lock seemed to turn. He sat back for a moment, then lifted the lid. It opened readily. There were retaining hinges on either side which seemed shiny enough to be new. He knew this could not be so. Perhaps the impression was given because they were free of dust.

On the inside of the lid was a piece of fabric with an embroidered number '7' somehow attached. Within the storage space itself were some pages of sheet music. Unlike the hinges these had dust on them. Picking up the first Adrian blew some of the powdery residue away then stiffened involuntarily. He was holding what seemed like a copy of Clara Schumann's piano concerto.

Adrian did not know anyone who hadn't at some time either been taken aback by a coincidence or who hadn't at least registered one. In the past the coincidences in his life had always been what they said on the tin. Chance occurrences of no significance. How often had he assuaged someone's anxious over interpretation with the words 'it's only a coincidence' as though that made all other possibilities unworthy of consideration? He placed the music respectfully to one side and looked at the other contents.

There was some more music all mostly for piano but were the early drafts of two violin pieces roughly outlined. He did not recognize these but knew in that moment that he would try to play them later. The very bottom of the storage area was unexpectedly covered in faded green velour like material. Perhaps it had been all the recent movement and struggling with the lock that made this come away at one end. There was something else underneath.

Careful removal of the covering revealed a small bundle of papers held together by faded green ribbon. Without knowing why, he hesitated for a moment before picking this up. It seemed to him to be in the form of diary entries but, if that was the intention, it was flawed in that there was only a day and month but no year. In so far as he could make out, the entries seemed to be written in conventional ink rather than biro.

There is something about reading the unpublished diaries of another without their consent that had the flavour of the voyeur about it. But it was not this that jolted Adrian. It was the date. Sunday 9th September – exactly today's date. How often does it happen that a calendar repeats itself in this way, he wondered? When put together with finding the Clara Schumann concerto which he had just played with Gabriel Barrowman, coincidence began to lose its entitlement to a fair trial.

Now, with full alertness to the irrationality of the belief that something at least unusual if not unnatural was going on, Adrian looked back at the page. Apart from the date, the diary entry, if that is what it was, appeared to be written in some form of code. He looked at the succeeding pages. They were dated but not sequentially. Whatever was being recorded did not occur every day but at approximately weekly intervals. The content was always in the same encoded form. Though without any idea of how to break a code he got himself a pen and pad and sat back on the settee. The one person he knew who could assist with this was from the past that was locked in another piano stool somewhere long ago and the key, he hoped, forever lost.

Adrian's efforts as a code breaker did not last long. He got up, put the music on the shelf of the piano, and went to the kitchen. He would use this piece that Gabriel knew so well to teach him to read music. The tea he made only set his head buzzing even more. He was like a man whose efforts to avoid sitting on the anthill had somehow caused him to knock into a hornet's nest. Now the beauty of his pupil conspired with the conundrum of the code to eclipse clear thinking. His head felt like Stalin's opinion of Shostakovich's McBeth, full of quacks, hoots, pants and gasps. Certainly it was presently more full of muddle than of music.

For the second time in two days Adrian left the cottage, again without locking it, to go for a walk. This used to be a part of his life that was important to him, whether alone or with another didn't matter to him as long as there were periods when there was no talking. He knew why he had stopped doing it. It was the same reason that he had felt the need to seek out somewhere else to live. Music was back in his life but with the penance of having to teach it, penance that was, apart from one pupil.

Today's walk took him along the path by the stream that welcomed him to the unpretentious chaos of nature's meadow. His mother would have thought that it was the waft of angelic wings that must have teased the grass to a curtsey as he passed but the smile visiting his face instead masked a clandestine image of his pupil. Then once again, with satanic sharpness, his mind's scythe cut smoothly through the bucolic scene, leaving fold after fold of blossoms that would surely die. No ceremony here, no perfumed ritual nor mass for the mourning, nothing but the cold, sharp sounds of an atonal and unforgiving reality.

Chapter 6

A B C D E F G

Adrian was rediscovering walking. He used to keep going till some instinct only as old as his feet told him to turn back. When he got it wrong it was like a law of diminished returns. Little warning pricks on his left heel were usually the first warning. He remembered his father reading him accounts of the myths as bedtime stories. His mother had not approved. The Bible was the only text needed.

The tale of Achilles was an early one that had stayed with him. Achilles's mother may have had the intention of making him invincible when she held him by the heel and dipped him in the Styx but she, like so many mothers since, had a lot to answer for. To be human is to be vulnerable. Of course he had always been able to accept that. How often were the words 'I'm only human' heard when someone had behaved badly or succumbed to temptation. The myths were a powerful code. He knew that he had to work hard to stop his regular excursions into them becoming a self-aggrandizing retreat. The sins of the more distant past are always more manageable than our own.

Today he had walked only for about half an hour when the other code was calling him back. There had been no epiphany in the fresh air, nothing had come to him to suggest any particular means of breaking it. His solitary thought had been that the Victorians had a flower code to pass messages of feelings, even of love. Apart from the now clichéd red rose he could remember only that daffodils represented unrequited love and purple violets told the recipient that the sender was occupied with thoughts of fondness and love for them. And of course he knew about green carnations, especially from Coward's operetta 'Bitter Sweet' and Oscar Wilde's wearing of the well-known symbol.

None of Adrian's musings had helped. They were merely what he did, not a strategy. He knew to crack a code, certain basic information was required such as who had created it and why.

His sense was that this particular coded challenge, though old, was unsophisticated, more designed to stop a casual reader from getting what it said than to stand the scrutiny of enemy codebreakers.

As a boy he had made up various secret codes. These were simple substitutions and wouldn't have taken an adult long to crack. To his mother, who had found one, instead of seeing it like the written equivalent of speaking in tongues, she declared it to be satanic. When she said 'there is no point Adrian, God always knows what is in your heart' he hadn't doubted it. It wasn't God he wanted to hide it from. She was standing in front of him. What might her opinion of him have been if she had known the lewd thoughts that preoccupied him when he was about the Gabriel's age? Such things hadn't any place in her plans for him. She had insisted on knowing what it said.

There was now a wryness to Adrian's smile of remembering as he recalled telling her it was just random letters he was going to leave for his teacher to find and waste frustrating hours trying to decipher. She had been angry at the disrespect this showed but had accepted it. The only cost was a handful of Hail Marys at his next confession when the telling of fibs was acknowledged. Fibs sounded so much less serious than lies. A casuist already at that age, he now thought.

Back at Magus Cottage a cheese and chutney sandwich being carried through to the living room was an unlikely continuation of parental defiance. Adrian again picked up the encrypted material. After some time he began to wonder if it was true that musicians were good at code breaking. If it was, then perhaps he wasn't a true musician. Maybe claiming to be one was just another deception in a life already rich in them.

None the less Adrian persisted despite knowing that inspiration was as rare as happy people in a therapy group. Another whole pad of paper. Two further hours devoid of success or enjoyment. He would have to come back to this. The violin music was retrieved from the piano stool and placed in front of Clara's concerto on the piano. Several attempts to play it proved as misguided as his code breaking. It just wouldn't work for him. Some days were like that. Old forms of negative thinking returned to him like a reflux. After a while he put down the violin and returned the music to the stool knowing he'd be drawn back to it, if only to understand whether it was the music or him. The chastising tones of his mother impatiently saying, 'sometimes not being able to give up is as much a sign of weakness as strength' he now heard as a parrot squawking from a perch to which it was attached by a golden chain.

As Adrian closed the lid the numeral '7' once more registered with him. Unless there were a number of such piano stools distinguished by numbers, what did this mean? He sat looking across the piano stool to the piano, imagining Gabriel sitting there like Pygmalion's enchanted ivory statue slowly coming to life and turning slightly towards him with a forever distant, possibly regretful, smile. His mother would have said he was bewitched. He fully recognized that he had been captivated even before the musical talent was revealed but what was less certain was what the boy might possibly have seen in him? Surely he must have been just like any other teacher. Yet the feeling was of a different level of connection, some redeeming purpose.

Passively Adrian watched as his absent pupil repeatedly played in short bursts, each time with apparently increasing vigour. After every demonstration Gabriel would turn and look back towards him with a questioning look in his eyes as if to ask, 'haven't you got it yet?' Then with an exasperated finality it registered with Adrian. 'The scales, seven notes' he almost called aloud, 'it's what it says on the inside of the piano stool. It's a mnemonic for the code'. When he glanced back at the piano stool there was no one there. Of course there wasn't, what was he thinking even to check?

Everyone knows, he told himself later, that our brains continue to work on problems when we are asleep, that we sometimes wake with a potential answer to some niggling or even more central question. There's nothing surprising or supernatural about it. Wherever the idea came from he immediately picked up the pad of paper and scribbled out the alphabet. Then under each letter he wrote a number. He would again try one of the oldest codes from his childhood, another simple substitution. Any letter from the original would be replaced by counting backwards seven letters. In this way the word boy would be rendered UHR. It wasn't long before Adrian experienced a moment of exhilaration, maybe even joy, as the first word emerged. He had the right key.

It was obvious that this exercise was going to take some time. Clearly someone more computer literate would create a programme to complete this task. That was unimportant. He was getting somewhere. It was some two hours before any consideration was given to having a break. There had not even been any thought of having anything to eat. Even the earlier sandwich was unfinished. Though there now was food in the house he simply made himself some toast which was hurriedly consumed then back to his task. He was speeding up a little by remembering the substitution for commonly occurring letters, the vowels to him now being TXBHN.

The more of the first entry that emerged the more Adrian could see the why a code was used. From some of the explicit comments he decided that the writer was more likely to be a male. He was now locked into the task.

When the phone rang he ignored it. He did this three times before feeling he had to answer it. It was Andrea Linkleader. Could she come early for her session in the morning? She had a dental appointment which had been arranged at short notice. Adrian hoped he was not sounding too impatient. He gave her the option of rearranging but she was keen to keep the frequency of lessons going. The piano, she said, was more and more important to her. She was listening to more music on the radio and watched any piano on TV. Her husband had complained that she was becoming possessed by it. It was agreed that her session would be brought forward by half an hour.

The call had reminded Adrian that nothing was yet prepared for her lesson. He wasn't that far from the end of the first dated entry. It would be good to finish that and get up earlier in the morning to sort the lesson out. So it was that his efforts continued for another hour, then it was time to sit back and read. It was astonishing. Not quite pornographic by the standards of the world he used to occupy but clearly exuded sexual feelings. He cringed as he realized that the subject of desire was having music lessons. She was the code maker's pupil.

He read his transcription:

'She arrived graceful as ever. I am enchanted afresh and blush that she might detect this. This gracious child has the face of a goddess and is of such slimness of frame that it is a wonder she is not fragile.

I am of the opinion that it will not be long before she turns to have the body of a woman. How spoiling that would be though I am more usually of a mind to wonder at the workings of nature. One day I know she will be the possession of another who will take all comfort from her.

I have spoken again of this matter with my good friend Samuel who counsels that all men have such feelings and that they will pass, yet I know in me that daily they grow stronger. I am suffocating in the delight it is to be in her presence. Her flaxen hair, her eyes of such green that the emeralds recoil in jealousy, her skin with the fragility of a newly opened flower and her long neck, swan like in its elegance. It would truly take a Rembrandt to seek to capture the essence of such a one as this, to do it full justice.

There are days she wears garments of such flimsiness that I believe I can see the form of her body beneath and at such times, as she sits at the piano and her skirts ride up a little I see the delicate turn of her ankle. This very day, when for the first time it was necessary for me to help correctly position her feet on the pedals, she bestowed on me the most sublime smile of thanks.

God willing she will develop feelings for me though I am myself but still young and an impecunious teacher of the piano and her guardian a man of much wealth. Yet does she fill my nights with the delights of her form and my dreams with the memory of her loveliness'.

Adrian read his transcription of the code maker's illicit desires twice. Having got up and placed the papers in the piano stool, he found himself locking it, lest anyone should think this about one of his own pupils, then he prepared for bed.

It was the night of the day of his first lesson with Gabriel Barrowman. Sleep was not going to be easy with Shostakovich playing mockingly in his head periodically giving way to a flamboyant rendering by the master himself of 'we all wear a green carnation now'. He wanted to spend time thinking of the duet he had played with Gabriel. How could it have been possible? No plan, no agreement, no rehearsal. But what merger, what playing?

Deliberately trying not to think of something is at best a contradictory thing to do. So no surprises that this held for the ornate piano stool and the sexual shadow of the deciphered diary entry. While he wasn't even sure he wanted to read the rest, he still felt a need to find out more about the writer of those words. Had what he was describing taken place in this very house?

In the image storm of such half dreamed reworkings one inevitably composes a medley from the fragments, perhaps in an effort to create the coherence, preferably harmony, they would otherwise lack. In this way is manufactured the raw form of something that might be crafted and developed, so as to generate at least the illusion of a greater sense of control. But that was not happening.

Earlier he thought he had heard a sound but had dismissed that as unlikely since it was coming from above him. Now he sat up in bed, almost sure he had heard something. There could be no sleep if he didn't find an explanation. In this village intruders just wasn't an option.

Adrian got out of bed and reached for his dressing gown but it was not in its usual place. He walked along the corridor to the stairs up to the attic not registering if they creaked as they normally did. Once more the door at the top opened silently. Standing, looking something like a silhouette of himself, he became aware of the cold state of his nakedness. In the attic space he could make out the frame of the window with the paleness of a part-moon furtively in the distance.

Remaining there for some time simply looking around, it seemed ridiculous to think there had been anything there. It's often hard to be sure of the direction of a sound. He could have been mistaken. If there was something it must have been outside.

It was just as he reached the conclusion that he'd probably made a mistake that, for a moment, he thought there was a movement, perhaps more a shadow passing. There was no sound. He tried the light again. Still nothing, even when the switch was flicked up and down several times. It wasn't easy at first to say what it was made him think something was different. Being careful not to trip over anything he moved across the room towards the window. Then he saw that the coat stand on which the keys had hung was lying on its side near the window. Perhaps, in his haste to get the keys, it had been destabilized and had later fallen. Surely that must have been the sound he had heard. But what was it that had made him think there was a movement. There was nothing else he could see. Was it possible that it was a random rearrangement of the clouds across the moon which had been somehow displaced and relocated in his thinking? Whatever it was, there was nothing to be done now. Beginning to feel the full extent of the cold, he moved back towards the door but as he got there it banged shut. A sudden draught, surely that was it, nothing more. None the less he stopped with the irrational unease that is twinned with the dark. The night has the power to conjure the primeval in us. Being naked makes everyone feel more vulnerable. For a moment the fear was that he might somehow have been locked in but the door opened readily then, just as he was leaving, the light flickered a few times and came on fully before again going out. The reasoning man in him checked the switch. It was in the 'on' position. Obviously a loose connection, much ado about nothing. As he turned to go downstairs he had a sense of more movement behind him but, when he looked round, there was again nothing. The genie of irrationality never willingly returns to its bottle.

Back in his bedroom his dressing gown was where it always was. He must have been half asleep when he tried to find it before going upstairs. Now in bed, sleep still wouldn't come. His head was overflowing with thoughts, firstly of Gabriel and then of the code maker's pupil. Somehow that other piano teacher was coming to contaminate his thinking. The feelings of that man for his pupil were just inappropriate. The appreciation of exceptional beauty was one thing, lusting after a young girl quite another. He began to wonder about the moral jeopardy in which that innocent child had found herself and with someone entrusted to teach her, especially one who should have been introducing her to the liberating gift of music. Had that teacher ever strayed beyond the attraction? It was one of those curious situations in which one wants to know something yet paradoxically does not want to find out, like waiting for a test result for some condition, especially one that could be incurable.

He spent an hour trying to put all this out of his head. To get to some level of sleep. Tomorrow there could be more decoding and of course there was Andrea Linkleader, who had a right to a full and pre-planned lesson. It was no good, he wasn't going to get to sleep. Swinging his legs out of bed and standing up he put on his dressing gown. Once downstairs the sense that having a hot drink would help, evaporated into uncertainty. Conventional wisdom, those words that he so despised, would have it that tea or coffee would be more likely to keep him awake.

Adrian went into the living room and sat on the settee looking at the piano stool. Struggling to put the possible contents of the next pages out of his mind, he chaotically planned the lesson for Mrs Linkleader. He admired the fact that she stuck with it though progress was slow. There was no doubt that she practised on an electronic piano keyboard at home. He had never himself adjusted to those. They had their place though and were both affordable and relatively easy to store.

Gabriel, on the other hand, could practise on the upright Bechstein his missing mother had inherited. He didn't know much about where he lived with his father. He really didn't know much about either of them or for that matter Celia, the daughter of a bishop, who had found it in her to leave that beautiful child behind. How could she when he was finding a few days absence painful? And that message, 'men will always find you beautiful and women strange'. What a thing to say to a boy of that age and what did it mean anyway? Did she find him strange? Ok, so he was a bit, even very, different but that's another matter.

Throughout his life Adrian had a dislike of judging people. Never, even when in a sense it had been part of his job, had he strayed into making this personal. Then came the time when he himself was judged. Even that was before the tragedy that had befallen him. There had been the fuss. The painful, intrusive publicity. He couldn't stay there anymore. Not by himself. When they were together he felt, really they felt, they could do anything as long as the other was there. Then Adrian had found himself with a detailed map of the country trying to find somewhere to go, somewhere he could be alone, somewhere no one would recognize him. So it was that this village had been chosen, then Magus Cottage. Now, according to Siobhan Walsh, there was some sort of story about this cottage too.

When he had made the decision to move here Adrian hadn't given much thought to how he would live. There had been an appeal to the cottage but to go so far as thinking it was drawing him to it was the sort of thing his mother would have said. None the less it had what at the time he had called a good feel to it, and could accommodate his piano. Only just, he now remembered, when it came to getting it into the room. His landlord hadn't looked at all happy. He seemed to think he should have been told there was a piano. A dog yes, thought Adrian, if he'd had one of those, people knew to ask about pets but who could have issues with a fine piano?

The love of music had been with him from the beginning. It was not the first time he had taught, quite enjoying it with individual pupils. Giving music lessons seemed the natural thing to generate some income. But he had not considered the problem of recruiting pupils in a small village. Asking parents to send their children to the home of a male stranger and then giving that stranger money. A tall order.

These extra waking hours were as unproductive as his time with Julie Moyer. At several points Adrian found himself diverted from the task of preparing for his ten o'clock now expected at nine thirty. Then with one final effort he decided that he had done enough. He would now get himself ready for his day. But the shower could not wash off the contaminating thoughts a previous teacher had for a pupil.

Chapter 7

Toothache

Not unexpectedly Andrea Linkleader was not her usual dedicated self. She arrived, hand to her left jaw like an improbable model for Rodin though, happily thought Adrian, she was fully clothed. Periodically she reassumed this pose, each time apologizing for interrupting her own playing. This was simply not going to work as a lesson. For a while Adrian played for her, demonstrating things that he thought she could practise on her keyboard at home. He offered her something to drink but she couldn't bear the thought of putting either hot or cold liquid in her mouth.

Adrian knew it's always harder to cope when there's nothing left to try. His mother had abhorred the evils of alcohol but had always kept some in the house for medicinal purposes. The only situation in which he had ever seen it used for was toothache. She would soak some cotton wool in whisky and get him to hold it on the affected tooth. Now he suggested this to Andrea. She looked disbelievingly at him but then nodded. He didn't have any cotton wool. He considered using kitchen paper but felt this would disintegrate. Reassuring Andrea he would be back in a minute he went up to his bedroom to get a clean cotton hanky. As he went into his bedroom things just didn't feel right. For one thing his dressing gown was no longer hanging up but lying on the unmade bed. Maybe he'd misremembered that. It wouldn't be the first time. Then there were the very few toiletries on the chest of drawers. Surely he hadn't left them like that. He shook his head. There really wasn't time to puzzle over it. What was he allowing to happen to his own thinking?

Back downstairs he soaked a fold of hanky in whisky and gave it to Andrea telling her to hold it to her tooth. She did as he suggested and gave a muffled thanks then, looking steadfastly at him, held it in place. They kept up this uneasy silence for a short while then Adrian asked if she would like him to play for her. She nodded.

He went to the piano and this time pulled up the ornate stool favoured by Gabriel. He played Grieg's piano concerto. It had always seemed to him to have a relaxing quality to it, indeed even in his previous incarnation he had often recommended recordings of it to others who were stressed or had difficulty sleeping. To him the music had a rich poetic quality that evoked soft lyrical delights but with a reflective, gently melancholic second movement. He found it difficult to understand why Debussy had once called Grieg 'a pink bon bon wrapped in snow'. There was to him a calming strength to this masterful work. When he had finished playing more than half the lesson time had elapsed. Andrea applauded, "wonderful" she said, "I don't know if it was the whisky or the music but my tooth isn't hurting so much". He half turned round on the piano stool and thanked her. His offer to continue the lesson was declined.

"I'd give anything to play like that. Who wrote it?"

He explained that it was the only piano concerto that Grieg had completed.

"Why?" she demanded, "if only I could write like that I wouldn't be able to stop myself".

"Well" responded Adrian, "my view is that he didn't do more in that vein as he produced that one in the euphoria of the birth of his daughter Alexandra".

"He should have had more kids then" retorted Andrea.

"He couldn't, they couldn't" he responded. For some reason he felt he couldn't tell her that Alexandra had died just over a year later. Instead he went on to say, "but he continued to write other great music. In Denmark, he's a national hero".

Andrea responded, "I didn't know he was Danish".

Though this comment unnecessarily offended Adrian he couldn't afford to alienate any student.

"Perhaps" he said "you're thinking because he had a Scottish granddad they should claim him".

"I didn't know that either" she replied, "I did meet a Scottish bloke the other day. He doesn't stop talking that one. He'd come to collect our lawnmower for repair. It had just stopped working. Franklin's always services it. Nice fella though, the Scottish bloke. He saw my keyboard. He said he had a son who came to you".

"He does" said Adrian, immediately reminded of the interconnectedness of village life, "have you ever met Gabriel?"

"I haven't but Mrs. Ruddick knows him. Well I say knows him, knows of him. Her girl's in the same class. Apparently he's a strange boy, that one".

"He's gifted" said Adrian breaking his own rule about not talking about his pupils to others. He immediately wanted to get off the subject, "the Barrowmans are new to the village. You must know everyone. How long have you been here?"

"I was born here then left" she replied, "I only came back when I was pregnant with Adam. I wanted to be near my mother for support then she went and died on me".

"That's sad" said Adrian.

"It was a blessing in a way" responded Andrea, "she was in a lot of pain. They couldn't do anything for her. She did live to see Adam though. That's something I suppose".

"Did she live with you in the end?" he asked.

"No she died in her own bed in her own place. That was up this end too. This is the original part of the village you know. The water pump was up this end. As you know that's only an ornament now".

"To my shame I've never gone fully into the history of the village" he said "but I've only been here seven years. That makes me a new boy".

She smiled at him, "unless you go back generations you're an incomer. Sometimes a family has lived in a place so long they say anyone who takes over is cursed, like this place". She immediately looked embarrassed at what she had just said and apologized, "sorry Mr Grayling, I really didn't mean that to come out that way. Just the sort of things the old folk say, you're an educated man. None of that would worry you".

"It doesn't, you're right" said Adrian, "but it does interest me. I don't really know the history of this cottage. I know there have been a few tenants before me but none have ever stayed. Do you know anything about it?"

"Just a bit. Only the gossip" she said, "now if you really want the lowdown you'd have to talk to Old Kennedy but he doesn't say much to anyone nowadays. He's like a walking history book except that he doesn't walk much either these days and he doesn't always make sense. His granddaughter's the only one who visits and that's not very often".

"What's old Kennedy's first name?" asked Adrian

"Goodness" replied Andrea, "now you're asking. I don't actually know. Everyone's just called him Kennedy as far back as anyone can remember and now just Old Kennedy".

"And this house" asked Adrian, "what do you know about it?"

"It's not haunted if that's what you're afraid of. It was. They did one of those things with priests and bells and the like, to get rid of it".

"An exorcism" said Adrian feeling incredulous.

"Yes, that was it" she said, "what you called it".

"What was it?" he asked, "what did people feel was happening here that they needed all that medieval stuff?"

"It's not really my place to talk about it. My mother used to say if you talk about curses they come after you. She was a bit funny like that. Believed a lot of stuff. What do you think?"

"Things like that are true only if you believe them" said Adrian, "people don't believe true things, believing something makes it true for them".

He was going to go on to say that's the big limitation of belief, its disadvantage over its arch enemy evidence. Evidence defines something as true even if no one believes it. He didn't really want to get into that sort of discussion anymore and certainly not with Andrea Linkleader. Sometimes he missed it though.

"Well I'm not sure I understand that" said Andrea, "but anyway if you must know, the Sinclairs were the family that lived here for generations, no more than that. What people said is that every so often one of them wouldn't turn out to be like the others".

"Not like the others" interrupted Adrian, "in what way?"

"I don't really know all that detail. Don't get me wrong. They weren't like monsters or anything. It's always been said they were very beautiful. All the Sinclairs were but every so often there was one… well it was like some sort of changeling in the form of an angel. But everyone knew the Sinclairs were an irreligious bunch at the best of times. The thing is some of them weren't very beautiful inside. My mother used to say they were unnatural, 'otherlings' she called them".

"So what was it, what was so unnatural about them?"

"I don't know" replied Andrea, becoming a little more uncomfortable, "I've no idea how they were so unnatural. It's just the way things were talked about in those times. The Sinclairs were used to frighten children you know like, 'if you keep doing that you'll turn into a Sinclair', or the 'Sinclairs will get you'. You know the sort of things they say. I'd never do it to mine, scare them like that".

As Andrea talked she suddenly called out in pain and put her head back to her jaw, "see" she said "even my teeth don't like me talking about them".

"We don't have time for more music" said Adrian "but we can experiment again with the whisky". He picked up the hanky she had used before and again dipped a portion of it in the whisky.

"Thanks Adrian" she said, as she positioned it back in her mouth but at exactly the same time she almost physically jumped, as the doorbell sounded in the hallway.

"Christ, that scared me" she said, "that'll be my husband to drive me to the dentist".

She picked up her handbag to get some money out. Adrian half-heartedly tried to protest that she hadn't actually had a lesson. He was pleased when she insisted on paying.

Mr Linkleader was a plump man who should have had a round face to go with this but instead his whole head struck Adrian as more like a cube. The effect was almost comical. Andrea introduced him, "this is Mr Linkleader" she said but obviously assumed he would know who Adrian was. Adrian for his part stretched out his arm to shake hands,

"Adrian Grayling" he said.

"Mr Linkleader is a builder if you ever need one" said Andrea, "a very good one".

"Excellent" said Adrian, "always good to know".

"Mr. Grayling's interested in this house" went on Andrea.

"Really" said the builder, "it's for sale is it? Well who would have believed it? I thought that family would let it rot first".

"No, not to buy it" said Adrian, "I'm interested in its history".

"You too" said Linkleader, "it stood empty half the time till you took it on and now everyone wants to know its history".

"Who else?" asked Adrian.

"Some woman" he replied.

"Do you know her name?"

"Sorry mate. I'm no good with names. Anyway I've got to get Mrs Linkleader to the dentist".

"See you next week" called out Andrea as they left, "and I'll bring the hanky back, washed of course".

"You don't want to go believing all that stuff she'll have told you about this place if you ever want to sleep at night that is" added Mr Linkleader.

"I'm not a superstitious man" said Adrian.

"Maybe you should be" replied Mr Linkleader.

Chapter 8

The Water Pump

The regularity had gone from the days of Adrian Grayling. After the first difficult years having moved to the village things had settled into a pattern. As his savings had dwindled providentially he had begun to have more pupils for music lessons. Generally these would take place after school hours or weekends with younger ones or in the mornings with adults. Most of his child pupils were girls and both of his adult pupils women. In so far as he knew he had built up a respectable reputation for some degree of success. Pupils did move up grades and their parents mostly wanted them to continue their lessons.

The first part of the afternoons had largely been his own time. He did what little housework there was to do, read and listened to music. He had even tried a little composing. The pattern that was established had itself become his bulwark against the past which would otherwise have laid siege and overwhelmed him. Now that was changing. There was a sense of something new and dangerously disruptive at work. His name was Gabriel. He felt he was becoming obsessed with this pupil. He tried not to think that he was being somehow possessed by him. That sort of thinking was worthy of Andrea Linkleader or his mother.

He had now come to accept that, in village lore at least, something had happened here. However long ago he had no idea. Something of its time that had worried people enough to want an exorcism, though in his experience that was not likely to take much. But it had to be something that persuaded the church to go along with the ritual, that is if it was the full thing, a major exorcism. No, he felt that his reaction to his pupil was the very human reaction of any sensitive mortal being exposed to sublime beauty. There was nothing creepy about it, certainly nothing perverted. Beauty was beauty. Not everyone was gifted with the capacity to recognize it. Mere intimations of beauty could lead the unwary to think there was something supernatural about it. It certainly wasn't unnatural in the sense of that which would turn it into some sort of freak show. Gabriel was simply an extraordinarily beautiful boy. There was nothing synthetic or in any way inappropriate about how pleasing it was to look at him. No, what he was having difficulty with was not the fact of this boy's appearance, it was more than the aesthetic, it was straightforwardly its intrusive impact on him. When he lay in bed at night the image would come gently into his awareness and from there to his dreams. Often too in the forgiving light of the music room he would look around and see him sitting at the piano, half turned towards him, a smile ruefully latent on his face. But perhaps most powerfully of all he longed for the pupils arrival for his next lesson.

Today was Tuesday. Timothy Paulson had come and gone. He could hardly remember the session. He knew some people found religious devotion in the young something enchanting, even reassuring. He had long since found it artificial, unctuous, at best saccharine and inherently insincere. Why couldn't Timothy be like other kids? There were superheroes aplenty out there. When Adrian had mentioned superheroes, Timothy had immediately described Jesus as a superhero. As he did so Adrian thought he could hear the ancestral voice of the child's grandfather. Ok so he hadn't met him but he'd heard enough about him. When Adrian had politely asked in what way Timothy found Jesus a superhero the child had beamed up at him, "he dies every day to save others and comes back to life. He has the power to see through people. He willingly bestows the gift of everlasting life even to the poor and fallen, he…".

Adrian managed to interrupt the flow. "and he fed the multitude with bread and fish. So Timothy, tell me what do fish have?"

"Scales" responded the child.

"Exactly" said Adrian, "did you know that in honour of that miracle since then people learning music have practised scales which is what you are going to do today".

Lessons with this child often seemed to drag. He was sure this one must have been more than an hour though it had been planned as a normal session. Timothy had wanted to sit on the piano stool used by Gabriel. Adrian had rather clumsily refused to allow that. He then tried to recover the situation by explaining that the stool had special qualities, something that would bestow everlasting grace on the person who played as they sat there. "You are too young for that but perhaps one day, if you practise" he had explained. Timothy had seemed impressed and motivated.

In keeping with the flavour of the session the saintly child's aunt had been late picking him up. Now Adrian was free to do what he wanted with the rest of the day. It was a long time since he had walked around the village. He obviously hadn't been very observant before. So Magus Cottage was in the old part. It had previously all seemed to him of one time. But yes, as he went along he could see it a little more clearly. He nodded to a man with a small dog on a very long leash. "Good afternoon sir" the man had replied then added, "it's strange times we live in" but moved on without saying anything else or giving Adrian a chance to check what he meant. As he went passed the shop down towards the Mitre he stopped to examine the ornate water pump. Victorian he thought. He took hold of the handle but it wouldn't budge. A voice behind him said, "if you're that desperate the pub's just here".

"Hello Siobhan" he said before turning round, "I normally hear your bicycle bell".

She was leaning on her bike. She now rang the bell.

"Oh there you are" he said almost as though she was one of his child students.

She smiled, "so are you going to buy me a drink then?" she asked.

"I would" he said "but you're not going to believe this".

"You've no money with you" she hijacked his sentence, "fortunately I do" she went on.

"I couldn't".

"That's what they all say. It started with a simple twenty pence debt and spiralled till you were in the control of the lenders. Come on. It's only what men have always done to women".

"So that's what men have always done to women. I was wondering" he responded.

She took him by the left arm with her right hand and, wheeling her bike with her left, steered him toward the bar. He simply let her do this. She leaned her bike against the wall and went in. There were only three or four others there. He did not recognize any of them. They sat in the corner seat he normally occupied.

"What are you going to have?" she asked.

"A half of Antique Ugly" he said reflexively. He wasn't in the habit of drinking at all at lunchtime and seldom enough during the evening. He was still musing on how he'd got from just going for a quick walk round the village to sitting in a bar with an attractive woman buying him a drink when she returned with a large glass of white wine for herself and a pint of Antique Ugly.

"Doesn't anyone in this village understand the concept of half?" he began ungraciously, then said "thanks Siobhan".

"I did ask for a half but she said you always have a pint. I didn't know you were an habitué" she said.

"I'm not" he said then realized he was sounding defensive. He picked up his glass, angled it slightly towards hers spilling a fractional amount and said "cheers".

"Slainte" she responded bringing her glass into contact with his, "this was a bit of good luck".

"Sometimes I think the Irish make whatever happens, their luck" he said.

"Talking about that" she said, "I had a dream about you the other night. After I saw round your place, and thank you for that Adrian".

He took a sip of beer and asked, "seeing round or the dream?"

"Both" she grinned, "and don't embarrass me by asking what the dream was about or I'd be saying 'Hail Marys' for a month".

She's flirting with me again, thought Adrian. It was a long time since he had been in a pub with any woman let alone one as sparky and attractive as Siobhan Walsh. He was enjoying it. He wasn't sure what was in it for her but she had kissed him last time.

"I wonder what the collective noun would be for a month of Hail Marys" he said, "maybe a veniality".

The inaccessibility and poor quality of his effort embarrassed him as soon as he said it. He was out of practise. She laughed anyway. That was at least a good sign that she wanted to please. Flat jokes are a greater damper in any social setting than flat beer.

"Since you're the music teacher with a secret story, I would have thought a sinphoney would have been the word" she said looking straight at him, then added, "sometimes I think of you all alone rattling around in that cottage. Don't you ever feel in need of company?"

He didn't want to say 'no' and have to explain further, he certainly didn't want to get into explaining why he's alone, so he said "sometimes. What about you?"

"You've asked me about that before" she replied "I'm not alone. I'm staying with Beckie. Maybe you're not sure if I've a partner? It'd be very prudish of you to care. It's my life Adrian. That would be a decision for me".

"Sorry Siobhan" he said "that was a bit clumsy. It's just that you're a very attractive young woman. It's natural for me to wonder about your motives".

"Thank you for the compliment" she said "but let's just think about it. We've already established that there'd be no point in being after you for your money, so the only things left are free music lessons and your body. The problem with the music lessons is they'd take too long".

"And you think my body won't?" he said.

Siobhan laughed, "well if you take as long as you do over a pint you may be right. Drink up, let us eat drink and be merry".

"For that shall abide with him of his labour the days of his life, which God giveth him under the sun. Ecclesiastes 8 v 15" said Adrian finishing his pint in one go. He was about to stand up when Gwyneth brought the same again to the table.

"Hello Adrian" she said, "and it's not even Thursday. Nice to see you out actually enjoying yourself for a change. Now don't go taking advantage of this young lady".

"Thanks Gwyneth" said Siobhan, "just put it on my tab".

"Already done" said Gwyneth then returned to the bar.

"You had arranged this?" said Adrian looking at the pint of Antique Ugly before him and Siobhan's glass of white wine.

"I didn't want to have to go to the bar twice" she grinned, "and since you were kind enough to owe me for a drink I had to reciprocate".

"That doesn't make sense" he said.

"That's because you haven't drunk it yet" she replied "anyway we've lots to talk about".

"Talk about?" he queried.

"Yes" she responded, "it's good for my reputation to be seen with an attractive, ever so slightly older man". She picked up her glass and again said 'Slainte'. He responded in the same way. She then asked, "no progress on finding the cellar?"

"No" he said, then added "not that I've actually been looking. It's just that I've never seen a door. What makes you so sure there's a cellar anyway?"

"I need it for my story" she said "and I've talked to people about your cottage".

"Anyone in particular?" he asked.

"People generally but there is one in particular I think I need to talk to. I don't know if you'd know him especially as, when I ask people about you, they say either that you keep yourself to yourself or that you're a recluse who gives music lessons. You've become a nearly invisible man in a village in which me riding my bike too fast is news. I can't think of you as invisible but there is something. I haven't decided which rumour to start".

"You haven't said which one in particular you asked about my cottage?" he repeated.

"There's an elderly guy everyone calls Old Kennedy" she said.

"Yes, the one who was never Young Kennedy but was previously just Kennedy".

"You do know him. Perhaps you're not such a recluse after all".

"I know of him. From one of my piano students, the builder's wife".

"Daniel Linkleader" she said the distaste dripping from her words, "that bodger, still handy with his hands if you get my meaning".

Adrian had an almost cartoon like image in his mind of the plump, cube headed builder, "so you were the beautiful woman asking about Magus Cottage" he said.

"Is that what the creep said?" she asked, the source of the compliment apparently immediately devaluing it.

"So did you learn anything?"

"Only that some of the cottages did have cellars. It was usually the ones with attics. Topping and tailing he called it".

"That's what they used to call it when I had to share a bed with a visiting cousin when I was a boy".

"Male or female?" she asked.

"Always male", he responded, "you obviously don't know my mother. All women were lustful beings bent on seducing men".

"That's a bit of a generalization. I only seduce the attractive ones. You can call me Jezebel".

"First Kings Chapter 16" he said reflexively.

"Kings will do so long as they're not too old" she grinned, "you seem to know a lot about the Bible".

"Not me" he said, "my mother. Fanatical".

"And your dad" she asked opportunistically.

"More subversive. A worshipper of Baal" he replied, "so Daniel Linkleader didn't say anything else?"

"No"

"Nothing about the Sinclairs?" he asked.

The look on her face when he mentioned the Sinclairs was revealing, "the Sinclairs?" she asked "what do you know about them?" He thought she was trying to sound casual.

"Not much but from the look on your face you obviously know something. All I know is that they originally lived in Magus Cottage and there were rumours about them, so what's your take on them?"

"I don't know much more than you" she said, "there are some local stories but I suspect there's more to be found out. Old Kennedy might be able to fill us in if he talks to us, or me at any rate".

"Why just you? Why do we both not see him together?"

"I don't know Adrian. It might be a bit overwhelming for him. He's only expecting me".

"I didn't know you already had an appointment with him".

"My friend Beckie knows him through her dad when he was alive. Her Dad and Old Kennedy had known each other for yonks. She's got an emergency key for his place. She keeps an eye on him. She arranged for me to see him on Thursday morning".

In that moment Adrian knew that there was no point in pressing matters. He was not prepared to sacrifice his time with Gabriel Barrowman.

"Why don't we meet afterwards to discuss it" suggested Siobhan, "we could meet here at lunchtime?"

"Make it the evening and I'll buy you a meal".

"It's a deal" she smiled at him "and I'll bring my purse. Just in case".

"Sorry about today" he said still sounding a little embarrassed, "I was just walking down to the water pump and you came along like a beautiful water nymph and lured me away. Thursday I will pay for everything".

She put her hand on his and smiled her easy smile at him, "maybe you won't need to pay for absolutely everything" she said. She raised her wine glass "till Thursday at seven" she said.

Adrian repeated her words then added, "Thursday's child has far to go".

"Not very" she responded, "just down the road and I have a bike. I was actually born on a Thursday though".

"It ought to have been a Monday" said Adrian.

The rapid fire of duelling compliments, innuendo that would make double entendres seem of virginal simplicity and of small talk about big things, continued with such effortless fluency that he had not wanted it to end. It had been a long time since Adrian had enjoyed the company of another in this way. That night he had another dream. Not as he might have wished about Siobhan. After years of not recalling any dreams now they were coming more frequently. Twice recently he had woken in the night to an unknown but familiar sounding tune coming, he thought, from the attic. The first time it had been sufficiently convincing for him to go up there but again nothing. Dreaming perhaps? He must have wrongly thought it was the music that awakened him rather than wakening from the music. But what was that piece that sounded more like a lament?

Chapter 9

Tzigane

In Adrian's mind the water pump and Siobhan were now as inextricably linked as the image of Gabriel Barrowman was to some sort of classical ideal of beauty. He had returned from the pub with Stephen Dunstone's Water Nymph music playing quietly in his head. He liked harp music but had never played a harp. Sometimes it was just the right instrument. Maybe it was the association with Ireland that now brought it more to mind.

The two pints of Antique Ugly had a less disruptive effect than the previous time he had less. He smiled to himself when he thought of the implications of that. It did have character. Strong but not overpowering. Maybe he should suggest that they change the name to something more mellow like Siobhan's Harp. Though any amount of alcohol at lunchtime made him sleepy he was determined not to succumb. Flirting with Siobhan had made him feel younger, more like the old days. And he had found himself aroused by her. When she had touched his hand and said he would not have to pay for absolutely everything in that lighthearted way of hers, the deliberate inviting, sheer obviousness of it, played tantalizingly with his feelings. How long had it been since he last allowed himself to believe good things would happen again though he still remembered how ingenuous flirting had accelerated to something tragically sublime.

Adrian had been in two minds about whether he would ever go back to the coded diary in the piano stool. He sat looking at the ornate outline of the object for some time before picking up the keys, getting out the previous decryption and reading it again. Once more it troubled him. None the less he got his pad and pen and sat down and began work.

The plan was to try to concentrate on a word by word basis like some cryptographers calque. It was a process that started slowly but speeded up somewhat. It was only when he had finished the entry that he rather more threw than put his pen down and began to read.

'*She has arrived this day looking more wan and lovely than before, her hair full flaxen fair it was, inviting my hand to touch it. She did not seem to mind when I picked it up and let it again drop to cascade around her neck. I told her I would buy for her a ribbon of the deepest crimson for her lessons with me to keep her hair out of her eyes. Nor did she protest when I brushed an imagined piece of dust from the delicacy of her shoulder.*

Just touching her in this innocent way reaches into me with such force that it aroused in me feelings such as I have seldom experienced before.

Today I told her I had a need to hear her singing voice for the proper evaluation of what we should do next. It pleased me greatly to say we. She would, I said, need to stand for the best effect to be achieved. Oh joy. I do not understand why I had not thought to ask her to sing before. So it was that this angel stood before me and sang notes of such innocent delight as she is yet pure. She could not know the ecstasy of gladness she caused in me, how moved my body and how enriched she made my very being. No mortal man, made as we are of flesh and bones, could fail to surrender to the temptations of this goddess, planted here among our kind. To resist would be to deny the naturalness of our existence and the sanctity of true love. Why should another have her who could not, in all earnestness, begin to match the fervour in me? Why should it be that mere position or rank or crude fullness of purse should have such unjust ascendancy?

I can see in this maiden a wholesome need of one with youth and vigour to bring to a timely fulfillment the complete and enduring expression of her translucent beauty. It is as though she is the very incarnation of Jonson's words for she has surely drunk to me only with her eyes and I have pledged with mine and if she would but leave a kiss within the cup I would have no need of wine.

One day I will have her to sing his words to me. Though her years be tender I have it in me that her heart has a fullness of womanly understanding and, while I live, no man shall harm a hair of her golden head. God, in his infinite wisdom has brought us together and no man shall put us asunder.

I have this day adorned my piano with the reddest of roses I could pay for, to express in their natural language what I cannot yet rightly do in mine. My good friend Samuel tells me that young maidens are to be had for the price I paid for these roses with only the knowing of where to go and without the pains of delay and cost that I can ill bear.

Though he has not yet said it with his accustomed and true frankness, for he would not trust it to the page for fear of ill use or misunderstanding of his words, should anything befall the object of his desire, I can tell he has the full knowing of that of which I speak when I talk of my insufferable pain. Ofttimes a savagery walks with true beauty and carries with it a desperate cruelty that does not let a man speak plainly of his heart's desiring. Those who have never known a love such as this, seek to guard against better men achieving the bliss that nightly beckons to me when she comes and stands in spectral anticipation by my bed. Such men have satanic aims about them for love is the true and enduring enemy of evil.

Her lips I know will have the tenderness of dreams about them, her nakedness has not yet been brought to nature's intended true caresses and, in the abundant starlight that overflows from her eyes, I can see pleading for what will come and it brings the sparkle with which she means to light my way to her heart. Oh lucky maiden who will feel the rich fulfillment of love that would take up the sword and die guarding against any cause that brought but one tear to mar the perfection of her skin. Yet do I hold fire on the making of my true vow known to her till I am ready and she will embrace me in all freedom.

I have but one desire, to offer her the everlasting protection that all such perfection should have as a birthright.'

Adrian stopped. He had read the fruits of his decoding. He did not feel he needed to check it. The meaning was already clear. He did not know the name of this young man but he had come again to detest him because he shamed beauty with lust. He wondered once more if he should burn this material but instead again placed it in the piano stool and locked it.

The words however would not let him be. There could be no hiding from them. He needed someone to talk to as a diversion but he had no good friend Samuel. Spending time with Siobhan had reminded him how alone he was, of what had changed since it all happened. One continuity was music. From before the time that memories were separate things and since then at all important moments in his life, that had been his great solace. Despite this he had only recently tried his own hand at composing. He wondered if it was the process of creating that got him thinking of how things could be.

Now he again got out the work for violin that was slowly in progress. He tried to play what little he had achieved. It was to him all just too derivative. It lacked flair, certainly originality. Sometimes he felt he would never produce original work. There was just too much of other people's music in his head. That must, he thought, be true of all composers. All great works must have reflections and echoes. He put down what he self mockingly thought of as his score and went back to the piano stool and retrieved the part written work from there.

Once more he found it impossible to get into playing it. On the page it looked a bit like Tzigane which he knew to be a difficult piece. He had never fully mastered it to his own satisfaction. His playing felt and sounded sluggish. It crawled miserably when it should be a frenzied, abandoned dance. It was sometimes said that Ravel had worked closely with the violinist Jelly d'Aranyi when she had commissioned it. Adrian knew that Ravel shared with him a certain slowness to work. He had put this down as due to a perfectionism in them both though a seriously misplaced one in his case. Ravel might not have produced that much but what he had was masterful so that he had been able to say "my only mistress is my music".

If he was being honest Adrian could not make this claim, important though music was to him. Religion had once also been important to him. Unlike Ravel whom he knew to dislike the showily religious in music, he could still listen to that but as music not as an act of worshipful surrender.

He put his violin back on the stand and sat down again at the piano. He needed to reclaim some sense of musical competence. He had not forgotten the decoded second diary entry. It would not let him. In it had been mentioned 'Drink to me only'. That classic mix of old folk song and poem had long been a favourite. Could that be a coincidence? It was in danger of being contaminated. He didn't want that to happen. It needed to be repurified. He found himself drawn to make an arrangement for piano.

Only once he had completed this was Adrian willing to stop.

For a second time the unplayable piece was now safely in the music stool. But securing the piano stool did not succeed in locking his thoughts. His past life had begun to creep up on him like someone with amnesia slowly able to recall things. Perhaps he shouldn't fight it. Why not just let it in again? Get angry with it. With himself. He was well aware that, once upon a time, he had counselled people to come to terms with the past. He no longer liked thinking in that way. It was too much like the terms of a surrender, victory for an old enemy. The past in this moment was a many headed hydra that needed to be slain before the future could be his kingdom. But he was no Hercules. Now glancing back at the piano stool for another timeless moment of his present, Adrian saw Gabriel sitting there still wearing a smile like a sad halo.

The supernatural was another ancient foe but one that seemed to him independent of time. He stared languorously at the now unoccupied piano stool for such a long time that the space between his pupil and he became filled with the scented softness of incense that held him in a place between the worlds of memory and dreaming.

Chapter 10

A capella

It was Thursday morning. His Wednesday had seemed to drag. He could remember little musically of Julie Moyer's contribution to the session though that was hardly surprising. She had again wanted to rehearse for her improbable recital and had asked him to play on the Stradi she had bought for him, 'to give her inspiration' she had said. He had gone along with this. He had played the solo violin piece from Schindler's List.

"You remembered" she had said, her cloying tone seeming to him like the stickiness of spilled orange juice congealing on the floor.

"Yes I remember it" he had replied, though he had no idea what in particular she was talking about.

"How many lessons ago was it that I told you how much I liked that film?" she asked. It was only then that he made the connection.

"The John Williams' score" he said evasively, "truly shows the emotional tone music can add to a film but for me it was the playing of Itzhak Perlman that made it one of the most moving pieces I have ever heard in a film".

"I am so pleased you remembered it" she again gushed, "you are such a sensitive man. Not like some others I could name. I could stay here forever just listening to you".

Finally she had left. 'Forever' was over for that week. It had been necessary for him to position himself carefully away from her as she seemed to be posturing to kiss him as she departed. And he hadn't at all liked the sound of that 'could stay forever' bit.

Now it was almost time for Gabriel to arrive. Last night he had again dreamt about this pupil. In the dream the boy was in trouble and needed help. He was frantically stretching out his hand toward Adrian who was desperately trying to get to him but Gabriel always seemed to be moving further and further away accompanied by a musical crescendo that never achieved a climax.

His other problem was that he had great difficulty in planning what they should be doing today. There was something about this boy that made each session potentially like a final one. What was missing, he realized, was that he didn't actually feel he knew him. His private agenda was to learn more, his musical agenda to see how far he could be stretched.

When the bell rang Adrian immediately opened the door. Gone was any pretence of not waiting there. He looked once more at the boy.

"Hello" he said then repeated himself this time adding his name and the question "how are you today?"

The handshake was accompanied by the searchingness of Gabriel's long stare.

In the piano room Gabriel no longer waited to be given permission to go to the piano. Now he went directly to it and sat on the stool that looked as though it was made for him. He immediately began to play, his fingers looking more as though they were dancing to the tune rather than playing it. He could not see the look on Adrian's face. It was the strange tune he had dreamt he heard from the attic.

"Beautifully played" he said, "but I can't quite place the piece. What's it called?"

"I don't know" replied Gabriel, "my mother used to play it to me. She might have written it herself".

"Another of her talents" said Adrian, "sometime, if you didn't mind, it would be good to see a photograph of your mother".

Gabriel did not respond.

"Did your mother ever sing?" asked Adrian.

The boy turned towards him, "she sang to me" he said.

"Can you remember what she sang?"

"The one she often sang to me was called 'A song for Celia' but she sang many others".

Given how he had felt about the decrypted diary entry Adrian had not wanted to inquire if Gabriel could sing but now found himself asking if he sang for his mother.

"She liked me to sing the same song to her" replied Adrian.

"Would you mind singing it for me?" asked Adrian tentatively trying to mask the anxiety that had taken root in the soil of coincidence, "hearing your singing voice could help with a full evaluation of what we should do next".

Without further prompting Gabriel got up and walked to the end of the piano, then resting one hand on it, he looked straight at Adrian who positioned himself to play the arrangement he had made. However Gabriel began to sing a capella. If Adrian had been entranced by the physical beauty of his pupil from the moment of first seeing him, now with the addition of the singing, the captivation was unbreakably complete. The boy's voice had an exceptionally innocent, evocative quality with the purity of tone of each note transcending the one before. Added to this was the ecstatic look on his face.

> Drink to me only with thine eyes,
> And I will pledge with mine;
> Or leave a kiss but in the cup,
> And I'll not look for wine.
> The thirst that from the soul doth rise
> Doth ask a drink divine;
> But might I of Jove's nectar sup,
> I would not change for thine.
> I sent thee late a rosy wreath,
> Not so much honouring thee
> As giving it a hope, that there
> It could not withered be.
> But thou thereon didst only breathe,
> And sent'st it back to me;
> Since when it grows, and smells, I swear,
> Not of itself, but thee.

When he stopped singing Gabriel remained standing perfectly still, less as though waiting for a reaction and more with a sense of completion. It took some time for Adrian to have recovered sufficiently to speak at all as though fearing his voice would break the consuming spell.

"That" he said quietly "was the most beautiful singing I have ever heard, sublime, celestial, I feel amazed and humbled. Who else has heard you sing?"

"Only my mother. Till now I have never sung for anyone else".

"What about your father?"

"I do not sing for my father because it hurts him. He says it is too much like my mother".

"Everything about you is beyond beautiful" said Adrian, "I want to hear you sing and play forever. Gabriel tell me about your mother".

"I do not know about my mother" he replied, "I think she might return when she again needs me to play for her. I must be ready. That is why I come to you".

"I do not wish to deceive you Gabriel and I do want you to come more than is right for me to say but I cannot promise that it will bring your mother back. I do not know how that will work".

"It will work" came the simple repetition of the statement, "now you must start to teach me how to read music".

For the remainder of the time they had, Adrian got Gabriel to play Clara Schumann's concerto. As he did this he pointed out the meaning and impact of the notations. He was aware of his pupil's single-minded focus on learning and the ability he had to remember what was taught. All too quickly for Adrian the session was over. As his pupil left they again shook hands. Adrian's fear was that he would be unable to let go. Once more Gabriel held him with his gaze, "thank you" he said, "next time I will again sing for you. Today you looked at me like my mother did when I sang for her. It is strange. It is a good thing".

Adrian sat for a while after his pupil had left. He did not know if the coming of that boy was the greatest blessing or the cruellest curse in his life which had known immense joy and the depths of the most profound, all engulfing, insufferable despair. And yet he was still here. The writer of the diary to whom he had a reaction but who had no name, had said that only a Rembrandt could do justice to the girl who came to him for music lessons and whose fate was presently unknown. It was hard to disagree with that in the case of his pupil too.

There was something else embedded in the choice of Rembrandt who could, to Adrian, not only capture all the subtlety and complexity of the human face with preternatural sensitivity but whose integration of light and shade had at first bewildered him. Then many years ago in a museum in Amsterdam, in a moment of quiet epiphany he had been endowed with the rare for him insight that went against everything he had previously believed. It was suddenly clear to him that light and dark are not opposites but expressions of a single reality. That thought had changed his thinking on many things. He remembered too that he was not alone then.

Images of Rembrandt portraits floating into his consciousness did not drive the thoughts of Gabriel Barrowman from his head. What they did however was generate a need for him to have some form of representation of this boy. Perhaps having a photograph would give him more control over when thoughts of his pupil came to him. Adrian was aware that any image of a child could be misconstrued. The right thing to do was to ask John Barrowman if he could do this. It was perfectly natural that he wished to have a photographic record of all his pupils. It would also be another opportunity to reinforce that Gabriel was an exceptional talent. There would be nothing lurid or clandestine about it.

There was however another difficulty. It worried Adrian that the motivation Gabriel had for taking lessons was to be ready for when his mother had need of him to play for her so she would return. He felt that his duty as the boy's teacher was to help him want music itself be the important thing, everything else a secondary aim. Yes, it was true that there was also a wider social duty to help Gabriel achieve the public success his talent demanded. But this was something which could undermine his own life. It had always appalled him that some of the greatest works of art, probably including Rembrandts, were locked unseen in temperature controlled vaults as investments. But he knew that if he encouraged Gabriel to share his gift, the public would want to know who discovered the talent, who taught him, nourished and refined the skills. That he really could not allow.

Chapter 11

A Sweet Far Thing

It was well into the afternoon before Adrian could allow himself to think about Siobhan Walsh and the evening to come. It was only now that he fully remembered that she had an arrangement to see Old Kennedy. That should have taken place at the same time he was being held in willing thrall by the face and voice of his pupil.

It seemed to be happening more and more to Adrian that whole blocks of time were being devalued, relegated to the rank of intervals at a concert, filled with forgettable refreshments while waiting for the music to begin again. All of Wednesday had been in that category and now most of this afternoon.

At six pm he had another shower and shaved again. He decided not to put on any aftershave. That might seem too much like a teenager trying to impress and, though that was exactly how he felt, there were some necessary, practical limits to honesty. Sometimes a condoning smile of insight was all that is required or should be permitted. By quarter to seven he left the house and walked toward the Mitre. How pathetic, he thought, as he touched the water pump and said the name Siobhan.

There were more people than he expected as he entered. He was horrified to see a reserved sign on the table he normally sat at for his meal. He was looking around for another when Gwyneth called out, "it's reserved for you. Siobhan arranged it. We don't normally do reservations". His delight at the news was beautifully counterpointed by the fact that half the pub now looked round at him and knew who he was meeting. "Sit down" Gwyneth called out again, "I'll bring your beer over".

In less time than if he had tried to order at the bar, a pint of Antique Ugly arrived at the table and an ice bucket containing a bottle of Cabernet Sauvignon and two glasses.

"Siobhan?" he asked.

Gwyneth smiled, "she'll not be best pleased if you've invited someone else. She said you're running a tab".

"Like the perfect gentleman" came Siobhan's voice, "any man worthy of his oats would do it".

"Oh it's oats is it" said Gwyneth turning and smiling at her.

"In a manner of speaking" responded Siobhan, "I've heard of the oat cuisine you serve up. We shall be sampling some of that".

Adrian hated it when women got into this sort of conversation about him. He could never quite decide if he was expected to join in. Ok, he thought, so the pun was quite clever. He had known someone else who could as effortlessly do that. And he remembered the laughter and then that final image of her that would not go away. The voice of Siobhan again pulled him back to the Mitre.

"You're busy tonight. Did my publicist arrange this?"

"Siobhan Walsh" replied Gwyneth, "you still living in a fantasy world. No, there's a visiting theatre group in. They want to see our upstairs room. They're trying to bring theatre to the masses. But you're ignoring this handsome young man and, unlike you, my life is not entirely given over to pleasure. I'll bring you a menu".

Now Adrian could look properly at Siobhan. Her auburn hair fell loosely about her shoulders, her skin had the clean looking healthiness that comes from no regular use of make-up and her dress, which had coloured buttons up the front, hung freely on her, its pattern picking up the green of her eyes. He found himself thinking that whereas Gabriel's skin had a miraculous translucent fragility to it, Siobhan's radiated a vigorous health. Christ, he thought, I need to stop myself thinking this. With what I have in mind I shouldn't be comparing them in this way. He picked up the wine bottle and poured a glass.

"Good" she grinned, "I think I'll have one of those as well".

"My wild Irish Rose" he said, "you can have anything you wish".

"So you see me as a sweet far thing do you?" she said then seeing the look of confusion on his face added, "Yeats. The problem is that the English have never made sense of the Irish but then I suppose that's because the Irish have always had the sense not to let them or maybe just to dream".

"And what do you dream of Siobhan?" he asked.

"I told you I had a dream about you" she said, "and funnily enough when I went to see Old Kennedy today he talked about dreams. Mind you he talks in riddles. Sometimes he doesn't seem to make sense but if you stay with him and go with the flow then refocus things, he's actually very interesting. I think I'll make him a character in my story".

"So what did you get out of him?" asked Adrian.

"Your cottage is made of gingerbread" she said then smiled, "sorry. 'There's always been the same family borned there and ended their days there' by which I take it he means it's been in the possession of the one family and its descendants like forever. He even seemed to be saying that they may have built it, at least the original bit. A lot of stuff seems just to be local rumour and speculation built up over the years like there being some sort of curse not so much on the cottage as the family. Over time people have come to think that a kind of evil stuff went on there. People died. Children went missing. In so far as I can make out with talk of ridding the place of demons there seems to have been some sort of exorcism. I didn't think they still did that but it could have been a while ago. He seemed to go a bit off the rails and started talking about what sounded like a local version of Gorgons that if you looked at them somehow they ruined your life. Well I suppose it's better than being turned to stone. Several times he peered at me and said 'you're a woman'. Somehow I don't think that was a plus for him. I told him that a man now lives in the cottage and that he wanted to find out more about it. By the time I left he'd agreed to see you in the morning. If he remembers that is. Anyway if you can be there at nine".

"Tomorrow?" questioned Adrian, "I see a kid before school. I don't think I can get finished in time. Do you think he would notice if I was half an hour or so late".

"I wouldn't put it past him" responded Siobhan, "there are clocks everywhere. Most aren't working and the ones that are all tell different times. Anyway it's up to you whether you go or not".

"Thanks for doing that Siobhan" said Adrian pouring her another glass of wine just as Gwyneth arrived to take their order. Siobhan surprised Adrian by having a starter followed by a steak.

He had the same. "Good" said Gwyneth, "keep it simple for me. And another bottle of the Cabernet and an Antique?"

"Sure" said Adrian. When Gwyneth left the table he said to Siobhan "another thing I got wrong about you. I had you down for a vegetarian".

"I am" said Siobhan "it's just that I haven't yet cut out the middle man. So what else have you got wrong about me?"

"That you were beautiful when the truth is you are more than that. You are also sexy and witty and you raise my spirits".

"Thank you kind sir" she said, "I'll hold you to that".

He was about to say something in reply when John Barrowman came up to the table.

"Sorry to disturb you while you've got company Mr Grayling" he said.

Adrian thought he looked worried. He introduced him to Siobhan then asked "what can I do for you? I can tell you Gabriel is the most gifted pupil I have met and he has a voice that would make an angel jealous, if angel's actually sang and that's disputed".

"Oh I know Mr Grayling" said John, "I know well what Gabe's like and his mother before him".

Adrian interrupted "you must call me Adrian" he said.

"Thank you" said John, "the thing is my landlord has given me notice. He needs the place back for his niece. I haven't been able to find anything else in the village. If I don't we'll have to move on. Pity. I like my job but more important Gabe likes it here and he likes you and wants to learn more music".

"That's terrible news John" said Adrian, suddenly feeling the detumescence of his world was falling apart. Not to be able to have his sessions with Gabriel, to hear him sing. Just to look at him. "Have you asked around, put an advert in the shop window?"

"Of course I have" came the despondent reply. The best is the chance of a place outside the village in about a month or so. They're waiting on probate but the son will probably hang onto it and rent out afterwards".

"Are you sure it's just for a month or so?" asked Siobhan.

"Yes. That's all I need. Why? Do you know somewhere?"

"I don't but Adrian does" she replied, "he's got a spare bedroom and there's the attic. It'd need cleaning and sorting out. I could help you with that".

John Barrowman looked at Adrian as though for confirmation. Magus Cottage hadn't occurred to Adrian.

"Yes. That's a great idea Siobhan" he said, then turning to John added "it is in a state. That part of the cottage hasn't been lived in for years".

As he said this his mind was as opportunistically crowded with possibilities as the attic was with unremembered things. The unsettling of dust. The attic cleared without need for exorcism. To have Gabriel under his roof for a whole month. The sense that had been growing in him that something was not quite as it should be, that change was coming, could now be embraced rather than feared. Change didn't have to be bad. His world could expand without altering the perimeter. What was out there from before would still be out there while things transformed within. And most marvellously of all, he could keep his pupil.

"That would be great" said John, "I can get some time off and come and sort it out while Gabe's at school. Thank you so much Mr Gra... I mean Adrian".

"And I meant what I said" added Siobhan, "I could help with the clear-up. It's a fascinating old place. All of this ok with you Adrian. It won't have to interrupt your teaching and at the end of it you have more of your place to live in".

John Barrowman made a note of the times he could come to work. When he had finished he once more profusely thanked Adrian for his kindness and acknowledged all he was doing for Gabe. He then told Siobhan how much he appreciated the suggestion in the first place. He apologized again for disturbing their evening. Adrian had almost forgotten till that moment how long he could go on about things.

When they had the table back to themselves Siobhan smiled at Adrian and put her hand on his,

"That was great Adrian. You could see how much he appreciated it. I hope you don't mind that I suggested it. And think what your attic will be like later not to mention a spare bedroom you can actually use".

They enjoyed their steak and finished the wine. There was no denying it that Siobhan was good company. If she was a musical evening there would have been a dizzying range of changes of style, tempo and direction, the baroque would give way to jazz, then classical or even country and western. There was no unfilled moment. He couldn't have said what they talked about, he was enjoying it too much. She had proved once again that the English didn't make easy sense of the Irish. But why bother when being with her as much expanded his feelings as John Barrowman was shortly to his living space.

When Adrian went to the bar to pay, Gwyneth grinned at him and said, "I don't know what musical chord you play, but it's not just the fair maidens but the good-looking blokes that dance to your tune. John Barrowman has insisted he will settle up".

Adrian's protest, feeble enough at the best of times, seemed weaker still tonight.

"No" said Gwyneth, "he really did insist".

Another drinker standing at the bar turned and said, "you can pay for mine if you are so desperate to get rid of your money". He then stopped and looked at Adrian intently, "don't I know you from somewhere?" he asked.

"I don't think you can" replied Adrian, "I've a good memory for faces. I've never met you before".

"I don't mean like we're old friends" said the man, "just know you from somewhere like the telly or the newspapers".

"You can't" said Siobhan taking Adrian's arm and adding flirtatiously, "I wouldn't have forgotten you" as though she and Adrian had been together for years and she would know everyone he did, "you with the theatre group?"

"I don't have the talent for that" he replied, "but I work with them. I suppose a bit like a roadie".

"Don't knock that" said Siobhan, "without it there wouldn't be a show. Will you be doing it here?"

"I hope so" he said.

"Leave him alone" said Gwyneth winking, "you've got a bloke. Let someone else get a look in".

As they left Adrian could hear him saying "I'm sure I've seen him before. Is he local?"

"Yea" she said, "he's the piano teacher".

There seemed to be a welcome shared assumption built into things that Siobhan would come back with him. He could see that she flirted with everyone but it was, he felt, more purposeful with him.

Once they were back in Magus Cottage, Siobhan converted the assumption to an action. She took his head and, pulling it to her, kissed him with a force he had seldom experienced before. His hands moved down her back pressing her body against his. He was sure she must be able to feel the firmness of his erection against her. Now he held her from him and began slowly to unbutton her dress to the waist. She was not wearing anything underneath. The erect tautness of her nipples made him want to suckle them. His hands gently slid her dress from her shoulders till it fell to the floor. Now he knelt before her, kissing the firmness of her stomach then lowered her panties which she stepped out of.

Seeing a lover totally naked had a disproportionate effect with him like an accelerant in a fire. It had been like that for as long as he could remember, even after the allure of the forbidden had gone.

Siobhan watched smiling as he unbuttoned his shirt then she again kissed him, her hands now under his shirt. She played with his belt line then, as her fingers traced it round, kissed his chest and undid his belt. With the slightest of glances upwards, as though checking his reaction, she unzipped his trousers. As she knelt in front of him she pulled down his trousers and pants with one smooth motion. Kneeling in front of him she removed his shoes and socks. Now he was wearing only his open shirt. He gently tried to pull her head towards his penis but this was resisted. She stood up and again kissed him.

"Bed" she said and took his hand.

She led him upstairs as if it was her house and he did not know the way. Once in the bedroom he discarded his shirt and they both fell naked on the bed in each other's arms.

It had been many years since he had made love. It was only recently that it had again begun to feel right. In fluctuating nighttime fantasies during this period, when he thought of sex and love, the music in his head had been Schumann's Romance written for Clara. But now with the association Clara had for the purity of Gabriel Barrowman this no longer seemed right. His body had been ready both a lot earlier and more frequently than he had been mentally prepared and he had known again the release of onanism. Now he found his hands in contact with another's flesh.

Tenderly Adrian explored Siobhan's liberated, melodic nakedness. When he took her breasts alternately in his mouth, her nails dug into his back till he almost called out. His right leg parted hers and he contorted a little till he felt the moistness of her yielding vagina. The music of the adagio from Strauss's Sinfonia Domestica should have been the backdrop for this reawakening but his sense of wasted years and despairing acceptance that all happiness has a price in pain, now unconditionally caused him to surrender to the raw thrusting immediacy of the act. It was her Irishness that brought Isolde to mind and it was Wagner's majestic music that reached a climax with him. Even as he emptied himself into her body he thought he saw in the doorway a ghostly Gabriel Barrowman smiling forgivingly towards him before fading from view.

He stayed in Siobhan for a period of time too long to be sustained and too short to be useful. He slid out of and off her in one easy movement and they lay side by side, her glistening skin speaking of what he took to be its own satisfaction. There was something different to him in the smell of post coital sweat and in the undeserved exhaustion of so short an exertion. Sometimes he would glance towards the door to make sure they were still alone.

After a time Siobhan pulled the duvet up over them and went to sleep. Adrian did not know and would not ask what she thought of all of this. His pressing awareness was of wanting it to continue. He first watched then tried to match, the regularity of her breathing. His thought became of when he had done this with another but she was now gone.

Chapter 12

Seven

When Adrian got out of bed Siobhan was still asleep. He collected most of their clothes from the hallway. There was no point in trying to calculate how long it had been since that last needed to be done. For no particular reason the feeling had a degree of embarrassment about it. He brought Siobhan's things upstairs and left them on the chair by the bed then stood for a moment just looking at the chaos of hair on the pillow and the eyes that moved under their eyelids suggesting she was dreaming. Hopefully it was a pleasant one.

His own sleep had been erratic whether because of the unaccustomed exhaustion of sex, the three pints of antique ugly combined with the glasses of wine or the guilt that routinely lay in wait to mug any passing pleasure, there was no way of knowing. It was also somehow unsettling to think that, at Siobhan's suggestion, he was about to have, not just an ordinary house guest for a few weeks, but the only pupil who had ever disturbed him to that degree. And to make matters worse imagining that this boy had observed him in flagrante delicto had not just bothered him but had come to alarm him the more when he realized it had actually excited him.

Adrian quickly showered before going back downstairs and putting the kettle on. He returned to the piano room and was about to look at his card index to do some planning for Paula Byrnes' lesson when he remembered that she was not actually coming. She was being a bridesmaid at a wedding where no one apparently approved of the groom. For some reason it made him feel sorry for this man he had never met. Perhaps there is a different sort of empathy engineered into gender.

"You're up early" said Siobhan's voice behind him. He turned round hoping she was still naked but she was fully dressed.

"You look lovely dressed or naked" he said, "though selfishly I have a preference for the latter. I'm up early because I was going to prepare a lesson for a pupil I'd forgotten isn't coming".

"Well that should mean you should make it to your rendezvous with Old Kennedy".

Siobhan immediately saw that he had forgotten this too.

"What am I going to do with you?" she said.

"What would I do without you?" he responded.

"I'm not here forever Adrian" she said, suddenly more seriously.

"None of us is" he replied drifting into the evasive faux philosophizing he knew too well that he relied on to avoid confronting some reality or other.

"Breakfast?" said Siobhan.

"Please" he responded.

"I meant I would like some" she smiled then moved closer and again kissed him.

They ate a breakfast of scrambled eggs and grilled bacon in the kitchen, Siobhan commenting that the smell of grilling bacon was such an aphrodisiac to her that she fully understood why so many religions forbade the eating of pork.

"You are right" said Adrian, "religions are always more about the control of pleasure than the worship of a deity. The real battle has always been between Apollo and Dionysus not between good and evil".

Siobhan smiled at him. She reached over and put her hand on his. He thought she was going to squeeze it but she just rested it there,

"A bit of a pompous way to put it but you said that as though it had a very particular meaning for you Adrian. The more time I spend with you the more I come to the conclusion that there's a lot of other stuff to learn. I think you are a man with secrets who has found himself living in a cursed cottage. My problem is I can't decide if it's you or this place that I should be writing about. I don't suppose there's any point in my asking you about your life before you came here".

"You're right" he replied picking up her hand and kissing it, "you would only know what I told you. The only real honesty in my life is music".

"Last night seemed fairly honest to me" she said "so what music do you think about when you see me?" she asked.

"You" he said, "that can only be Stravinsky, you are so much a Dionysian, it has to be the Rite of Spring, particularly the Ritual of Abduction".

"That's strange" she said "I wanted to be a ballet dancer. I still love the ballet. I've seen that one. But doesn't the young girl chosen, dance herself to death for the old men of the ancestors".

"Yes" he said "you do, in an act of propitiation. But don't look so worried Siobhan. You have re-energized this soon-to-be old man by your beauty. If I could compose you would forever be locked into a rhythm that would pulsate with the elegant rawness of your life force".

"I like it when you talk dirty" she smiled "but I still have to go. Perhaps I could re-energize you again another day if you agree not to go on about age".

"Agreed" he said, "what about tonight?"

"Not tonight Napoleon" she said as she stood up, "why don't we have a drink tomorrow in the Mitre and you can tell me all about what you get from Old Kennedy. Or had you forgotten again? This morning at nine."

Adrian now stood up too, "I hadn't forgotten" he said, "it seems a long time to wait for tomorrow before I see you again".

They kissed. Adrian would have had it last longer but Siobhan broke off and, not for the first time, precipitately parted with a wave that both tantalized and trivialized.

He arrived at the cottage occupied by Old Kennedy at precisely nine o'clock. The rusty front gate pointlessly squeaked a warning of his arrival. There was no bell. The heavy knocker in the shape of a hand and wrist did not seem to make much impact on the thick door. Deciding how often and how hard to knock in situations like this can be a problem. He didn't want to anger or rush the inhabitant.

In due course the door opened. A very small man, with hardly enough body structure to sustain the wearing of clothes and with a head that looked as though it may never have seen hair, was standing there squinting up at him through glasses with one lens missing. A heavy blue pullover hung on his upper body like on a wire coathanger and below that was what looked like pyjama bottoms that ended some inches above his slippers which themselves gave the impression of being on the wrong feet. The impact stopped short of being absurdly comical instead achieving a degree of pathos.

"Yes" he said, the voice a bit deeper than Adrian had expected, "what is it? Do you know what time it is?"

Adrian reached out his hand and said, "I'm Adrian Grayling, the piano teacher".

He was going to go on to explain but Old Kennedy interrupted with the words

"Why would I want a piano teacher?" He peered past Adrian before going on, "I'm expecting someone".

"Yes" said Adrian, "Mr. Kennedy, you're expecting me. Siobhan Walsh, the Irish woman who came to see you arranged for me to come to talk to you about Magus Cottage".

"Irish woman" he said "I know no Irish woman. What would an Irish woman be doing with a piano teacher in my house?"

It was obvious that this was not going to be an easy morning and he immediately wondered what weight he could possibly put on anything he was told. None the less he persisted.

"The Sinclair cottage" he said in an effort to locate himself in Old Kennedy's thinking.

"This isn't the Sinclair cottage" said the impatient voice "that's further up the road on the left. It's where that piano teacher fella lives now".

"That's me" said Adrian.

"Well you should know it then. Anyway what's a fella like you doing in a place like that? Is it the music? That's it. It's the music. You're not the first you know. My advice to you is to go".

"Could we talk about what you know about the family that lived there and Magus Cottage?" he asked, "I'm really interested to find out and everyone says you know it better than anyone".

There was a moment's indecision then, without saying anything, Old Kennedy turned and walked back in. Adrian too hesitated then followed him, closing the door. The room to which he was led was not unlike his own teaching room in size and height. He counted at least seven clocks of different ages and sizes perched on a variety of objects including two of them on the mantlepiece, one on either side of a faded photo. It was too gloomy for Adrian to see what was in the picture. He knew there was a granddaughter who visited. Perhaps something to do with that.

As Siobhan had said a number of the clocks appeared to be working but none of them was close to the actual time of day. The curtains on the windows were pulled almost completely shut, allowing just enough space for someone to peer out and for a chute of light to reveal but not disturb the dust. Places and music were so routinely associated for Adrian that the silence here immediately unsettled him.

"Sit down" Old Kennedy more instructed than invited then placed himself with his back to the light. Adrian sat on a settee that seemed unusually firm. "I know you from somewhere" said the old man.

"I don't think so" replied Adrian, "you may have seen me around the village. I've lived here for seven years".

"Seven" said Old Kennedy as though the number had special significance.

"Yes" said Adrian, "I've lived in Magus Cottage for seven years".

"He was seven when I first saw him" said Old Kennedy, "I rue the day".

"Saw whom?" asked Adrian.

"The Sinclair boy" said Old Kennedy impatiently, "you should get out of that place if you still can. Young people nowadays don't believe in that sort of thing but there is a curse".

"Would you be willing to tell me about the curse and how it affected you?" asked Adrian pleased that the opening confusion on the doorstep had given way to a degree of focus.

"No" replied Old Kennedy, "they say you spread a curse by talking about it".

"I'm willing to take that risk" said Adrian, "Mr Kennedy, it's important for me to know more about the Sinclairs".

"There have always been Sinclairs here" he replied regretfully, "long before there were Kennedy's or any of the others and no good ever came of any of them I know of, except maybe one or two. My advice to you is get out and if they try to get you to stay don't listen and above all else don't look at them, especially the young ones".

"I don't understand" said Adrian, "why should I not look at them? What would happen?"

"Just don't do it" said Old Kennedy.

"Was there some sort of story about a child who died?" he asked.

"People die" came the reply, "some children went missing. It was all a long time ago. Just leave it at that".

"I really would like to know more" said Adrian.

"Not from me" replied Old Kennedy his tone firmer and now looking towards Adrian added "everytime this is talked about it brings it all back. It spreads the curse. I won't do it. Go please".

"Could we talk another day perhaps?"

"Maybe. Not today. Just don't look at them".

Adrian left and made his way back to Magus Cottage. Old Kennedy had looked even more tired and frail as they shook hands. He had obviously been drained by his memories of something he thought had happened but Adrian knew better than most how that worked. Still logically it didn't mean there was anything in what he believed. People are too easily persuaded by things they fear.

As he got to Magus Cottage he saw a small car parked there. He didn't recognize it. When he drew level John Barrowman got out.

"Hello Mr Grayling… sorry Adrian" he said, "sorry I didn't phone. Would it be ok if I made a start on sorting things out in your spare room?"

Adrian shook hands with his visitor.

"Hello John" he said, "no problem. Let me show you around. Gabriel at school I take it?"

"Sure. He never refuses to go but I know he doesn't want to be there" replied John, "when I told him we would be living with you for a while he smiled just the same smile his mother had. I could tell he was happy. That's not always easy with Gabe".

In so far as Adrian could tell John Barrowman was most impressed by the temporary accommodation on offer. Certainly his thanks were both repeated and effusive. He could have no idea how much Adrian Grayling was looking forward to having Gabriel live under his roof and how pleased he was that the beautiful boy seemed to want to be there.

Chapter 13

Sophrosyne

John Barrowman immediately became focused on the task of preparing the bedroom. Adrian was happy to leave him to it. He sat downstairs looking towards the ornate but unoccupied piano stool by the waiting piano. Recently he had again found himself drawn to making another transcription yet still had been reluctant to start. What was preoccupying him was the thought of having Gabriel living under the same roof, the imagining of various everyday scenarios. There would be breakfasts, getting ready for school. The image of Gabriel, his youthfulness highlighted by his school uniform, moved gracefully across his awareness. There would be the anticipation of his return. Making sure he had done his homework. Absurdly he found himself thinking that it was a pity, at nearly fourteen he was too old for bedtime stories. With mellowing fondness Adrian remembered this gentle transition from the waking world to the bower of dreams. A narrative lullaby.

There was something about the melodic extremes of lullabies that appealed to Adrian, their form nested as they were in tonal simplicity. Though it had achieved a clichéd appreciation he still liked the musicality of the Brahms lullaby especially the arrangement for cello and piano which he found perfectly relaxing even as an adult. Thinking of this eased his thoughts towards Gabriel's music lessons; both the official paid for ones, his privileged and private time with his pupil during which it would be legitimate to get the boy to sing for him and the other opportunistically snatched moments where so much incidental learning of lasting value can take place. He had always sought the sophrosyne and in this child he had a chance to mould it.

Adrian shook his head as though to dislodge these thoughts and stood up. He can't go on thinking like this. Socrates had said that beauty is a short lived tyranny. But he didn't feel tyrannized so much as entranced and once in such a state no one chooses to leave it. He now smiled to himself as he remembered the philosophy seminars during which he and the other young men had been introduced to Plato's Symposium and to Phaedrus. The suppressed giggling within his group as Alcibiades says that Socrates obsessed about beautiful boys, following them in a daze and the madness that stems from love when one is reminded of true beauty by the sight of a beautiful boy.

Hearing such things talked about openly and from revered sources was not simply empowering, it was liberating and validating, effects enhanced by the context in which this ancient learning was being imparted. He could not believe that he was the only one present who was having impure thoughts. He had rightly anticipated the veritable hailstorm of Hail Marys' that had come his way.

Thinking about his own impure thoughts led Adrian to wonder what might have happened if the unnamed piano teacher found himself living under the same roof as the young girl who was his pupil. It seemed to be this that finally moved him to go to the piano stool and retrieve the coded diary.

Adrian worked steadily interrupted only by occasional sounds from upstairs as John Barrowman moved objects in preparation for the arrival of Gabriel. Finally Adrian picked up the completed section and sat back to read it:

So is it that she has come to walk in quiet grace and lonely splendour through my days of cruel difficulty to put her from my mind and my nights when there can be no forgetting.

Samuel tells me I am truly smitten, that I have fallen with completeness under some enchantment that has no breaking. She comes and my day lightens, my heart quickens and I can but consume the wonder that is her form and fall drunken to the eternity of her thrall.

Oh my divine one, you wear the beauty of Helen like a smile of forgiving. She who was stolen by Theseus, won by Menelaus and then taken again by Paris, yes would I launch ten thousand ships or more and burn all the towers of Illum for such a prize.

Sometimes I can see that she knows full well the delight she has become to me. Now do I learn too late that all great beauty is born with the hunger for worship and that cruel loneliness is the price the unrequited pay.

Today did I venture to reach forward and, with my shaking hand I did gently touch the fairness of that unblemished cheek but she did but sigh and with her hand did brush the place I touched as though some unwanted flying thing had landed there. Sometimes it comes to me that I must be more like Paris and take my prize by force. Then so be it, only the gods can stop me. She would, I know, come to bask in the warmth of my true love and in time to return it.

Adrian looked with distaste at the entry. What sort of man would be so animalistic as to have these thoughts and be so deluded about love to consider that course? And this was but a child, and shame upon shame, his pupil. To admire the beauty of any other at any age is both a worthy and honest thing, he thought, for true beauty sings out and should not be denied but to consider such vulgar possession by the exercise of undisciplined strength was nothing short of a brutish betrayal. Therein lies rape and degradation for both victim and perpetrator.

Looking again at the next written entry, Adrian was beginning to feel a need to learn the lengths to which this piano teacher would go and the fate of his young pupil. He might have set about a further transcription had there not been a knock at the door. An apologetic John Barrowman stood there.

"Sorry to disturb you Adrian. I've finished for now. Would you like to see what I've managed to do?"

"I'm sure you'll have done a good job" he responded then, seeing the look on the face of the other, got up adding, "but seeing is believing".

He had always felt that was one of the more ridiculous things that people say. John Barrowman smiled,

"Yes" he said "I agree but Celia used to say that we see so little of what is there. She used to talk about seeing without looking".

"She sounds like a most interesting person" said Adrian as he followed John Barrowman along the corridor and up the stairs. Once in the bedroom Adrian had to reconsider his dismissal of seeing as believing. The transformation was indeed considerable.

There was not a spot of dust anywhere. The room smelt of air freshener or polish. The window had been opened. The chest of drawers to one side of the bed had clearly been polished and had come up very well. The dustsheet that had covered the bed was neatly folded on the chair that itself looked as if it too had been polished. Adrian vaguely remembered that there had been an old suitcase on the chair but none was to be seen. The bed had a mattress but as yet no bedding.

"Well what do you think?" asked John Barrowman.

"It's amazing" replied Adrian, "it really is".

"And I did a quick tidy up in the bathroom while I was at it just to get the feel of it. I'll try not to let any of Gabriel's stuff or mine get in your way. I really am most grateful for this opportunity and of course if it's all right with you I'd happily keep the whole house clean and tidy to compensate you a bit for the inevitable inconvenience – especially having a child in the house".

"Gabriel will be no trouble" said Adrian with more defensive immediacy than he intended, "I shall enjoy having him around. But you remind me. I'd like your permission to take a photograph or two of him. I like to keep photos with my pupil records. I always get the parent's permission for that".

"Naturally you have my permission" said John, "I'm just pleased he's taken so well to you and of course that you think he had some talent that you can bring on".

"It's more than talent John. He is the most gifted child I have ever worked with" said Adrian who knew how close he had come to adding 'and the most beautiful'.

"Tomorrow if it's ok I could make a start with the attic" went on John, "not while you've a pupil of course".

"That would be fine with me" responded Adrian, "it's Gabriel tomorrow. So you don't mind him missing school?"

"It's complicated" said John, "he had seemed to be settling but he really doesn't like it. He's just not on the same wavelength as the others. He was always a sensitive boy. One of them called him 'weird' the other day. Though he doesn't say anything I know he takes that sort of thing to heart. He feels he learns more from you in one session than in a whole week there. If I had the money I'd pull him out of school and employ someone like you as a personal tutor".

"School's important" said Adrian, "I'll do what I can for him and encourage him in every way, not just musically. I feel a strong duty, a commitment".

The two men came back downstairs Adrian to the piano room while John prepared a pot of tea he had insisted on making. When they were seated John again launched into an elaborated outpouring of thanks. Adrian steered the conversation back to Gabriel,

"He is an exceptional boy" he said, "what was he like when he was much younger".

"The same" said John, "he's always been the same really except when he was littler, looking like he does wasn't a problem. Everyone thought he was cute. A lot of people thought he looked more like a girl. He's an only child and was very close to his mother. Sometimes I think too close".

"Celia going off like that must have had an effect" commented Adrian, "does he ever talk about her?"

"He's never been one to say much. But I knew it got to him. You have to read him not wait for him to say things. He keeps everything to himself like she did. I could tell he couldn't understand why she went, well join the club there. Maybe he felt it was his fault the way I did. He was afraid something had happened to her. If we heard a siren I could see it unsettled him".

"I don't mean to intrude but I would like to know a little more about her" said Adrian, "I think you said she is the daughter of a bishop".

"She is" said John, "I don't think either her mother or her father much approved of me but once Celia made up her mind about something there was no stopping her".

"What was it you felt they didn't approve about you?" he asked.

John looked at him as though the answer ought to be obvious, "Scottish, a working-class man who was no great shakes at school and from a Catholic background".

"Perhaps the bishop had forgotten that Jesus was a carpenter" said Adrian.

John smiled, "maybe. The thing to me was I don't think they understood their daughter. Not that it was ever easy to understand Celia. I don't think I ever did. Then Gabriel came along. We hadn't planned to have a baby, well I hadn't anyway but once he was here that's all there was in her life".

"But she could still walk away and leave him?" queried Adrian still unable to mask his puzzlement.

"I know" said John, "sometimes she used to say she felt he was sucking everything out of her. She called him her Lilith whatever that meant. At other times she said she was getting too close. She even said there would come a point at which they'd merge. Then they would destroy each other".

"In what way do you think she meant destroy each other?" asked Adrian.

"I don't know" said John, "she'd often say the strangest things, sometimes after she'd been playing music for hours. Gabriel would be with her. Sometimes they'd play together. If you just came in and heard them both laughing the way they did it'd have been easy to think they were mad or acting mad".

"Did they sing together much?" asked Adrian.

"Sure" replied John, "but not when I was in the room. If I'd listen at the door I'd often not be able to tell which of them it was. Why do you ask?"

"He has an extraordinary singing voice, unique. I don't think I've ever heard a purer tone and the feeling he brings to it like he was delivering a thousand years of sad experience".

"Will he be alright?" asked John his tone suddenly more concerned than Adrian had picked up before.

"We'll have to make sure he is" said Adrian, "it's the one last important thing".

Chapter 14

The Eyes of Alchemy

Adrian was disproportionately pleased when Gabriel arrived for his lesson by himself. In the night he had again been preoccupied with thoughts of him. He had started to be concerned that perhaps his father would come with him. Of course Adrian wanted the preparation over as quickly as possible so that they would be under the same roof but he had come to value his teaching sessions with Gabriel over any other part of his time. It was exclusive, sacrosanct, indeed hallowed. It would not be the first time in his life that Adrian could be accused of worshipping beauty.

Today his pupil was dressed all in white. He wore a white shirt with the top three buttons undone, white flannel trousers that looked soft but held their shape, white trainers that showed no sign of ever having been walked in. The enchanted delicacy of his pale features was framed by the impossible shiningness of his black ringlets. Could he have been told by his father that Adrian wanted to take some photos? He dismissed this thought. It was simply not possible for Gabriel to look less than perfect whatever he was wearing. Adrian had never detected in him the slightest hint of hubris. Contrarily he was indeed more of an essence, perfect personhood without the contamination of ego, a transcendent purity of form that bathed the eye of the beholder in a pleasurable warmth.

When they were inside Adrian explained that he would like to have some photographs for his records if Gabriel did not mind. Once again the faraway smile that spoke of unfathomed private places were the surrogate for consent. This was to Adrian a special task that required a proper old-fashioned camera with a tripod and changeable lens. He had only his phone. It didn't feel quite right. How could that do justice to his subject? It seemed to trivialize the opportunity. None the less he took a number of full length photos then some of the upper body and others of the head only. He also tried to take some of Gabriel sitting at the piano. When he attempted a shot of the reflection in the piano it was spoiled by the intrusion of his own image taking the picture with his phone.

The effect did not simply ruin the picture. It robbed the scene of its enchantment. Included was the ornate piano stool containing its transcribed diary entries that both profaned and betrayed, with the inherent ugliness of lust, the spectral innocence of a child entrusted to a teacher to be enriched and liberated by the magic of music. And worse still for Adrian, he immediately felt a devaluing even sullying of the aesthetic purity of the motives and feelings he had towards his own pupil, this irredeemably beautiful boy.

It seemed however that Gabriel either read his teacher's new reluctance or for other reasons thought the photographic interlude was over since he positioned his hands on the keys and played a single note signalling it was time for music. Adrian pulled up the other stool, "thank you for letting me take the photos" he said. He was fully aware that he had taken more than could ever be required for record keeping purposes.

The boy made no acknowledgement for the thanks. Instead he said,

"I dreamt of my mother last night. She was smiling and beckoning to me to come".

To Adrian the word 'beckoning' had a strangely antiquated feel to it for a young boy but then this special child had a way of making age an irrelevant notion.

"You may have dreamt that because you would like her to be with you. It must be important to know that she misses you" said Adrian.

Gabriel did not look towards him. Instead he began to play the Clara Schumann that his mother liked. He played with such delicacy and verve that Adrian could only listen. He should have got out the sheet music and pointed as Gabriel played but he didn't. He knew that he was losing control of things. What ought to have concerned him more was that he did not any longer seem to mind.

When Gabriel stopped he sat perfectly still. Adrian could see his reflection in the piano lid. The smile on the beautiful face was of such sublime serenity that Adrian could not do anything, lost as he was in pleasurable paralysis. It had been a performance for an absent other with no need of applause. He could not have said how long they sat there. The thought that beauty is its own immortality and a talisman for all others against mortality was all that was needed. It does not age as we do. It is the eye's alchemy.

After the unmeasured time of a dream Gabriel again spoke, "she is singing" he said.

"What is she singing?" asked Adrian.

"It is a song she sang for me. She said it was about me"

"Would you sing it for me?" he asked.

Gabriel stood up. He made no comment or protest. Instead he once again moved to the end of the piano, rested his hand there and, in a tone that matched the whiteness of his attire, began to sing, surely to an audience of other angels.

The Minstrel Boy to the war is gone
In the ranks of death you will find him;
His father's sword he had girded on,
And his wild harp slung behind him.
"Land of Song" said the warrior bard,
"Tho' all the world betrays thee,
One sword, at least, thy rights shall guard,
One faithful harp shall praise thee".
The Minstrel fell! But the foeman's chain
Could not bring that proud soul under:
The harp he loved ne'er spoke again
For he tore its chords asunder;
And said, "No chains shall sully thee,
Thou soul of love and brav'ry!
Thy songs were made for the pure and free
They shall not sound in slavery".

When he stopped Adrian did not move or applaud. How well he knew that song. It had been requested by the person he had loved most in all the many lives he had lived, to be played at her funeral. He knew the story of the Irishman who wrote it, knew that he had become Byron's literary executor, knew that he acceded to the decision to destroy the memoirs and knew too of the enduring love of Byron's life, the beautiful John Edleston, a chorister at Cambridge whose voice had first attracted his notice. And now this voice, this face, this boy.

A helpless Adrian Grayling sat, as very often before, so lost in the musical philosophy and literature of others that he no longer felt the entitlement to his own life. He did not see the tear that strayed from his eye but it did not pass unnoticed by his pupil who gracefully moved towards him and gently removed it with a finger then kissed him on the cheek.

There are kisses of greeting and of respect, of passion, coy simplicity and of childhood sweetness, kisses of duty and of betrayal, of praise and parting, of wonderment and delight. Then there was the kiss of the everlastingness of that moment. The music in Adrian's head was the opening aria of Handel's Xerxes. To him there was no other piece of music so skilfully simple in its delivery of harmony and rhythm allowing itself to be immersed in all the delights of the forbidden promise of the countertenor voice.

Then came the words of his pupil, so quietly carried by a voice that they seemed to be emerging from the music, "sometimes my mother too cried when I sang to her. She said she could not bear to think of my voice changing, that such a thing would be like Eurydice stepping on the serpents that took the joy from Orpheus singing. She did not say what she meant. I did not ask".

Adrian smiled at the boy. He knew what his mother meant. "Thank you for singing to me" he said, "I knew someone once who had asked for that to be sung at her funeral though at the time she requested it she was young, healthy and beautiful. The Irish have that side to them. To the poetic among them death seems to be life's companion not its foe. She looked at the ocean and did not see water but a welcome. The Minstrel Boy spoke to her. She always felt it should be sung by a beautiful boy whose voice had not yet changed".

"You loved her?" said the boy.

"Like none other" he replied.

"My mother said that a love that did not hear its name cried for the eternity of that silence".

"Your mother" said Adrian, "the woman who gave you life, was a very special person Gabriel and she made you special".

"It is time for me to go" said Gabriel, "the day after tomorrow we come here. I want you still to play for me, to help me absorb more of my mother and I will sing for you".

"Yes" said Adrian "we will continue. If I had my way, forever".

"Twenty-one lessons" replied the boy.

When Gabriel had gone Adrian returned to the piano and sat. His pupil had sung The Minstrel Boy a capella. Now Adrian played the traditional Irish air to which the words had been set by Thomas Moore. He vainly tied to conjure up an image of Gabriel singing it at the end of the piano. He played that tune over and over again but could not separate the words from the music. He thought of Byron and the disguised love of John Edleston whom Byron had considered the one he loved above all others, he thought of what the burned memoirs might have said of love's beauty to end the eternity of that silence and, as he thought of Gabriel, he remembered that kiss.

The music now surrounding him was Sibelius 'The First Kiss'. What indeed, he wondered, would heaven make of the first and perhaps only kiss from Gabriel. In his heart he knew the angels would look to see the reflection of their own bliss, a heavenly validation that he believed would be as right as it was unlikely. What he now felt that Runeberg had got wrong was that death turned away. That he knew it only does that in order to look back again when it is least expected and most undeserved.

Adrian now found himself playing the Clara Schumann but was overwhelmingly aware that he had not and could not reach the heights his pupil had achieved. He was not only the most beautiful pupil he had ever had but the strangest and most remote. With true parental blindness his father had only been able to see that he was a little different. It was hard for Adrian to pinpoint what it was about this child that had caused him to talk to him like an adult. Almost a confessor. Since Ciara's death he had not spoken about her to another. No one in this village knew that she had ever even existed let alone what she had meant to him. There was a knowing attunedness to Gabriel that spoke to him of hidden knowledge, of more mystic times.

Though it was still morning Adrian had found himself drained by his time with Gabriel. To him, in that moment, there was no distinction between emotional and physical exhaustion. Perhaps it was the reawakening of things long safely locked in slumber. He had sipped from a goblet of the waters of Lethe, the ameles potamos, the wonderful river of unmindfulness, as Socrates had the hemlock for a different oblivion. He got up from the piano and made his way upstairs. It was still too many hours before he was due to meet Siobhan in the Mitre. He did not get as far as his bedroom but turned instead into what was to be Gabriel's room to be shared with his father. There was as yet no bedding. He lay down on the mattress and closed his eyes. The image above him was of a Gabriel whose smile floated in a lake of elsewhere. The bed was much more comfortable than he had thought it would be, much more invitingly so, drawing him to the succubus of sleep. Siobhan had been right. This was a good room. It is wrong to think that we go to sleep or even that we fall asleep. Sleep silently and irresistibly claims us, perhaps possesses us, drains all resistance from us, demands unconditional surrender. There is an unspoken paradox in the exhausted struggling to stay awake. He knew more than others that sleep can be both friend and enemy. It can be of comforting rest or the unleashing of fears, memories, imagines.

Adrian lay there, his head crowded, heavy and overflowing, a prisoner of sleep's capacity to construct its own world of wayward understanding. Imagines, is that really a word he wondered, the question joining the ranks of the not quite asked but still there. But he had heard it before, he felt sure of that. A word, the word, definite or indefinite article? Then Somnus playfully ricocheted his thoughts around his head till they became a tunefully hummed arrangement of Brahms, bathing him in a warmly welcome simplicity, transporting him once more to the seminar room where he and his companions were being introduced to the Symposium and to Phaedrus whose name itself could be savoured. How long ago had it been and how close to pointless all that sometimes seemed. But it had been his life. Then. It had taken the gradualness of time long spun for him to recognize the complexities and possibilities of mortal feelings, to appreciate more the pleasure the subversive teacher, the one they then thought elderly, was getting from introducing these young men to the ideas.

'Imagines' his teacher was saying, 'was the name Philostratus gave to his writing. He was born nearly three centuries before what we date as the birth of Christ'.

The distinctive softness of the Scottish accent continued, 'Philostratus was like a one man academy of art appreciation. There is dispute as to whether some of the paintings he described even existed, certainly in the form he wrote about them but there was no denying he talked a good picture. In one there was the personification of 'Sleep' which wore a black and white coat and carried boxes of horn and of ivory in the same colours, containing either good or bad dreams. No doubt for him the good dreams were of the beautiful boys to whom he wrote such wonderful letters'.

This teacher had shocked each of them in their own developing way of recognizing such things but all of them grew to love him and to learn from him. And in turn he loved them, some more than others. None that Adrian knew of felt wronged, devalued or misused, any more than he believed had the acolytes of Socrates. They had basked in his lifetime of experience, had learned the comprehensiveness of adult culture, grew to know what it is to be valued, even loved, and the joys of helping others reach a fuller autonomy. And there was another thing he now believed this priest had tried to teach them, perhaps as important as any of the others, that in time everything becomes its own mythology.

As Adrian fully surrendered to sleep something else from the writing of Philostratus connected him to Gabriel via the sweet simplicity of the Song for Celia. It was his letters that Jonson had so fully harvested for some of the most significant ideas in the poem including all of the powerful first line, 'Drink to me only with thine eyes', and the image of the kiss left in the cup. But it was the face and voice of his beautiful boy pupil that hypnos hijacked and used to transform Adrian's enveloping dreams.

Chapter 15

The Cloths of Heaven

The lights of the Mitre beckoned though it was still daylight, rendering the thought of the Antique Ugly all the more welcoming. It had acquired its own allure as had other things since that first meeting with John Barrowman. If asked Adrian would no doubt have confirmed his view that, to say there could be anything fateful about a meeting was primitive reasoning. There was just too much about such thinking that involved a surrendering of responsibility. He had come to think of outcomes instead as a narrowing of reality to the observer's point of view or perhaps that what we see as reality is the outcome of that narrowing. Surely that's what all meaning, even belief, had to be, a narrowing till only one of the unending possibilities can be seen or perhaps felt. Apollo narrows, Dionysus expands. They are not, he had come to believe, separate things any more than the elemental forces of nature that physicists constantly reinvent, are separate.

Adrian had only known how long he had remained sleep's hostage by how cold he felt when he awakened on the bare mattress of Gabriel's bed. He had sat up with an adrenalized suddenness, unsure where he was or how he had got there. He had looked around at the unaccustomed, perhaps even unnatural cleanliness of the room. He couldn't remember any of the dreams that had invaded his head, just that there had been a phantasmagoric dance of all the demons. He used to think that sleep was creative, that it manufactured the content of the dreams. Now it seemed to him that dreams were the coloured strands of the unweaving of reality by the dark.

The Mitre was busier than he expected. As Gwyneth saw him enter she began to pour his Antique Ugly. "I'll bring it over" she called to him.

"Thanks" he reflexively called back. He had recently begun to feel more a part of the village community. He glanced across at his table to find Siobhan already sitting there a book and a bottle of wine on the table in front of her. This time she was not wearing the same thing. For a moment he was taken aback. Like Gabriel in the morning she was dressed in white. Also like Gabriel the first few buttons of her blouse were undone. As she saw him approach she smiled, he thought in genuine pleasure as much as welcome and tossed her head back causing her to lean away from him and allowing him to see that she was not wearing anything under her blouse. He found himself becoming aroused. He was going to kiss her cheek but she kissed him fully on the lips.

"You look ravishing" he said when she released him.

"Thank you kind sir" she replied, "but if we could leave the ravishing till later and deal with the famishing now".

"They are both a kind of appetite" said Adrian, "remember mortification of the flesh, 'Mortify therefore you members which are upon the earth; fornication, uncleanness, inordinate affection, evil concupiscence and covetousness, which is idolatry'. Paul's Epistle to the Colossians".

"Christ Adrian. What a chat up line? And another fun evening was had by all. I think I prefer 'go forth and multiply', that's going to be 1st Epistle of Siobhan to the people she intends to sleep with, well with the relevant precautions against the multiplying bit. It's a good job you like to act out the sins you rail against. Your mother has a lot to answer for".

"Sorry" said Adrian, "old habits".

As he said this Gwyneth arrived with the Antique Ugly and the menus. "Eating at this time" she said, "another early night I suppose".

She grinned at Siobhan.

"Mortifying the flesh" responded Siobhan.

"No, more a hot flush" responded Gwyneth.

Both women laughed. Gwyneth went on, "on his tab?"

Siobhan nodded, "he doesn't know that I know that John Barrowman paid for the last one so he still owes me a meal" she added.

As Gwyneth went off Adrian glanced at the book on the table, "what are you reading?" he asked.

"Reading?" she replied, "writing. That's my notebook. I've started on the story I'm setting in Magus Cottage, well at least notes for it".

"Have you decided on what it's about?" he asked.

"A piano teacher" she grinned, "he tries to sell his soul to the devil but the devil turns him down. Says the way he's going on he'll get him anyway in due course. The only way would be for the piano teacher to prove that he can be good for twenty-one months. Then he could be considered a worthy prize. Any lapse and the twenty-one months starts afresh. The piano teacher accepts. However he changes his mind but the deal's been made. The story's about his struggle to find temptation for that period. Then an Irish princess comes along and tries to save him from the Devil by enticing him to sin again and again".

Adrian had been horrified when he heard the words 'piano teacher' and then reference to the Devil. He had tried to hide his reaction. It had taken him some moments to relax back into the alternative universe of her intention. Only an Irishwoman, he thought, could find a way of making sin a means of avoiding the Devil. He had always thought that women would make good priests, especially Jesuits.

The arrival of food and second pint of Antique Ugly further mellowed the evening. She was good company, attractive, witty and clearly intent on using all senses of her own clutches to save him from Satan's. He told her that Gabriel and his father would shortly be moving in. "I hope it doesn't cramp our style" she said.

"Why should it?" he responded, "they've their own room".

"But presumably they share the bathroom and the rest of the house. We weren't exactly quiet or restricted to one room last time as I recall and we operated more of an undress code" she said.

"It was your idea to invite them" he said.

"We hadn't exactly hooked up then" she replied.

"It's not for long" said Adrian, "and hopefully my twenty one-months will start again later".

Siobhan smiled and poured herself another glass of wine, "Slainte" she said, "may the Devil never take you".

The evening continued with the now expected convivial mix of sexual innuendo, literary references, the perils of freelance writing and the magic of music. They did not notice that they were being more closely observed than usual. The man from the travelling theatre group was looking more at Adrian than Siobhan, in his hand a cutting from a paper, folded so as to reveal the photo not the text. It appeared that he was more trying to compare them. He asked Gwyneth what she thought. She said that Adrian Grayling looked nothing like the man in the picture. "Bit of a coincidence" said the man, "the same first name too".

"Adrian's not exactly an unusual man's name" she replied.

"Well" said the man who had identified himself as a roadie, "if it is the same one he is an unusual man. That woman he's with looks young enough to be his daughter".

"Well she's not" insisted Gwyneth "and I tell you it's not the same man. She's a friend of mine and he is. We look after our own here. You wouldn't want starting rumours to cost the group you work for the hire of the venue".

"Sorry" said the man, "I'll take your word for it. Let me buy you a drink to apologize".

"Thanks" said Gwyneth, "I'll put a double gin on the side and I did mean what I said".

She noted however that he repeatedly glanced back at Siobhan and Adrian. She would like to have known who the man in the photograph was and what the article was about. The roadie had said he is an unusual man. That covers a multitude of sins.

At the table by the window Siobhan's white shoed foot was working its way up Adrian's left leg. He couldn't quite see how she was doing it while retaining a look of un-involvement but however it was, he was responding to it. She had drunk the bottle of wine by herself. As he glanced around to check that no one could see what was happening, he caught the eye of a man at the bar who seemed to be staring at him but this man immediately averted his eyes back to Gwyneth.

Adrian looked back at Siobhan who was smiling at him. While Gabriel's smile expressed something disturbingly private and remote, perhaps lonely or even otherworldly, Siobhan's was more openly connected to her more immediate intentions and had an invitingness to it.

"What are you thinking?" he asked her.

"That I want to be a virgin again" she replied, looking at him with the softness of a dew drop on a blade of morning grass, "I want the fearful excitement of that first time again, I want the promise it holds to take me tenderly in its arms and to cherish me, I want it to be as gentle as a child's sleep and as welcome as tomorrow. You'll think me silly but I really want to be a virgin again. I don't just want to sleep with a man because I like him in the same way I might choose to have another glass of wine. I want to be seduced. Before you say anything Adrian think, 'of night and light and the half light; I would spread the cloths under your feet. But I being poor, have only my dreams. I have spread my dreams under your feet. Tread softly because you tread on my dreams'. Be my Yeats" she said, "take me. Swaddle me in the cloths of heaven".

Her words still had the capacity to take Adrian by surprise. Could she be joking or, as her fellow countrymen were so fond of saying, was it the drink talking or was it some fantasy of seduction she wanted him to join in. If Lady Lamb could have a fantasy of being a page boy and dressing as one why should Siobhan be denied her imagined moment? She had looked so innocently pleading as she said those words.

He took her hand and in a gentle whisper said, "would you come and be as one with me beautiful maiden? I have not far from here a bower, full safe and sanctuary it is for all the dreams and longings of our kind, a quiet place where flows the blissful river of music that will carry you with unmeasured time to your promised land of perfect rest on a bed of sweetly scented petals and there we each shall have our heart's content".

He felt a little foolish as he conjured these words unsure if he was creating or quoting or even if what he said made sense. Somehow the smile on her face told him that it didn't matter. He paid and they left. He thought he heard the man at the bar say to Gwyneth, "it's him, I'd swear it".

Normally any hint of his past intruding would have continued to alarm Adrian but as he walked past the water pump holding the hand of his personal Naiad, the fear abated and in his head and all around him was the music of Debussy's Prelude to the Afternoon of a Faun. It lured him through layer after layer of orchestration and became again that wonderful cornucopia of clarinets, cor anglais, crutales and fellowship of flutes. That the love there was unrequited did not raise frustration to the point of anguish. The virgin by his side had chosen him.

In Magus Cottage no tearing of clothes in the hallway, no naked rush to the bedroom, no blinding urgency to steal the moment but rather a respectful tumescence of anticipation. He invited her to sit, having positioned one of the piano stools so that she could see him. He then sat on the ornate stool and placed his fingers as he had seen Gabriel do and adopted the same posture. Then he began to play 'The Song for Celia' and to sing the words to her. He knew his voice lacked the purity of his pupil but perhaps that was because he lacked the chaste simplicity of that boy, his own thoughts never straying far from his surrender to the more wanton and licentious. The art of guilt is to be always a retrospective show.

Adrian looked towards the white muse who sat with her hands clasped on her lap. Now with abruptness he felt his own skin assuming a pallor that must surely match what she wore. The girl who sat there seemed to him not to be Siobhan but one transmogrified into his imagining of the pupil from the transcribed diaries. He stared. Insanity, he thought, occurs not when the impossible assumes the mantle of the real but when the real denies itself. 'Then saith the damsel that kept the door unto Peter, Art thou also one of this man's disciples? He saith, I am not'.

It was not the crowing of the cock but the distant sounding of the church bell that seemed to restore Siobhan who stood at the moment that he got to his feet. He reached out his hand and she took it in hers. "Come" he said. No further words were required as he led her from the room along the corridor and up the wooden stairs. Once in the bedroom they stood facing each other. He held both her hands for a few moments then said,

"I am suffocating in the delight of your presence, your hair, your eyes, your skin which has the fragility of a newly opened flower. It would truly take a Rembrandt to capture the essence of one such as you".

She made no resistance as he slowly, gently began to take her clothes off. They did not kiss till she was fully naked, quivering before him. She did not assist but, still standing there, watched as he removed his own things. Once more he took his time in doing this. When he too stood there naked she looked at him coyly as though it was the first time she had seen a naked man, or perhaps one fully aroused. Then they kissed. As they did so he picked her up and placed her on the bed then lay beside her.

The music that accompanied them when they entered the bedroom was Strauss's Salome, Dance of the Seven Veils. At that point it seemed somehow appropriate that Strauss had specified that this should be a decent work as if performed on a prayer mat. To Adrian once again this injunction was quickly seen as delightfully misplaced. The eroticism emerged from its cocoon and the quickening pace and coruscating chords and surges of sensuality could not be denied. His caresses of her tender body were gentle and unrushed and she responded with quietly welcoming acceptance. When they had first made love she was an equal partner managing his body and her own pleasure. Now in the reborn virginal state of her imaginings she was more submissive to his approaches and desires only passively accepting her growing arousal. When, after a period of a length that he could remember only once before in his life, she allowed him to enter her, she gave a startled gasp and whispered a prolonged sigh that developed and grew to a joyful moaning with her fingernails digging into his back. He had often wondered how the soloists in Schulhoff's Sonata Erotica achieved what they had to do. It was an underrated piece.

As he came and she experienced him sharing all that was in him with her, she made a cry that managed somehow to be both shrill and muted and arched her body a little. Then after another period he rolled off her and they lay side by side, she gleaming in contentment and he still panting a little. Both of them now slept.

Adrian had the sense that she was already awake when he woke. For a moment he had wondered if he had dreamed the whole thing particularly Siobhan's fantasy of being a virgin again. The different pace to this encounter had reminded him more about how things used to be with a lover and a beloved, often with the man in the role of lover. It was hard for Adrian to say whether being the object of desire or the desiring one was the more privileged. Nowadays of course emancipated women sought to be simultaneously in both roles. He knew even when it was two males that historically the male in the implicitly more passive role of the penetrated suffered a greater loss of status. Of course in some societies it would have been a boy in the role of object of desire. There had long been a premium on beautiful young males and none, he thought, more beautiful than his own Gabriel. It was, he insisted to himself, perfectly possible even right that another could be admired for their beauty. He was unsure when the erotizing of beauty had begun or whether, when the object was of one's own species, it was any longer possible to separate the two. Yet we do it so easily with other species. To say a racehorse is beautiful is not to lust after it. Likewise with any beautiful object. Even the metronome on his mantelpiece he thought of as beautiful. If he said of either that he found them beautiful his good taste might be lauded. But if he were to venture to say of Gabriel, only that he was beautiful, the condemnation would be swift and final.

Adrian now turned towards Siobhan. He could immediately see that his instinct had been right. She was awake. She smiled at him as he positioned himself on his side then said an unnecessary 'thanks' before asking,

"am I the only virgin you've deflowered with more than once?"

"Taking the innocence of a virgin must restart my twenty-one months before the devil can claim me and as for deflowering the same person twice…" he said. She smiled again.

"I will be renewed again" she said, "of my many fantasies that's one I've never acted on before. I had a boyfriend once who wanted me to dress as a schoolgirl. I wouldn't. We parted. What do you think of that Adrian? A schoolgirl! A bloody Lolita".

"You are a beautiful woman Siobhan" responded Adrian now lying back on his pillow, "I'm sure you were also beautiful when you were younger. Boys and men looking at you would not have been able to avoid seeing that. Nor would other girls or women. Often people use 'schoolgirl' as shorthand for young".

"It's one thing to think it" responded Siobhan, "but Nabakov has Humbert running off with her. They have sex Adrian. She was a child".

"I'm not condoning rape" said Adrian, "it's just that I distrust doctrines. It's simply assumed that no sexual contact with people under sixteen or eighteen can be consensual and it's dogma that it's always bad, harmful. But girls can consent to sex when they are sixteen and still at school. Mostly I think what people are worried about is not age but age difference. Try telling most younger teenagers that they are too young to give consent. What concerns me is that we always manage to create groups of people we want to stone to death".

"I don't want to talk about this anymore now" responded Siobhan, "I don't want to spoil things. Is it tomorrow John Barrowman and his son move in?"

"Yes" said Adrian, fully aware what Siobhan would say if she knew how chastely beautiful he found Gabriel.

Chapter 16

Adante con moto

Adrian knew that he was less and less interested in his other pupils. There was only one who mattered. He mechanically prepared for Paula Byrnes. Getting up early in the morning was not the problem, even on one with a grey, indecisive drizzle like this.

Once he had felt it was important work, opening a gateway to the riches of another world, the only common language in the shared history of mankind, one that was his almost constant companion even before it was felt that he had some talent for it. For a long time he hadn't even considered that everyone did not have their lives accompanied by different music especially at times of heightened involvement. The cinema had confirmed for him that it must be so, as did hearing people sing or hum as they went about even boring seeming tasks. Surely there had never been a society or culture that did not practise music of some sort or in some form. Perhaps it started with people imitating sounds and rhythms from their natural world with the voice at first being the only instrument.

The history of musical instruments had fascinated him. He was drawn to the theory that it was probably the case that songs at first told stories, after all hadn't one written in cuneiform not been found in Syria. That must have dated it from nearly three and a half centuries ago. It was to him fairly self-evident that song would have flourished for millennia before writing, which itself had to be a truly important development though he was aware that there are some suggestions that the earliest need to record things in marks on walls etc. was for accounting purposes. It was ever so, Adrian thought, and despite the advance payment for Gabriel's twenty-one lessons, he still had a living to make.

The idea of some things being 'ever so' both depressed and reassured him. Clearly there were some continuities such as eating that invited easy explanations. Sex too. The continuity of the species had required that. He had always considered it obvious that early man probably did not make the connection between coitus and conception, maybe not till they slowly discovered that they could breed animals. Before that it must have been an instinctive matter that brought not just pleasure but comfort and release. Long before pheromones stood accused, physical features must surely have played a role. He wasn't denying the other factors but just couldn't get away from the notion that within any group some others will have been seen as more desirable. Maybe beauty and health have always gone together so that evolutionally forces influenced partner choice in that way.

Adrian now again thought of Siobhan, the reborn virgin, who had not long ago walked into the soft rain of the early morning with his only umbrella erect for protection. How nearly had he come to allowing the hard logic of his views on age to bludgeon her adherence to the fragile modern consensus?

Predictably on time Paula Byrnes had again bounced into his hallway without even a wave goodbye to her mother who had smiled what she probably intended to be a look of shared understanding to Adrian. The lesson had consisted of some of his prepared material and much excited chatter from Paula about her role as bridesmaid including her annoucement she would have four bridesmaids when she got married and named those of her friends she had decided would be best suited to the role. She had not yet determined who she was going to marry but knew it would definitely not be Timothy Paulson who was in her class and described a 'yukkie'. Adrian had said nothing but was inclined to agree.

Adrian had tried to capitalize on her fascination by playing a version of Mendelssohn's Wedding March but this didn't seem to be recognized. Paula simply showed little interest though she thought the name Mendelssohn was funny and as for Felix, well who would name their baby after a cat food. He explained that Felix had started composing at age twelve but it was only when he told her he had played in public concert at age nine that she took a little more interest.

He decided not to mention how easily the portrait by Carl Begas of the young Felix Mendelssohn at age twelve could be mistaken for a young girl. He knew this was the age Felix had been introduced to Goethe who was astonished at his skills and who invited him back a number of times with Mendelssohn later setting some of Goethe's poems to music. Whether Goethe's fondness for young boys and girls was an influence here did not seem relevant to Adrian, he had recognized the talent. Adrian had smiled to himself as he remembered that Goethe had said that he liked boys a lot but the girls are nicer, 'if I tire of her as a girl, she'll play the boy for me as well'. Fantasies, fantasies Siobhan. What on earth would his emancipated virgin have thought if she knew that Goethe had also said that 'pederasty is as old as humanity itself and one can therefore say that it is natural'.

Adrian was quietly delighted when the lesson ended and Mrs Brynes arrived on time. He was even more pleased that she had remembered she had not paid for the previous lesson.

"How was the wedding?"

His feigned interest was intended as her reward. He normally didn't make small talk with the parents or show an interest in their lives outside an occasional comment on progress. He wasn't sure he was very good at it. Since the very recent addition of Siobhan to his world with an increase in visits to the Mitre, these conversational dark arts had been practised a little more. He wouldn't say he wasn't enjoying it.

"Great which is more than I can say for the weather" said Mrs Byrnes.

"And Ivan?" asked Adrian smiling.

"Jury's still out. He did get rather drunk afterwards but Clara looked lovely" she replied, then added, "I did her hair".

"No wonder she was lovely" said Adrian.

"I'm going to marry Mr Grayling" chirped Paula, "amin't I?" she said looking at him.

Adrian hoped that the horror he felt at the suggestion in the presence of the child's mother wouldn't show,

"Well" he said, "you've got to grow up and become a famous violinist first and by then you'll have lots and lots of handsome young men of your age whose hearts you can break".

"Do you really think she's got that much talent?" asked a beaming Mrs. Byrnes.

"Talent alone is never enough" he replied, not wishing to deceive but delighted the issue of Paula marrying him had passed without further comment, "a love of the instrument is very important and practice, practice, practice comes into it".

He felt like adding "and don't give up on the hairdressing option".

A happy Mrs Byrnes and Paula walked down to the gate which she had parked blocking.

"See" he heard her saying, "what do I tell you. Keep practising".

Adrian returned to the piano room and put his violin back on its stand. He was boiling the kettle when the phone rang. It was John Barrowman. He wanted to begin moving his things in that afternoon and hoped it would be ok if he and Gabriel started to stay from tonight. Once they were in he would finish sorting out the attic as a sitting room for them. It did not take long for Adrian to agree to this arrangement. The thought of it actually happening made him feel weak. The sheer physicality of his reaction surprised him.

"I've one other thing to ask" said John, "we'd never get the piano up those stairs. If it was long-term I could take the window out and rig a pulley to hoist it up. That'd work. I'd reinstate the window. But it's only for a few weeks and that's a lifesaver in itself. Would it be ok if I stored it at work and sometimes, if it's alright with you and not too much of a nuisance and if he didn't play it too loud, if Gabriel could practise on yours. I want him to keep it up. Coming to you is the best thing that's happened to him since Celia left. He never says much about anything but I know he really likes you. He's probably bored with me. Who wouldn't be? Celia was. I'm not sure why she married me…".

It was difficult for Adrian to identify a pause where he could get a word in,

"John" he finally said, "stop it John. Do you think for one moment that I would not want the most gifted pupil I have ever had to practise? It is a pleasure to watch him play, to listen to him. If I didn't need the money from the other pupils I would have only Gabriel". He stopped himself saying more.

"Thank you so much" said John "what a blessing it was for us to come here. I thought it might be helpful because of his mother's connection with the village and then to meet you. I'm so grateful. I just hope someday I can properly repay you".

A sort of anxious excitement informed the next few hours. It was a feeling he had not had to quite this extent for some time. Of course somethings had always made him nervous, even, at times, fearful. But the nearest he could place what he presently felt was to some sort of performance anxiety like many of the finest virtuosos experienced, sometimes to such a crippling degree that they gave up public appearances. Indeed he knew that many of the history's greatest composers probably suffered from what would nowadays be regarded as mental health problems, Mozart, Beethoven, Schumann, Mahler, Brahms, Brucker, Berlioz, he could add almost endlessly to the list.

He had never really taken to the trend of posthumous diagnosis any more than he was happy with the transient sexual and behavioural mores of today being used to condemn historical figures or, for that matter, even those in the present day. 'Judge not, that ye not be judged. For with what judgment ye judge, ye shall be judged: and with what measure ye mete, it shall be measured to you again. And why beholdest thou the mote that is in thy brother's eye, but considerest not the beam that is in thine own eye'. How often had he found himself quoting Mathew 7 verses 1-3.

His was the sort of unease that made getting a focus to anything difficult. He went from room to room vaguely tidying. He went upstairs and again entered Gabriel's bedroom which to him had seemed to have remained dust free. The Catholic church used the word 'Incorruptibility' when divine intervention meant that the body of a saint like Saint Bernadette did not decompose. He resisted the temptation again to lie on the bed in which Gabriel, the uncorrupted, would sleep but rather stood staring at it. How would this arrangement really work out? That beautiful boy, that embodiment of musical purity, physically with him everyday. And now, with the agreement that he would practise on Adrian's piano, he would have even more privileged time with him. An almost physical sense of pleasure flowed over him afresh when he thought again of the words, 'he really likes you'. Those four words meant much more to Adrian than John Barrowman could have realized. He savoured the sound of them.

Not just 'likes you' but 'really likes you'. Indeed their importance to him took him a little by surprise. He remembered the kiss. Outside the dreary drizzle into which Siobhan had set-off had continued but his day had brightened with an inner light and heat that was sustaining and energizing. Only people without benefit of inner sunshine can be troubled by the ordinariness of weather. Gabriel liked him. The barometric bullying could not dampen the pleasure those words gave him.

The music in Adrian's head as he stood looking at the empty bed was Mendelssohn's Fourth Symphony. The exuberant allegro vivace of the opening movement enraptured him. The excitement of the build-up of strings made him visualize dancing. He knew that when he composed it, the twenty-four-year old Felix wrote to his sister saying it was the jolliest thing he had written. It always had the effect of accompanying moments like this. It could almost create them. He liked too the andante con moto with its hint of wistfulness. Some people, he knew, had speculated that it was influenced at one remove by Goethe's Faust. He didn't feel he knew enough here to make up his mind. It was the effect he enjoyed.

Shopping had to be done. He would be providing for Gabriel and John as well as himself. No longer would counting the slices of bread do. He should have asked John what sorts of things Gabriel liked. It was clear that he didn't overeat but he had to be sustained. Adrian was not quite sure how The Handy Stores made money. Perhaps some people paid a subscription to become one of the select few able to hear and dispense village gossip. It seemed to him that, practically every time he strayed into that sanctum, the High Priestess, Fiona Bellows was leaning on the counter talking to another woman. He could tell that some were chosen. There were adherents and heretics in this temple of tittle tattle. It was social media writ small with only one core belief shared with its bigger brother – that fact checking was anathema, indeed the antichrist. At times the exchanges among the disciples seemed to take on a sacramental flavour with lowered tones, whispered voices and the paradoxical caution of checking around lest someone should hear what would shortly spread like a conversational cholera from a water pump.

Today again, as so often before, he felt that he was among the topics of conversation, occasionally the central feature. Adrian had his old straw basket with him. Why he kept it he didn't know though it was almost back in fashion as food wrappings were going out of favour. His mother would have approved of this trend, not the gossip. 'Small talk is for small-minded people', she would say, 'gossip is for the godless'. The image in his mind now was of one of Bruegel's beautifully rendered proverbs, 'one winds on the distaff what the other spins'. So often his mind took cover behind culture from the hectoring hoi polloi and the many who clearly considered themselves without sin.

"My" said Fiona, as he placed the unaccustomed articles on the counter, "Mr Grayling, what has that Siobhan Walsh done to you?"

Pathetically he could only think to say, "I don't know what you mean Mrs. Bellows".

He didn't bother to look round to see who was sniggering. So did everyone know that Siobhan was an occasional nocturnal visitor. Certainly they would have been seen in the pub together. The only comfort he could take from this was that they didn't know he had made her a virgin again. There is sometimes a small superiority and protective pleasure in secrets.

"Sorry Mr Grayling" went on Mrs Bellows, "it's none of our business I know and she is a fine looking woman. Between you and Old Kennedy it is then".

"Old Kennedy?" he queried.

"Oh didn't you know" responded Mrs Bellows, "she's probably just visiting and if it's true that she's writing a book about your place then that'd be it".

Another voice behind, "if she's writing a book about that place it'll be a ghost story then? Smart one that Walsh woman. Bloody stupid names the Irish have. That Beckie Miller did say something to my Andrew. Now her father and Old Kennedy they were an odd couple".

Adrian did not want to get further into this conversation. Nothing he said would make much difference. Sometimes he felt that nothing anyone said ever made a difference. Things were either heard as confirmations or denials and the tribal positions strengthened or weakened accordingly but not changed. Original thinking and alternative views were as valued as an embarrassing genital itch. He put his shopping in the basket with the only further comment from Fiona Bellows of "wine too" receiving from him a nod of confirmation of the obvious. The solitary thing that had gone up in his estimation when he paid were the prices. He knew from experience that there was always a price to be paid.

John Barrowman arrived first with his car as loaded as it could be including the front passenger seat where Adrian had expected to find Gabriel. John seemed to recognize what was happening before Adrian said anything,

"Gabe's back with the rest of the stuff. I'll get this stowed then go back for him. I can leave a fair bit at work. We don't have that much. It looks worse in a small car. We'll try not to be any trouble Adrian, I promise you that".

Normally in a situation like this Adrian would not have considered helping carry things in. But some of this was Gabriel's. However having been resolutely turned down for a third time he sat in the piano room though he did not play. The music had not yet arrived. Perhaps it was the nature of his work that kept John Barrowman so fit. He was not even out of breath when he finished the last trip upstairs and set off again.

Adrian was watching from his bedroom window which, next to the attic, gave the best view of the road when he saw the little blue car again approaching. He could see that this time Gabriel was sitting in front. The car being small did not have the impact with Gabriel that it had with his father. It made John Barrowman look bigger but Gabriel's slight frame, perfectly proportioned head and exquisitely delicate features defined their own space. He was wearing black jeans and a white shirt with only the top two buttons undone. His face carried the mostly faraway expression he had seen before as he stood looking at the exterior of his new home though this time it also conveyed a sense of something being seen for the first time. He seemed to dwell a little longer on the attic window. Perhaps his father had talked to him about hoisting his piano on a pulley up there.

There was clearly no anticipation that Gabriel would carry anything upstairs. Normally Adrian would have found this inappropriate given the expectations of his own childhood but with this boy it had its own rightness to it and simply seemed so fitting. But then everything about him did.

Though they were probably only upstairs for an hour it appeared to Adrian to be an insufferably long time. He could see that he was going to have to work hard to establish his pupil's sense that this was not just where he was staying but his home.

John, who had brought a plastic crate of food, had asked if he could store some in the fridge. He had volunteered to cook for them that evening. Adrian explained that he already had thought of a simple pasta dish if, that is, they liked pasta. Amidst apologetic declarations that they were already putting him out, John confirmed that they did have pasta and indeed that it was one of the things Gabriel was a bit more reliable about eating. "Celia was the same" he had said, "fussy but still to me looked great on it but everyone else thought she was so pale".

That evening they ate together at the little table in the kitchen. Adrian had wanted Gabriel to sit opposite him so he would have an unfettered view of the loveliness but to fit everyone in Adrian and John sat at either end facing one another with Gabriel positioned in the middle so that periodically their legs touched. Adrian apologized when this happened but Gabriel never pulled back his legs if they made contact.

Adrian had opened a bottle of wine. He asked John if Gabriel should have some.

"He's never had wine" replied his father, "I haven't much either. I'm normally more a beer man".

"Not even communion wine" said Adrian.

"No, I'm not into that religious stuff much anymore. Never was really. Celia was, in her own way. Everything with Celia was in her own way. She said religions suffocated the spiritual. I didn't know communion wine was allowed to have alcohol".

"In the Catholic tradition" said Adrian, "like everything else the wine to be used is closely prescribed. It must be pure grape wine though in some special circumstances mustum can be used. Canon law says the wine must be natural, made from grapes and not corrupted. A quantity of water is to be added. If the wine is weak a small quantity of brandy if distilled from the grape may also be added. Sorry" he said, as though catching apology from

John, "I'm going on a bit. Sacramental wine is specially produced to meet the requirements".

"In that case I'll try some" said John, "you do know a lot of stuff Adrian".

"And my best pupil?" queried Adrian.

"Yes, if you think it's all right" responded John, relinquishing responsibility for his son to Adrian.

"I worked in Italy for a while" said Adrian, "there, children and young people drink with their parents. They teach primary school children about wine and wine making".

He poured a glass for John, then turning to Gabriel asked if he would like some. Gabriel nodded. He poured half a glass for him then himself a full glass.

Adrian watched as both his guests sampled the wine. He vaguely regretted not having bought something better so that their first experience would be even more rewarding. John took a good-sized mouthful, immediately swallowed it and said "not bad". Adrian looked at Gabriel who sat looking into the glass he was holding just short of his lips. It would, he thought, have been a perfect photograph. Because of his beauty, Ganymede had been abducted to be the wine pourer for the gods. Here, fittingly he was drinking the wine himself. The only true God is beauty.

As they ate the conversation continued. Apart from the fact that it was largely banal, Adrian could not have reported much about it. He had to concentrate on being careful not to be too obviously staring at the risen Ganymede. John was the sort of man who could take a long time to say he had finished talking. Then there would be the apologies for having talked for too long. Gabriel for his part never volunteered anything. His style was the antithesis of his father's, responding with the minimum of words to any questions asked. It made what he did say all the more important to Adrian.

When he had eaten what he wanted of his pasta Gabriel asked Adrian, not his father, if he could be excused. The old-fashioned nature of this again registered. He also asked if he might play the piano for a little while. Adrian could only acquiesce in this though he would have preferred him to stay. Teacher and father watched the boy move with unhurried grace from the table.

As Adrian produced the fruit salad he had prepared himself from the only fruit he could find in the shop, the sound of beautifully executed piano music seeped softly through and seemed to fill not just the kitchen but the cottage, suffusing them in a wash of delight. He couldn't quite place the music but it was certainly familiar, if only vaguely so. Somehow it didn't matter. Music should be something to respond to, not to know about. What was missing was being able to see the pianist as he performed.

Making conversation with John began to irritate Adrian. Even if what was being talked about had any interest it was not what he needed. He wanted to be where Gabriel was. Finally he persuaded John that they should have their coffee in the other room and listen to the playing. John first delayed things by insisting on stacking the dishwasher having first washed each item thoroughly.

Finally, coffee in hand, they could join Gabriel. As they entered he looked up for a moment but, like a professional in a piano bar, did not interrupt his playing. John continued to talk as they listened. Adrian tried to read Gabriel's body language from his back. He longed to be at the piano with him, seeing those graceful fingers and the perfect reflection in the piano lid.

After a too short time John announced that Gabriel would be tired and they should have an early night. Gabriel responsively stood-up. He waited till his father had again thanked Adrian profusely for his generosity then quietly said 'thank you'. Leaning over Adrian kissed him on the forehead, "goodnight Gabriel" he said. The gentle sweetness of the smiled reply was counterpointed by the lingering look at his piano teacher.

Adrian needed to distract himself from the moment. "John" he said, "tomorrow I'll see if I can get a foldaway bed from somewhere".

"Don't worry" said Adrian, "since his mother left he's come in with me. He's used to it".

With those words the two of them left.

Chapter 17

The Huntress

Adrian had drunk more wine than normal. He couldn't be sure that wasn't why the night following the first evening with his house guests had proved so wakeful and restless. It had seemed somehow better to stay downstairs for a little while after they had gone up to the bed they would share. The piano stool from which Gabriel had provided a musical accompaniment to their evening had seemed symbolically unoccupied. That his pupil had tended to play the same piece more than once probably reflected limitations in his repertoire. More emphasis on teaching him to read music was clearly needed. There were already hints of good promise here. He had not played the Clara Schumann or either Song for Celia or The Minstrel Boy. Adrian embarrassed himself by hoping that this was because these were personal to them.

Once in bed Adrian felt sleep was punishing him by remaining in some distant hiding place, provoking him to search for it. Trying to sleep is such a paradoxical thing to do. The only thing in life that did not reduce to paradox, he thought, was beauty. Untouchable, necessary beauty. Adrian had often felt appalled by the intellectual desert around him. Had it not been for Gabriel he would have more profoundly regretted having relaunched himself into his immediate social world from which the only escape was through music. Wagner came to his mind at that moment, definitely to him the most imposingly philosophical of composers. Maybe that's why he liked his music so much and found it so aggressively challenging. Goya had got it right, the Sleep of Reason does produce monsters. Fantasy and the imagination may be the raw material but it is the discipline of reason that liberates it to take flight as art and music.

The first time Adrian had seen the Goya etching he had been immediately drawn to it and had returned to look several times. It had been reproduced in a book at school but this had been withdrawn from the library because someone had complained that it elsewhere contained some representations of naked bodies. This, they felt, to be inappropriate for boys. In an intellectually liberated world nothing is inappropriate, just not yet appropriated, he thought. As a younger man he might have graffitied 'Apollo loves Dionysus OK'. He didn't really think this was a fully requited love. His world then was not liberated. It wasn't still.

Adrian knew from experience that people often claim not to sleep when the likelihood was that they had dozed, at least sporadically. But to him the greatest negative in the absence of sleep is not being denied rest. It was being condemned to be confronted by one's own thoughts and feelings. Alone. With none of the quotidian distractions that protect from awareness of our insignificance and many imperfections. The angry awfulness of facing the paucity of our intellectual resources. The parading of the blatant banality of the ideas that come to us. Now it was cruelly clear to him that he was just like the rest of them. Not set aside. Different. Special. The astonishing demeaning clarity of his reverse epiphany hit him like fifty thousand volts of reality.

"Oh daughters of Zeus" he heard himself cry from the desperation of his own cross, "why hast thou forsaken me". His thoughts, once released, pursued him like hungry children in a Moroccan souk. We are driven mad for the want of sleep so that we beg pitiably for it like a starving man for a morsel of even rotted food. An imperfect idea is still an idea. Yet for all this he still clung to the belief that great art can elevate culture to a throne of exuberant excellence. Ok, so what if it achieves this by pointing the finger at our individual worthlessness. Perhaps this is its true purpose; control and incorporation through our sense of inadequacy. When he was not being tormented by such a sense of individual pointlessness, Adrian was sustained, to some extent, by a conviction that, to be exposed to great music or any art is to partake of it, to be nourished by it, to have the protection of its tribe, ultimately to have a god.

But biology too has a way of reminding us of the most common of denominators. Adrian needed to go to the loo. He slept naked but now that he had house guests he felt he should wear his dressing gown. Despite his need he passed the bathroom and stood at the door of the garden bedroom. There was not a sound from the shared room of father and son. He tried to be as quiet as the Holy Ghost. He didn't even flush the loo to avoid disturbing others. Back in bed he lay once more condemning the puerility of his own thought that nothing can have meaning when everything becomes a metaphor. It was all too like something from the endless sermons his mother dragged him to as a boy. Why have none of the churches ever learned that aphorism is not philosophy?

In the morning he didn't have his usual shower. With only one bathroom he needed to come to some sort of arrangement with the others. It was only the start of the first day and already he was feeling constrained. Had it not been for the thought of the sleeping boy he would have sought a way out of the situation. Downstairs he found John Barrowman already up and dressed. The kettle had been boiled.

"What" John asked by way of greeting "would you like for breakfast?"

"I usually only have toast" replied Adrian.

"I've some eggs that I brought, and bacon if you would like some. Gabriel's like you. Has hardly anything. Celia was the same. I always get up early. Though it's not a working day for me I wanted to get a move on with the attic. I like to keep busy. The sooner I've that done the sooner we can be out of your hair for more of the time. I really am very grateful for this. I've been wondering if I could install a little… something like a caravan shower up there too then you'd have nearly everything back. What do you think? Nothing that would require structural change of course".

Adrian reflexively checked the kettle for water before responding,

"Interesting ideas but it's not my cottage. I'd have to run anything significant past the landlord. In the meantime perhaps we could come to some agreement about the shower".

"Certainly" replied John, "Gabe can have a shower before bedtime. He usually goes to bed earlier than I do. It'd give us a chance to have a chat till upstairs is available. I enjoyed talking to you last night. I could put a telly up there. There is one other thing Adrian. I'd like to pay half the rent during the time we're here. Would that be all right with you?"

Though his first instinct had been to say it wasn't necessary, Adrian responded

"that would be helpful at this time".

He then felt that he ought to offer to assist with the final sorting out of the attic. He was delighted when John wouldn't hear of it.

Adrian sat having his tea and toast. He watched as John prepared bacon and egg for himself. What he was primarily interested in however was seeing Gabriel on his first morning in Magus Cottage but his pupil did not materialize. As though John again knew what was in his thinking he said,

"Gabe will be awake and up. He'll be sitting thinking. He does that a lot. His last school even thought he had a problem but they never knew his mother".

John had finished preparing his breakfast and sat down at the table with Adrian. The night had clearly bestowed hunger on him in greater quantity than delicacy. If hereditary was anything to go by Gabriel's grace must have come from his mother. As John entered a form of inelegant hand-to-mouth conflict with his plate Adrian asked,

"What sort of problem did they think he had?"

"Too self-contained, I think they said. No problem with his work or behaviour though they felt he put no effort in. When they wanted to refer him somewhere one of them said he was a little boy lost. He had no real friends. Generally the other lads didn't really take to him. Well he wasn't much interested in footie. I used to support Killie".

"Killie?" queried Adrian.

"Kilmarnock" explained John, "it's coming back to this village his mother came from that's making a difference and especially coming to you. I don't know what you've done to him but whatever it is, it's working. Keep it up Adrian".

"I don't know how much credit I can take" said Adrian, "but he has a gift. He has such natural grace and sensitivity to music and his singing voice, even a cappella, is astonishing, moving".

"A what was that?" asked John.

"Sorry" replied Adrian, "a cappella, that's just silly jargon for singing without musical accompaniment. He tells me his mother could sing".

"She had a lovely voice" said John, "I can't sing a note. But anyway I must get on. Don't worry about us. I'll sort us out and if there's any little thing I can do for you Adrian just let me know".

John was about to go upstairs when Siobhan arrived. She kissed Adrian on the lips then shook hands with John.

"I saw your car was here overnight so I assumed you'd moved in. I promised to help you sort things out. Am I too late?"

"I've only the attic to finish with. Thanks for the offer though. You've done enough in suggesting staying here till we get ourselves sorted out long-term".

"And is long term going to be in the village?" she asked.

"I hope so. I'll stay as long as Gabe's happy. Anyway I wouldn't dream of taking him away from Adrian here".

Siobhan and Adrian went into the piano room.

"So how is it so far?" she asked.

"It's only been one evening" he replied, "but I think it will work out ok. Gabriel entertained us, well me anyway, with an impromptu recital".

"Where is this kid that you go on about so much?" asked Siobhan "I've yet to meet him. I just saw him once from the distance".

"It's a Saturday morning" said Adrian "he's probably having a lie in on his first full day here. Don't worry, you will meet him".

"Just checking. I know he really exists even though the way you talk about him he could just be some fantasy figure" said Siobhan, grinning at him.

"He is real" replied Adrian, then added, "you're the only fantasy figure in my life".

"Well I won't be around in any form for the next couple of days. I've got to go back to my own place to check on things. I'll be back Monday, Tuesday at the latest. I was hoping we could get some time today before I go".

"Oh dear" said Adrian, "what a lovely thought but it might be a little difficult. Today's the first day they're here. It might be awkward".

"Awkward" said Siobhan sounding irked, "it's still your house isn't it. I'm not used to being turned down. There aren't many men I bother with. Come on, be spontaneous, let's just do it".

She leaned towards him and again kissed him. It was an art form in which she could run a master-class. He found his body responding to her as her hand ran up the inside of his leg. At that moment he had a sense that they were not alone. He looked across the room to find Gabriel standing passively in the doorway. He had no idea how long he had been there. He disentangled himself from Siobhan.

"This is Gabriel" he said, "Gabriel, come and meet Siobhan. She's a friend of mine".

Gabriel obediently stepped forward and stood in front of Siobhan. As he held out his hand, for a moment it seemed to her that he expected it to be kissed. They shook hands. There was a sense of formality to it that made her uncomfortable.

"Hello" she said, "good to meet you at last. I like your hair".

"Thank you" replied Gabriel, "and I like yours".

Siobhan laughed.

A silence that harboured uncertainty about what to do next, of lush embarrassment, dominated the space between them. Everyone knows that feeling. He knew the source of his own. In that moment his need was for her to like his pupil. He had first-hand experience of embarrassment used as an insidious weapon so that, even after all those years, it still resonated with him. As an adult it now seemed to him to carry the danger of loss, mostly of who he was, of the way he wanted to be thought of. And always there was the risk of shaming, of humiliation, things that can only happen in the presence of others, those with power. A childhood so overfull of his mother can do that so that it cannot readily be undone. But this was not quite all that he detected now. There was more a tension. In a way he later dismissed as fanciful the thought came to him that, if it was not dealt with, it could transmogrify into menace. He was about to intervene to diffuse the situation when Gabriel asked Siobhan,

"Do you think I am strange?"

"Strange" she repeated his word, "in what way strange? If you mean out of the ordinary then you are. Adrian tells me you are the most gifted pupil he has ever taught".

"My mother said women would find me strange".

Adrian hoped that he would not add that she also said men would find him beautiful. If asked he would not deny the beauty of this boy but knew how easily that could be misinterpreted.

"Why do you think she said that?" asked Siobhan, recovering enough composure to ask a more normal question.

"She did not say why" replied Adrian, "just that they would".

"You must always be yourself, value who you are" said Siobhan.

Adrian had the sense that she was trying to close down this conversation, to cage it in a modern cliché. He knew better than most that there's a way out of almost every situation but always at the cost of honesty.

"My mother told me everyone is many people" said Gabriel, "no one ever sees who you are. They choose".

"Your mother was a very interesting person Gabriel" intervened Adrian "and we will talk about her much more. But you must have breakfast. Come".

He led the way to the kitchen. He had hoped that Siobhan would not follow. He did not feel that Gabriel was comfortable with her. Perhaps it was because he may have seen her kiss him. Could this boy be jealous of her? It was a thought he felt did not do either of them justice. However Siobhan did follow them.

As his father had said Gabriel did not seem interested in eating. He was persuaded to have some toast. He sat there more nibbling than eating it. Siobhan suddenly asked,

"Will you be ok by yourself for a while? Adrian and I are going to go for a walk".

The question which did not faze Gabriel, surprised Adrian. Not only had going for a walk not been discussed but it somehow made him appear overprotective of his young pupil. Gabriel replied,

"I like being alone".

Siobhan took Adrian by the arm and steered him out. He glanced back to see Gabriel putting down the piece of toast.

They walked in silence for a while towards the woods. It was Siobhan who traded the silence for a few words,

"Christ, he is a strange boy" she said, "weird. And all that stuff about everyone being many people and choosing. I can believe it about him. It's bizarre yet his dad is so normal".

Adrian recognized that he was beginning to feel both angry and defensive with Siobhan,

"You haven't had a chance to get to know him" he responded, "you haven't heard him play or sing. His mother abandoning him had an effect, that's certainly true but he has an innocent beauty about him. When you come back next week you must come round again and get to know him a bit better. Perhaps we could all have dinner".

"I'd rather just meet you in the Mitre. I'm not comfortable with him" she said.

It was when they reached a clearing and sunlight freckled the canopy that, for the first time since Siobhan arrived that morning, Adrian began to hear the faint sounds of music. It was hard to pinpoint but it was there. It sounded a little like the unidentified piece Gabriel had played that was interrupted by the emptiness of his father's chatter.

"Let's not argue about it. Not about a boy" said Siobhan turning to him and kissing him.

He decanted his feelings into that kiss as she pulled him yet closer to her. Suddenly she freed herself and began, not so much to undress as to strip.

"Let's do it here, now" she said.

Already her dress was on the ground with her bra on top of it. Without taking her eyes off his and with only a slight bend of her knees she took her panties off. Adrian looked around fearing someone would come upon them but it was too late to try to control his body.

"Pretend you have just found me like this in the woods. A virgin alone and vulnerable".

He looked at her naked form. There she was, slightly quivering, in the open air of the woods on a brisk morning with shafts of sunlight suggestively penetrating above. In an instant he knew he had seen this before, the naked figure of Diana the Huntress in the Louvre. But it was the arrow in his own quiver that was now in command. The music accumulating in his head was Woolstenhulme's, Diana the Huntress, a piece best known to teachers of music. How often had he used this with slightly more advanced violin students. It had suited many classroom moments and now matched perfectly this woodland scene and how fittingly as Diana was sometimes represented as a virgin goddess. She again came to him and kissed him.

When she pulled up his top he raised his arms above his head in an act that combined obeyance and worship. She discarded the item and undid his trousers sliding them and his underpants down in one uninterrupted movement. He completed what she had started by kicking them off along with his shoes. Now both fully naked they faced each other, she in her radiant reborn virginity and he parading his arousal as an unequivocal proclamation of his intention.

Even consensual sexual acts are like a drama. Whether tragedy or comedy is always to be decided. Need exists. Tension builds. A resolution is sought. The outcome is not inevitable. Postures are adopted. Negotiations commenced. Breakdown. Recommencement. New positions taken. Combat engaged. The dance of the survival of their species choreographed anew through all eternity. The initial sense of crescendo from adagretto through allegro to prestissimo followed by the ritenuto signalling the requiem for effort spent.

Then the bodies of Siobhan and Adrian lay, still entwined but passion exhausted. They rested side by side, now more aware of the discomfort of their leafy bed of chance on the woodland surface. She looked toward him and, her tone softly emollient, said,

"Sorry Adrian, I didn't mean to be nasty about Gabriel. I know you like him and I could see you weren't happy with what I said".

Adrian sat up. He looked down at the glistening face and realized how much, apart from the hair colour, she did actually look like Diana in the Louvre painting.

"No need to apologize" he said "it's just that I've got a feeling he could so easily be misunderstood".

As he spoke there was a sudden sound. His reaction was exaggerated by fact of their nakedness. There was an 'after the fall' element to it all.

"Did you hear that?" he asked jumping up, "I think someone's coming".

She too stood up. There were times when Siobhan could assume a childlike quality. She was manifestly much less concerned than amused. She grinned at him and feigned panic, theatrically bending her knees a little and alternately covering her breasts and vagina with her hands. Adrian, who was momentarily peeved by her performance, grabbed his clothes while she more calmly picked up hers and followed him behind some bushes. She giggled as they both tried to dress quickly.

A large black Labrador which was not on a lead appeared closely followed by a noisily barking Jack Russell. The tail wagging Labrador immediately came towards where they were hiding. Adrian noticed that Siobhan had made the decision not to put her bra back on. He had never known why women with firm breasts actually wore them. She finished dressing faster than he did.

An elderly man appeared in the clearing as they came from behind the bushes. Siobhan tickled the head of the Labrador. "Hello Hector" she called out.

He turned towards them with a startled look as though he hadn't seen them.

"It's Siobhan Walsh" she said, "Beckie Miller's friend".

"Ah" he responded, "good-day to you".

He called the dogs to him and they set off again. Siobhan grinned at Adrian,

"The last time I was nearly caught like that I was a teenager playing strip poker. If Hector had been able to see properly the whole village would know by lunchtime. Not that it would matter. We're both adults. Oh I'd forgotten. You don't put so much weight on the age thing".

As they made their way back to Magus Cottage, Siobhan again brought up the subject of Adrian's house guests, wanting to check once more how long it was proposed they'd be there as though she hadn't been part of the original plan. Adrian heard music as he opened the front door.

"Listen" he said.

They both paused in the hallway.

"That's a fugue from Bach. I'm using it to help teach him to read music. I'm really glad he's practising. You're not very into the technicalities of music Siobhan but if you were you'd be able to tell the talent just from what he's doing – if you knew Bach that is. That boy has the mark of greatness about him. Churchill said that the price of greatness is responsibility but it's obvious to me that when it is a pupil who is great, the responsibility is with the teacher".

They entered the room where Gabriel was playing. As though sensing they were there he stopped playing the Bach and instead played the piece he had played the night before. Adrian went and stood by him while Siobhan sat on the settee.

After a period of about ten minutes he stopped. Siobhan applauded. Gabriel stood and turned around. He nodded appreciation for the applause. Adrian said,

"everything you play, even practise sessions you do beautifully. I don't know the piece you just played. What is it?"

"My mother wrote it" said Gabriel, "she called it 'Tears of the Teacher'. She put words to it but said I should sing them only if I ever had urgent need of her. Then she would come. She said it is a lucky one who finds a teacher to guide them in life".

"Have you ever wanted to sing those words?" he asked.

The boy nodded.

"How will you know when to sing it?" asked Adrian.

The pupil shook his head,

"I know when it is not the time" he said, "I sing it only in my head. If I sang it aloud I do not know if she would come back. If I sang it and she did not there would be nothing left, nothing. When I play it sometimes I feel someone is with me. Last night when I played it I thought there was someone else here. A girl in a white dress. She cried but when I looked round there was no one. Now I would like to go to my room".

"If there was no one there how did you know she had a white dress?" Adrian's question carried more of a need to know than a challenge.

"I knew" he said his voice sounding weary.

He turned to leave. "Gabriel" said Adrian gently. The boy paused and turned towards him. Adrian took both the child's hands in his, "Gabriel" he said again, "you must remember you can come to me, at any time of the day or night. You can ask me anything".

"You are my teacher" said Gabriel and for a third time kissed him on the cheek. Then with the merest nod to Siobhan he left the room.

"Adrian" said Siobhan "what just happened there? What was he talking about and why is he so sad?"

Adrian went and sat by her. "I don't know" he said, then added "there's something else. I'd been going to say something to you but the time hadn't seemed right. It just seems so absurd". He took the look on her face as puzzlement but it might equally have been concern. He went on,

"In that piano stool there, the old one Gabriel was sitting on, I found something. A diary that was written in code. I managed to break the code because it was musical. I haven't transcribed it all yet but what I read was about a girl in white who came to the diary keeper for piano lessons".

"A piano teacher" she said, "in this house. Adrian, what happened to the girl?"

"I don't know" said Adrian without questioning what made Siobhan think something had happened to her, "perhaps there's a clue in the other bits".

"Adrian" Siobhan said his name again in a tone far removed from her usual frivolity, "there is something I need to tell you too. About this place. I've been talking to Old Kennedy again. And there's something else. That story I'm thinking of writing might be true or at least have some truth in it".

Siobhan was about to say more but they heard someone approaching. An apologetic John Barrowman stood in the doorway,

"Sorry to interrupt" he said, "I'm going to make an early lunch. Gabe's in the room. I think he wants to be alone for a bit. He gets like that sometimes. Can I get you anything?"

"Not for me" said Siobhan standing up, "Adrian, I've got to go now. We can talk about this when I get back".

She kissed him, this time not on the lips but on the exact spot on his cheek that Gabriel had. She could have no idea how much that felt like sacrilege to him.

Chapter 18

Mother and Teacher

Adrian's mother used to say that he spent too much time thinking and not enough praying. Now in unintended confirmation of this he sat reflecting on the first morning with Gabriel under his roof. Then there was Siobhan's first meeting with his pupil. He had never had sex in the open air before. The risk, which had added palpably to the enjoyment, now seemed foolhardy. But what again was preoccupying this teacher was his pupil.

In his head Adrian replayed the tune of 'Tears of the Teacher'. Perhaps not in the highest league of great music but better than anything he could write and, the more it repeated, the more haunting it became. It was difficult for him to be fully objective. The association with Gabriel prevented that. Nor was it possible for him to stop himself thinking what the words might have been. Somehow he felt they would be like a cross between Celia's Song and The Minstrel Boy. Whatever they were Gabriel was hanging onto them, half hoping that they could magically summon the return of his mother yet fearing that they would not.

All that beauty, that enormous talent, yet this most gifted of pupils could say that, if he could not bring her back, he would have nothing. The loss of a beautiful loved object always comes at a terrible cost. Adrian knew that. He now had an unshakable sense that a world without Gabriel would be an oppressive, echoing thing, cold, grey and empty.

Feeling the torment of another. Unable to change it. The hell of powerlessness. The only thing left to Adrian was the medication of music. A child possessed by an overpowering longing for the mother who had apparently abandoned him. A mother with whom it was thought the relationship was too close. Adrian knew that the church of his childhood liked to be referred to as the mother church. It was also known as the mother and teacher but his own view of the maternal was less idealized. None the less he refused to hold his own mother wholly responsible for his life. Influential yes, a creator of directions yes. Responsible no. For so long that he could not remember when it had started, he had refused to denounce poor outcomes as the product of life experience. In this he was a modern heretic. It was simply an undeserved triumph of telos that had ushered in a new age of blame. Nor did Adrian accept that he was prone to overthinking though might be persuaded that the classical world and its myths came to his head more than to most people. Then of course there was the music.

How often had the example of St. Sebastian come to him, this martyr whose attempt to conceal his Christian faith was unsuccessful and, on being discovered, Emperor Diocletian ordered him tied to a tree and shot full of arrows, giving rise to the famous image of him by the artist Giovanni Bazzi, known as Il Sodoma, for reasons that left far too little to the imagination.

Yes of course there were endless other and more famous depictions of this scene most notably by Botticelli. Adrian had long found the look of Sebastian's face in that work just too casual for the theme, but who was he to judge? Here, his informing philosophy was simple, while it is always the binary that separates it is judgement that destroys us. Of course he knew that the Sebastian of these various representations did not die in this way. On being helped to recovery he confronted Diocletian with the evil of his ways and was clubbed to death for his trouble and thrown into a sewer. Such has long been the unfortunate fate of the tellers of unfashionable truths. Adrian had always dismissed as fanciful that the killing had been because the beautiful Sebastian had resisted the sexual advances of Diocletian but then he regarded much of his mother's church as mythic.

The image of St. Sebastian was none the less powerful. His attempts over the years to use the story to illustrate that there are many ways to understand outcomes, far from generating philosophical discussion of cause and responsibility, had brought the unthinking opprobrium of the microcosmic masses down on him. Perhaps the captain from the Praetorian Guard should have learned from Peter that denial is sometimes the best policy.

Sitting opposite the piano Adrian's mind was becoming both racingly energized and spillingly overfull, like a pint of Antique

Ugly in the hands of a drunk man. Now, but for a moment more fleeting than the flight of an arrow across his field of vision, he thought he saw Gabriel standing looking down at the piano stool. There was something about the look that reminded him of the face of St. Sebastian in the Giovanni Bazzi painting. In his head, the volume of Debussy's music on the martyrdom of the St. Sebastian was being slowly turned up. He had often said that the phrase 'what's not to like' could have been written for all of Debussy. His fondness for that entire corpus had never diminished. He simply found it absorbingly beautiful and this piece he thought of as much the better for being no longer so closely linked to D'Annunzio's self-indulgent and over-long play for which it was originally written. Surely further confirmation that he was right, sometimes it is best to divorce outcomes from sources.

Abruptly standing up Adrian got the keys. He would decode another entry in the diary that had apparently infiltrated his pupil the previous evening. He continued to work at this for much of the next couple of hours trying not to take in too much of the content till he would come to it afresh like sight reading a new piece of music. Finally he held the paper on his lap and read:

'She came again today, this pupil who teaches me the meaning of true beauty and who is, in truth, no more now a pupae but an ethereal creature. Whitely pure and wan I thought her to be in her long cocoon of gossamer such that, when I did position her by the piano with the window behind, it did render to my craving eye the silhouette of her coming form.

Samuel tells me that I should have a caution that what I see as divine might be a deceiving demon, some Lileth wandering from heart to heart, draining from each their true soul so that none can know completeness without her. He tells me that such beauty as I see could be of Satan's sister who craves only he and that I should free myself or forever gift my soul to her brother and surrender to her. When I plead that beauty is a pure expression of the divine he tells me that Lucifer, once an angel, kept that form forever and that I should look to all the once beautiful maidens whose husbands took them in passion but whose true nature shows with time, to mock them with the truth that the butterfly again becomes the caterpillar.

It is to me a certitude, as if plainly written by the wits God gave me, that there is no alchemy to turn to ugliness such a form as I discern beneath that dress of white, though I can have it that it may be that my temptress plays me like a fugue, for each time her beauty enters then my very being repeats its longing for the sight of her. She hath the key to my heart and has hidden it in her bosom that surely rises and sighs for me. Sometimes she deigns to grant the slightest of glances or, bliss be, launches towards me a smile of such sweet seduction that I could weep.

Never has a man been so tormented by goodness, so driven to a wild despairing love of another but yet cannot speak of it save to the noble Samuel, my honourable and faithful companion of this many a year. He tells me that Augustine himself asked whether things are beautiful because they delight or give delight because they are beautiful. I can tell him by all that is sacred in this world that it is my pupil who bestows beauty upon the very ground touched by her foot, nay more, even where her shadow falls, becomes sacred to me. Weekly I do know that she doth grow in fondness for me though her breeding will not let her yet speak of it. Today again she sang for me. Music is assuredly the true pathway to the soul of man and her voice an invitation to heaven. As she sang I came close to a full understanding of what it must be like to be of the distaff side and to suffer with the vapours, so weakly sad and close to madness did I become, so beyond all mortal reasoning and loss of control. Oh priceless child I fear that I will die for the love of you but if I do I will know that I have died for true beauty. Would that we lived in a time when our separate stations did not have such tyrant rule and you could choose to have me by your side. Gentle maiden, though your years may be tender your heart hath the knowledge of all the ages. Learn well this simple truth and take comfort from it. We will be as one and soon my precious infant, soon.

When it came time for her to go this day she again looked into me as if able to divine my desires and I would swear her eyes consecrated my love with her consent, though as yet no words of this have passed between us. Each day apart till our next time will be as a little death for me. If I could but sleep till then I would have it so'.

Adrian sat for a while with the transcript in his hand. He could not at that moment bring himself to read through it another time though he knew he would be drawn back to it at some point. Beauty, he thought, asks for nothing but appreciation of its presence but this man, whose name he did not know, had sexualized it; like a barbarian he had made crudely carnal what should have retained a more cerebral if not mystical essence. And he feared the music teacher had more than a betrayal of principle in mind.

Chapter 19

Chiaroscuro

That evening Adrian, Gabriel and John had again eaten together. He sometimes liked to think of meals as dining but this one was again in the kitchen. John had prepared a roast chicken. There wasn't actually anything wrong with the individual items or how they were cooked. They all just seemed so separate on the plate, like the parts of Adrian's life. It was in need of some flavouring, a few spices or a sauce perhaps, some additional element was certainly required to transform it from food into a meal. It was, thought Adrian, like music played by a robotic orchestra. For once he was grateful for John Barrowman's verbosity. He knew that he must have successfully nodded or given suitable verbal cues to listening since John showed no sign of annoyance or embarrassment or indeed stopping. Adrian could remember only that this prolix production was peppered with gratitude for being allowed to stay there even though he would be paying a share of the rent. The missing ingredient in the culinary experience found its counterpoint in the social. Here what was lacking was more readily identified. It needed intellectual content and especially humour. It didn't need to be particularly highbrow. An anecdote made amusing by the telling or an account of an unusual piece of music that had taken the listener by surprise would have sufficed or perhaps some reference to a painting that had touched or expanded the other.

Gabriel had said little and eaten less. His father's "he gets like that sometimes" had been too passively accepting to help. When Adrian had encouraged him, Gabriel had a couple of mouthfuls. Sometimes morsels matter like catching sight of a smile of support when giving an early performance. Gabriel seemed to eat only because he was given food. The pleasure of food in itself or of the social dimension simply seemed not to be there. He had however come close to smiling when Adrian told him about Prokofiev's 'For the Love of Three Oranges'. A cursed prince in search of three oranges and finding love along the way. With butterfly lightness a smile had almost landed on Gabriel's face when Adrian had said "so a lot to identify with". While he hadn't appeared particularly impressed when he learned that Prokofiev had written his first piece at age five what had really interested him was when Adrian told him that Prokofiev had been inspired by his mother playing the piano. He also looked intently at Adrian when he said in passing that Prokofiev had not fitted in with the other boys at the Conservatoire.

Before they had eaten John had shown Adrian what he had achieved in the attic. It was what he had come to expect from his meticulous lodger, clinically clean and ordered. What had really pleased Adrian was that the attic's atmosphere had been maintained whether John was aware of it or not. Perhaps it was seeing Gabriel standing centre stage and looking as though he belonged there that created the effect.

"Tomorrow" said John Barrowman "I shall collect the rest of my stuff from work and put it here, then Adrian, you'll be delighted to know, you'll have most of your living space back though we will still need to use the bathroom and kitchen".

"No please" said Adrian, "you are welcome and Gabriel must never feel he cannot come down and use the piano".

"Oh I think he knows that" replied John, "I know his talent makes him special to you. I'm just sorry I'm not more interesting. It was always like that, at school, then wherever I worked. I could know things but by the time I'd worked out how to say it no one was still talking about it. The funny thing is people still think I talk too much. Celia used to say that my conversation was more like musak. You're a musician, you probably don't approve of that. It's everywhere, well in big shops and even in lifts and toilets. I suppose it's there to increase sales but that wouldn't explain it in loos..."

Adrian interrupted, "don't put yourself down John. You are right that Gabriel's special, unique. But you have your own skills though you don't seem to value them".

Whether taking his cue from what was being said or from something in his inner world Gabriel now turned towards them and said,

"I think my mother would have liked it here. She would have absorbed things".

"She would Gabe, you're right. I'm sure she would have liked it" said John for the first time reaching out and putting his hand on his son's arm. To Adrian it appeared that Gabriel had remained still, perhaps even stiffly so.

After they had eaten John again loaded the dishwasher once more having first washed each item. They sat in the living room and Gabriel played the piano. When Adrian asked him if he would again play the piece his mother had written, John looked at his son and, a lonely sadness flavouring his words, said,

"your mother never talked to me about music". Then turning to Adrian he added, "Celia always said she didn't do requests. She said a request is a conclusion and art is always a question. She said it's a denial of the power of serendipity. She was always coming out with stuff like that".

As though confirming that there was little to be said Gabriel did not attempt to join in the conversation. Instead he unfussily swivelled back to the piano and again played 'Tears of the Teacher'. It was as though he had somehow picked up the vague melancholy of his father's tone.

Only one night had passed with his beautiful pupil living under his roof. While Adrian felt he might be getting a little more information about him he had a sense of knowing him less. This was the great paradox of the age. More information than had ever being easily available and less sense of knowing things. It was to him as though they were all dwelling in the Temple of Dagon when Samson collapsed the pillars on them. None the less there were to him some irreducibles and beauty in its many forms, was among these. In beauty he had found something in which the whole is not simply greater than the sum of the parts, beauty is the whole transformed to an indivisible oneness. It is a thing both necessary and sufficient in itself. He used to think that beauty aroused feelings in us that make us dream of souls. Having kissed the cold lips of unbearable loss it had now come to him that the soul was but a glass chisel, a fragmenting explanation for beauty.

The voice of John Barrowman reconnected him. Though the words, "I think I'll call it a day" were once more encased in a gush of gratitude, they delighted him. However, as so often in his life, the moment of relief was short lived when he discovered that he meant to take Gabriel with him. The solitary compensation was that once more he received a priceless goodnight kiss on the cheek from his pupil.

Adrian stayed downstairs long enough for both John and Gabriel to use the bathroom. He didn't do much with the time, apart from looking towards the piano stool on which Gabriel had so delicately perched and which contained, in its locked heart, the coded indelicacies of the thoughts of another piano teacher whom Adrian had come to despise. These thoughts unsettled him but unsettled was a word that could be fittingly used to describe his life since the arrival of his new pupil. Even the presence of Siobhan contributed to that effect. Though she made him feel alive and potent, it seemed to him that the timing was wrong. His mother, had she been able to conceive of such liaison at all, would have called it star-crossed but he knew that, to her, anything that was not in her own scheme of things she would have felt ill-omened. On top of all this there was the fact that he was not yet sure that Siobhan was who she claimed to be. He was hardly in the best moral position to condemn this.

Finally Adrian made his way to bed as though his body was a mechanical contraption that he manoeuvered clumsily. Everything once again seemed to conspire to make it unlikely that sleep would follow. Even when he tried to conjure music he did not find any, apart from a melancholic echo of 'Tears of the Teacher'. Tonight, fully armed thoughts patrolled Adrian's head. They raged in a psychotic bacchanalia of multicoloured transgressions. It was an orgy of exploding certainties and woeful wailing. Then the image took the form of a drowning Gabriel stretching towards him with desperate pleading, his reach falling short of sanctuary.

Sometimes in the past Adrian had thought that, were it not for the beauty he found in music, the only rescue for him would have been insanity but now, while his pupil had need of him, he had to survive.

Lying there thinking about the boy, other music slowly began to return to him, too indistinct to identify but with a softening effect, helping him mellow. There was no way of telling how long he had lain there in this way before more fully alerting. It wasn't possible to be sure but he thought he'd heard another sound. Adrian had lost count of the number of times since coming to Magus Cottage that he had wakened to what might be sounds, perhaps even music, seeming to come from the attic. It is strangely hard sometimes to know when one is awake.

Adrian concentrated. Nothing. Then the sound again. Was it the same sound? It was compelling enough to get him out of bed. He had left the door a little ajar because, when it was opened, it squealed a partial protest as though some creature, that could disturb his guests, was trapped under it. The corridor was lit by a yellowing light, stronger than a nightlight but not so bright as to fully wake anyone, the intention, like his past role which he now despised, was guidance not illumination.

Involuntarily Adrian's gaze tracked the sound like a hunter its prey. There, at the door to the bathroom, was Gabriel. He had stopped and was looking towards Adrian's bedroom. Had he too heard a sound or was he merely looking in the direction where his teacher should be asleep?

It was the first time that Adrian had seen his pupil fully naked. Though the light was from the solitary unprotected bulb, to Adrian at that moment a radiance shone not just around Gabriel but from him. His flawless skin, softly white it was, against the night black of his hair which hung in childlike ringlets to his slender shoulders, suggested virginal purity. The proportions to Adrian were Pythagorian. No longer merely a picture of perfection, the scene had metamorphosed into a manifestation of exquisite beauty that was both pleasing and beguiling. The pose possessed a self-assured naturalness which carved from the night a simple awareness of the space he occupied and then enriched it with the unselfconsciousness of his nakedness. There was something about the form of this boy that suggested an abandoned smile of saddened forgiveness. It forsook the empty anger of moralizing, leaving in its place a world liberated and suffused with a guiltless sense of acceptance of things and people as they are.

Adrian did not know how long he stood there feeling the joy of an uncomplicated entitlement to look. He felt what Zeus must have experienced when his eye first fell on Ganymede, or Apollo on seeing Hyacinthus, for Gabriel possessed all the beauty of

Narcissus but none of the self-absorbtion. Did his pupil know that his teacher was there looking at him, powerless to move, his freedom hijacked and held to an unpayable ransom?

Now the music that swarmed in his head was Sati's Gymnopedie which he knew to celebrate an ancient festival in which young men would dance with uninhibited nakedness. It was a deceptively simple piano piece that, to him, made playful use of mild dissonances to produce a gently melancholic effect that seemed to match the needs of the moment. More than most it changed with how it is played, especially the opening that never actually resolves. He now imagined Celia playing it to Gabriel.

He remained waiting at his bedroom door till his pupil re-emerged. The boy again stopped and looked briefly towards his door before turning and walking with graceful purpose towards the bedroom he shared with his father. When Adrian had first seen his pupil he had thought of Donatella's David but now felt that created too effete an image. In this moment of seeing Gabriel naked he was confirmed in the view that, though beautifully executed, Donatella's work failed to capture the natural fragility and vulnerability he saw in this boy. Another question now deposited itself in his mind. Had his pupil looked back one last time as he entered his room?

Adrian continued to stand there looking in the direction of the other door long after it was shut before returning to his empty bed. He knew now that sleep would be impossible so he lay there with the image of Gabriel potently occupying his mind in shades of light and dark. Caravaggio, that master of chiaroscuro, came to his mind. The boldly explicit images of naked boys designed to shock. At times the look on the faces of some of the boys, such as Cupid in Amor Vincit Omnia, seemed incongruous. None the less he could but admire the truly masterful manner in which the bodies were captured despite his sense that many of them were cheapened by appearing too much like boys for sale. He knew that some undoubtedly were.

Adrian's mother had always felt an affinity with John the Baptist. At times she seemed to see herself in the role. How she would have deplored Caravaggio's many representations of youthful John the Baptists if she had ever seen them but he remembered one with great fondness, a painting in which a naked and more sensuous adolescent John seemed immersed in a reverie and looking as sad as Gabriel sometimes did.

The problem for Adrian was that he sometimes felt too much like a tourist seeking beauty in the works of others but spoiling them by his mere presence. There were, he knew, many conceits in the arts but had come to believe there was but one deceit, that the arts can make us better when they can only make us different. He knew here he was at odds with Pythagoras who felt that beauty was necessary for the education of the soul. To Adrian, however, the soul was another of the conceits and that beauty had a lonelier task. It should have been beauty not fire that Prometheus was accused of bringing to mankind and for which he was tortured by the Gods. That would have been a more fitting Old Testament punishment since it is beauty that tortures mankind. He knew that the one person he had ever truly loved, had seen truth and beauty as the same thing. She had said with gently uncritical persuasiveness that he used his musings about beauty to camouflage truth from himself and that, those who deceive themselves, devalue everyone around them. And now she too was gone. It was in thinking this and with the sound of Gabriel hauntingly singing The Minstrel Boy, that he finally achieved some sleep, at least for a while.

Chapter 20

Rites

Adrian knew from Timothy Paulson that the giraffe was the most religious of the animals having evolved a long neck trying to see Jesus and that they only slept for a few minutes each night so they could pray more. Good for them, he had thought, in this another of his many largely sleepless nights. When he could no longer stand the thought of either Timothy Paulson or of trying to get to sleep, he got up. He had been sure he was the first to be awake but the sound of a car arriving with more Barrowman possessions told a different story.

John came in manhandling a chair from the trailer. He was followed by Gabriel carrying a wooden box. Last night had taught Adrian that the beauty of his pupil's face was matched by the perfection of his body. Today he was wearing jeans, an open necked shirt, and trainers. Gabriel had smiled at him and said a coy hello as lovers often have on first awakening with one another. What might he be remembering, wondered Adrian? Nakedness does not become everyone but Gabriel was a feast in the famine of his life.

The beauty of music can activate all the senses but added to this, with his pupil there was a sense of complete harmony. If only he could find a way to liberate him from the sadness that haunted his smile. Every instinct he had, told him that music was the panacea.

"Hello Adrian" said John, putting the armchair down, "this one's for the attic. I'll have to make several runs today. Super little car and great capacity now that I've borrowed a trailer. Best thing I ever did was putting the tow bar on it. It tows very well for just about 1000 cc's. I'll try not to get in your way. I brought Gabe with me so that you wouldn't be disturbed".

Adrian's immediate thought was that John could have no idea just how much Gabriel disturbed, even preoccupied him. The cheeriness of his response hopefully masked this. Though Adrian had been worried that Gabriel did not eat enough he was now more reassured that he had a slender rather than thin body which was healthy and unblemished. His offered assistance having been turned down by John, who seemed to manage things so much more efficiently by himself, Adrian remained with Gabriel.

When John came back down he immediately set about preparing scrambled egg and bacon for himself and Gabriel. Adrian regretted not having accepted the offer of bacon as he sat down with his toast. He asked them how they had slept. John immediately said he had slept like a log. This confirmed that his lodger's preference seemed to be never to use an original phrase when there's a cliché handy but at least clichés were of a prescribed length.

Breakfast was complete and father and son had set off again to collect more of their chattels when a less than cheery Siobhan arrived. There was neither the illuminating smile nor the customary kiss of greeting. Adrian had long ago come to consider himself as better at reading the moods and feelings of women than of other men. He had sometimes put this down to having to hone these skills to keep himself safe from his mother's unpredictable but fervent reactions. Today however no special skill was required. There was a problem. The cuneiform of her face spoke of consternation and, in a peculiar manner, matched the outline of her jaw which had assumed a wedge like shape and unaccustomed hardness. He led her into the piano room.

"What is it Siobhan?" he asked, "what's happened? Where's the beautiful bouncy Siobhan I've been looking forward to coming back?"

"It's you" she said, "you're what's happened. Or perhaps I should call you Father".

For a moment Adrian though she was pregnant but she quickly went on, "that's your official title isn't it? Father Adrian Mann, not Grayling? You kept that from me and what's this about killing a nun? I was so looking forward to coming back, then no sooner do I arrive than Beckie tells me that the whole village's talking about it".

Adrian knew that no one's past ever catches up without changing everyone's else's. He sat for a moment just looking at Siobhan. He wanted to reach forward to wipe the tear that had strayed down her cheek as Gabriel had for him but he knew this would not be accepted, at least not now.

"Siobhan" he said, "do you feel ready to listen? This is not going to be easy for me either".

"Oh I'm ready" came the curt reply "if I don't hear it now you'd only have a chance to make up something else".

"I assume this has all come from the man in the bar, the one with the theatre group?"

"Does it matter who it's come from?" she responded, "if it's true".

"I could ask Pilate's question, 'what is truth?'" said Adrian, "but I don't want to get sidetracked into definitions when what you want is an explanation and an understanding".

"Christ, now you are sounding like a priest. I should have known with all those biblical references you made. Just cut the crap Adrian. Tell me".

"Ok" said Adrian, "I am Adrian Mann. Grayling is my mother's maiden name. She was a fanatical believer, a convert to Catholicism. There's something about converts to any religion that breeds fanaticism. It's as though…".

"Stop it Adrian" demanded Siobhan, "I don't want to hear about the psychology of fanaticism. I want you to tell me about you".

"Sorry" replied Adrian summoning the placatory from his repertoire, "but however she got to be like it, my mother's fanaticism had an impact maybe a determinative one. She always wanted me to be a priest. I was dragged along to every mass. It wasn't that I didn't believe in anything, I just didn't want to worship anything maybe except music. That was the only thing that turned me on. Though I listened to all kinds it was classical that really moved me, meant something to me. And I had a feel for it. I don't think I had a gift like Gabriel does, he's extraordinary but I could play and I could more than just appreciate it, I lived for it".

"Adrian" his name said with the despairingness of his mother functioned as a reminder that he was digressing again. Looking towards Siobhan he went on,

"Learning the piano and violin were like a trade-off. The lessons for mass. I can't go into all the details now but I did end up going to a seminary. I don't have to tell you as an Irish woman that's like a cross between a university and a bootcamp for priests. And the goings -on there. It should be called a semenary. Till recently no one would believe it about the church now they'll believe anything. Anyway about six years later I went through the Rite of Ordination".

"This isn't telling me anything anyone couldn't get from Wikipedia" interrupted Siobhan, "I still want to know about you, what happened?"

"My belief was never strong. I learned I wasn't alone in that but some of the seminarians would make ISIL look like Islamic sceptics. They seemed to keep everyone in line. They were also part of the creation of the endless friendships, cliques and factions that flourished. Those came to have such enormous importance, but it was when I was out in the parishes that things really changed. To me there were three types of parishioner. The born and bred Catholics who attended as a form of routine and who largely did their own thing the rest of the time, the few truly devout and the underclass, no that's not fair, the needy and almost anyone in times of crisis. They required the ritual and had to have someone in persona christi. At those moments I meant something to them, something no one else could offer and that I didn't mean to any other".

"You're at it again Adrian" said Siobhan, "you say John Barrowman goes on a bit. Well physician heal thyself. What happened? What did you do? Who is this dead nun they talk about?"

"I don't think you understand how painful this is for me" Adrian's voice now carrying something of the anguish he was feeling, "in my lifetime the church had gone from dignified respect to public loathing. I was no better than the others. No, not about children, never that. For every priest that every touched a child there was the legion of the lustful and I marched with them. I used to joke about the crusade of the consenting. This isn't going to sound as I want it to but it wasn't hard to find women who responded. Then I met Sister Fidelma. She was about your age and had been a nun since she was eighteen. I was the confessor to the convent. I can't go into it all now and I know saying it quickly makes it sound too Mills and Boon. What happened was that we just fell in love with all the desperation of the damned. Ultimately I left the priesthood and she gave up the convent. We married. Not in the church of course. There was a scandal. That sort of thing could be managed more easily before social media. Now we have trial by Twitter and flogging by Facebook, a virtual but not virtuous avalanche of first stones hurled by the pressing of a key. People don't seem able any more to take time out of their busy lives to think for themselves".

Siobhan could see the impact telling her the story was having on him. She went and sat by him putting her arm around him. She kissed him on the cheek.

"I'm sorry Adrian" she said, "sorry about what you went through, sorry for making you live through it again. Some day when you're ready you can tell me what happened to Fidelma".

"Her name was Ciara Latimer" said Adrian, "she was more tortured by her infidelity to the church and breaking her vows than I was. In the end she couldn't take it anymore. She killed herself. A mortal sin".

"Christ Adrian, how awful for her, for you. That's why you came here is it, to get away from it all".

"And the Land be subdued before the Lord: the afterward ye shall return, and be guiltless before the Lord, and before Israel; and this land shall be your possession before the Lord.

But if you will not do so, behold, ye have sinned against the Lord: and be sure your sin will find you out".

Numbers 32 verses 22 to 23".

"All you've been through yet you still quote scripture".

"Remember" he said "that I am a priest in a church that unrepentantly plagiarized almost everything, all its essential and unique truths stolen from earlier faiths that they condemned, from the virgin birth to the resurrection. I don't denounce a work of art because I learn the artist was flawed. I condemn the hypocrites and I should know about that. I'm enough of a hypocrite not to find my own loss of faith such a problem, more a progressive opening of my eyes, a reacquiring of my own identity. What I found hard was the uncaring attitude of the church both as an institution and some of the individuals. The pressure disguised as pastoral concern on Ciara. But I shouldn't have been surprised. The church has always traded on the potential for guilt of the most sincere and sensitive. The church hierarchy has become nothing more than a manufacturer of moats for the eyes of others".

"Goodness Adrian" said Siobhan, "that was said with some feeling. I can see there's a whole different side to you".

"I loved that woman Siobhan, loved her in a way I never knew was possible. Now I know that love is loss waiting to happen. Sex isn't the ultimate expression of love, only semen".

"She was a lucky woman to have experienced the love you describe" said Siobhan.

"It wasn't enough to save her" he replied, "no one should be praised for love or take credit for it. It's involuntary. Duty, now that's hard. That requires character".

"I wish I could do something to help you Adrian" she responded.

"You already have. You're the first person I've been with since Ciara or talked to about any of this".

"Was she Irish?" asked Siobhan, "it's an Irish name".

"As the shamrock" he replied.

"So you're making a habit of it" she said then immediately regretted her choice of words, "sorry, sorry Adrian. I didn't mean habit like that. That was insensitive".

He smiled, "you do remind me of my old life in some ways but despite all my efforts I never need to be reminded of her".

Whatever else he might have said at that point was prevented by the arrival of John Barrowman and Gabriel. They came in carrying more items and stopped to say hello to Siobhan. When they went upstairs she said,

"Gabriel doesn't carry much".

"I think he carries too much" said Adrian.

Siobhan looked at him as though about to refuse the sacrament of the sacred aphorism. She seemed at the point of saying something different but changed her mind and instead asked,

"Are you going to tell John? They're bound to hear".

"I feel I have to" said Adrian, "from what you're saying all sorts of rumours will be flying around. If that newspaper cutting the man in the pub had is the one I think it was, it said that I had killed Ciara. They made it sound like seduction and murder".

"But it wasn't" said Siobhan, "horrific and tragic yes but not murder".

"When it comes to understanding responsibility" said Adrian, "words like proximate and distal used about causes are for the arcane vocabulary of a less-read paper. If I were to follow that reasoning I could say my mother killed her. That paper doesn't have readers but rows of open mouths squawking for lurid morsels to feed their wet dreams. It's true, Siobhan, the City of Facts has truly gone the way of the walls of Jericho, it has fallen and the Barbarians of Babel are in the ascendency".

"Adrian what you are saying may be right" said Siobhan, "but if you want people to listen, you have to sound less like a priest giving a sermon".

"You have a point Siobhan. It was always a bit like that even when I was at the seminary and in Rome. You're not the first to comment on it. And spending so much time alone or only with children since then hasn't helped".

Siobhan glanced at the clock. When she said she had to go he asked if she wanted to come back in the evening and perhaps spend the night. She kissed him on the lips and said she couldn't for a couple of days. She really needed to finish the piece on teen superstitions.

Though Adrian had long known that his past could catch up with him and of the risk of being forced to move on again he could not bear to think through the consequences of losing his pupil.

Gabriel was in his room, when he sat down to talk to John who listened more attentively to Adrian's account than he had ever achieved before. He seemed fascinated and intrigued, but he wasn't judgmental.

"I was brought up a catholic" he volunteered "but I never did have much time for any of it. Of course being the daughter of a bishop, Celia had been surrounded by what she always called the Anglican tradition though she had no time for the religion of churches any more than I had".

At this point John simply stopped. Adrian took the chance to ask, "and what of Gabriel?"

"He doesn't go to church or anything like that, if that's what you mean" replied John, "we never took him. Do you think we should have?"

"No. That's not at all what I'm suggesting. That's none of my business. I'm just interested in what makes him tick. I want to do the best for him, to bring on that enormous talent".

"Do you think he will be good enough to make a living at it?" asked John, "one day he'll have to at something. It'd be good if it was something he really liked".

"Oh he'd be more than good enough if it was what he wanted. Performing classical, any music really, is a difficult life. We'll have to work at making him emotionally robust enough to cope. And you can be sure there'll be detractors, jealousies".

"I'm glad he has you" repeated Adrian, "I wouldn't know where to begin. I never expected to be bringing a child up by myself let alone one with the special abilities you say Gabe has. He's not been really happy since his mum left Adrian, not till he started his lessons with you. You mean something to him. Something important. I know it's selfish but I hope all this stuff about your past life coming out doesn't spoil things for him, or you of course".

"It's not being selfish John" responded Adrian, "it's being a parent. Would you like me to tell Gabriel about this or would you prefer to?"

"Would you?" asked John "some of the kids at school will know. You'd be able to help him deal with it. They don't really like him or understand him. I don't think I understand him but I think you do. You'd probably have understood Celia. You'd certainly have got on with her".

"Perhaps" replied Adrian, "she certainly sounds a very interesting person. I still find her just leaving Gabriel difficult".

"She wasn't ever easy Adrian. She had her own way of thinking about things. You say you don't understand how she could just leave Gabe and I'd agree but I don't even understand why she got together with me. I don't know any music or read books or get into the stuff she does. She'd read poetry. That's another thing I didn't get on with at school. Well I suppose I wouldn't because of being a bit slow with reading and poetry's never about what it says on the tin".

"You're putting yourself down again John" said Adrian "and very few things are only about what it says on the tin". He could see that John seemed uncertain even troubled.

"Can I ask you a favour?" he asked.

Adrian nodded relieved that he was not in some way offended.

"This is the devil's timing with what you're going through but I might have to go away for a day or two overnight. Would you be willing to look after Gabe for me. He'll be no trouble. You'd just have to make sure he had something to eat and went to school. I wouldn't ask if it wasn't important".

Chapter 21

Chaperone

John Barrowman's request that Adrian look after Gabriel for a night or two had troubled and exhilarated Adrian in unequal proportions. On top of that he'd had to field two calls from parents asking him if the rumours were true. Timothy Paulson's mother had been quick to say that if she ever thought he was trying to convert Timothy to Catholicism she would immediately remove him and demand her money back for all his previous lessons. She was only keeping him there because Timothy liked him and he was the only music teacher for miles. She was reassured when he told her that her son had an impressively deep and unshakable faith for a boy of his age and that his grandfather would have been proud of him. The bit of hypocrisy that is about survival kept Adrian from uttering the words, insufferable brat.

The call from Mrs. Byrnes had been more concerning. Without specifying what she had heard she wanted to know if he would give his assurance that it was not true. Then she lobbed the deadly grenade of evidence free allegation by adding that she'd heard about priests and children. For a moment he thought Paula's comment about going to marry him was about to resurface. He had reassured her by explaining that he would be happy for her to sit in on all Paula's lessons if that would make her feel better.

As he put down the phone Adrian thought that the age of the chaperone had returned. He looked towards the piano stool. Though so far it had been a day that had taxed a system, trained and practised in the art of absorption of the feelings and needs of others, he felt an urge to decode a further entry. He just wanted someone else to have secrets and one that he believed was more reprehensible. There were not many entries left.

This one was longer than most. He worked steadily at it, again trying not to take in too much of its meaning till the first full read-through.

"As I sit to write this journal I am a thrice dejected man, first because my station in life is considered too lowly ever to plight my troth to this beauteous pupil, in the second part because she is considered by the generality of men to be too few in years for any, of whatever station, to be permitted to consider her and for the third part, I now have it more firmly in my heart that she would wish to be one with me if only these cruel barriers could be breached.

I have of late taken to following her carriage to where it is she dwells and do wait for many hours to catch but a glimpse of her. My friend Samuel, once so true, tells me that I am becoming demented by desire and that a Bridewell or Bedlam will be my certain dwelling if I do not have a caution. He hath sent to me, fair copied in his own hand, a poetic piece by the estimable Mr. Keats and asks what it is that can ail me alone and palely loitering. What, I demand, does it matter if no birds sing if my heart does.

It is an easy thing to see that I am woe-begone and that my brow is with anguish moist but that is not a lily he doth see on my brow and any rose she sets eyes upon can but fade before her beauty. And yes Mr. Keats has it aright that she is full beautiful with hair that's long but the only wildness I see in her eyes is their longing for me.

Oh wondrous will be the time when I can make for her a garland for her head. She hath looked at me as she does love but hath not yet made sweet moan. That day will surely come.

Samuel doth well know, I have no pacing steed yet would I have her all day long and her goddess voice would give sweet song. I have no need of relish sweet and honey wild but our eyes will speak of all the love that's in that child.

Yes did I follow her to her father's grot where I fear she weeps for me and sighs full sore, and though I have yet to shut her eyes with kisses four, know well my love that I have more.

I cannot now be lulled to sleep, for my latest dreams not woe betide, but is of thee my dearest by my side.

Oh yes there will be kings and warrior princes too, all deathly pale that you have spurned them all, So will their lips now be starved anew, For I have thee in thrall.

It had been many years since Adrian had first encountered La
Belle Dame sans Merci. It was a theme as ancient as lust and as
sure as loss. In the seminary his fascination with Greek
mythology had continued. He had pursued musical links. He
knew the story of Circe and Ulysses, the enchantress and the
warrior. In his head Vivaldi's wonderful music played. He heard
the cantata 'all'ombra di sospetto' which he had first come across
when learning Italian during his year at the Vatican. He had
translated the title as 'Shadow of Suspicion' but had come to
accept the more common 'The Shadow of Doubt'. It was to him
so beguilingly set for a solo voice with an accompanying flute.
Long before he had heard this piece he had loved the
countertenor voice. From this first hearing he had responded to
the duelling voice and flute which, to him, took on all the flavour
of a love duet.

That Vivaldi was an ordained priest and worked in a home
for abandoned children creating little musical ensembles from
among the girls had somehow personalized the depth of his
appreciation. Adrian wasn't sure if, even all those years ago, he
would have had the faith, at least in the socially cementing role
of the church, to make such a commitment. His life decisions
seemed to prove that obligations and vows meant little to him.
Now if only the church had women priests and if marriage were
permitted.

While Vivaldi's superlative music continued to charm, this
merely had the effect of counterpointing his distaste for the piano
teacher's thoughts in his secret diary entry complete with the
wilful misunderstanding of the poem. It was one thing to
recognize the beauty of another but of just what evil was this man
capable, or for that matter, any of us. He feared decoding the next
entry. This certainly wasn't something he could face today.

Adrian wasn't sure what made him look up. Standing in the
doorway was Gabriel who smiled towards him. The smile was of
simple but exquisite pleasure that seemed to be based on nothing

more than just seeing him. Had he been the shadow piano teacher he might have seen it as laced with unspoken longing. Adrian knew that Keats had also written:

'A thing of beauty is a joy forever:
Its loveliness increases; it will never
Pass into nothingness; but still will keep
A bower quiet for us, and a sleep
Full of sweet dreams, and health and quiet breathing.

This poem too he knew to have a mythical source being based on the account of Endymion beloved of the goddess Selene who found him so beautiful that she sought to have him endowed with eternal youth. Her wish was granted by Zeus who, in doing so, put Endymion into an eternal sleep. Still Selene visited him every night and had child after child by him. Thus, to him, Selene assumed the mantle of the succubus that he feared we all could become.

Sometimes the interconnectedness of his thoughts enriched Adrian's life and at other times bewildered him with their inconsequentiality. When he listened to music whether it be music that just came to him as with today's Vivaldi or that he had chosen to play, it seemed generally to have a benign effect. Without the musical accompaniment, the connections could variously taunt him about the trivia of this thinking or rebuke him for reinventing God as a cognitive kaleidoscope. Or was it that, when the seventh veil is pulled aside we are confronted with the horror that it is all simply a mask for our animal core that but feeds and fornicates.

He didn't want to believe that all symbolism is itself a veil, a ritual reincarnation of lust. The code the Keatsian piano teacher used was certainly a veil, his own incarnation as Adrian Grayling was a veil. What else, he wondered, beside the priestly pretences, might also be a veil? He looked back to the door where Gabriel stood. The one thing left to Adrian was the sense that, in beauty he had a transcendent absolute and in this pupil he had found its incarnation.

Adrian knew that he needed to stop thinking like this. He was beginning to register the possible ramifications of the story of

Father Adrian Mann being disseminated throughout the village, perhaps more widely.

He needed to hear his pupil play but first he sat with him on the settee and told him his story. The boy listened impassively. When Adrian finished Gabriel simply said,

"You loved her. Now she is gone".

"Not completely gone" said Adrian, "because I still remember her and she changed my life. And we are talking about her. I still mourn her Gabriel. Would you like to tell me more about your mother?"

"She had gone too" said Gabriel, "perhaps she will come back when she needs me to sing for her. She said one day I would find someone to teach me about the music of life. Now I have you. You are my teacher".

"There was a poet called Byron" said Adrian, "he once wrote,
'There's music in the sighing of a reed;
There's music in the gushing of a rill;
There's music in all things, if men had ears,
The earth is but he music of the spheres'.

Gabriel, poetry is there to say what we can't. He was a great poet and a man who loved deeply in many different ways that people did not always understand. His mum and dad did not live together for very long. She loved books and taught him to read. He did not like school when he first went there. He didn't really learn anything there".

His attempt to create some resonance for his pupil did not give any sign of having worked. When he had finished speaking Gabriel did not talk about school or Byron's mother but instead asked,

"Do you love deeply in ways that people do not understand?"

Though Adrian knew well enough from his life experience how easy it is to over attribute wisdom to children, he was none the less unsettled by the question. He paused for a moment before answering,

"I think everyone does Gabriel. Everyone has to find his own way of living and that means of loving. If they're being truthful each will have to admit to loving in many different ways, some public and some private, but if they do it honestly and the other wishes it, then love becomes its own purity".

"Did you love your mother?" he asked.

"Not I think in the way you love yours. My mother was important to me, very important but she lived through me not for me if you can understand that. She was only really happy when I wanted or said I wanted the things she wanted. I don't know why your mother left Gabriel but she wanted you to have music and she gave you a rare talent for it. It's the means of expressing everything important in our lives. I knew an old priest who called it the language of always".

"My mother would have liked you" said Gabriel, "now I would like to sing for you. If I sing for you, I sing for her".

With that Gabriel got up and walked to the piano. Adrian remained seated. His pupil positioned himself at the end of the piano and, with one hand again resting on it, looked towards Adrian and sang, 'The Minstrel Boy'. It was not just the feeling with which he rendered the song or even the lingering lines that spoke of the association of music and freedom but the fact that Gabriel sang it for him that mattered most in that moment. Feeling welled in him till he felt he would be unable to control it. When the child finished Adrian stood. He did not applaud but said, with as much sincerity as he had left in him,

"Beautiful Gabriel, beautiful".

Chapter 22

The Mephisto Waltz

Andrea Linkleader had come for her usual Monday morning lesson. It was clear that she was uneasy. Adrian wondered if she wanted to talk about the village gossip. He remembered to ask her how she'd got on at the dentist. To him the ordinary had become a hoped for antidote to the toxin of the new. There was reassurance for him when, rather like a child, she had pulled down her lower lip and tried to show him a filling. She was fine, thank you for asking. Wasn't the weather unusually good for the time of year. The bridge of platitude could have stretched across the morning and still not got anywhere. Adrian knew that things were in danger once again of moving too fast in his life. It was important to regain some control of the momentum.

"You've probably heard that before I came here I was in the priesthood Mrs Linkleader" he said, thinking that she might prefer that things were more formal, "and that is true. I once was, but I left. I'm the same music teacher I always was".

"I didn't know if you wanted me to call you Father" she responded.

"No" said Adrian, who had never been that comfortable with the designation, "Adrian will do nicely".

"But not Grayling" she more blurted out than said.

"Yes" he responded calmly, "you can still call me Grayling. I changed my name legally to my mother's name when I left".

"Why would you do that if you hadn't been guilty?" she asked.

"I wanted a fresh start. What do you think I was guilty of?"

"That nun" she replied, "they say you killed a nun. That's a sin isn't it?"

"And unlike most sins it would also have been against the law" he responded "if I'd done it. That newspaper article, the one I think is behind all this, said I killed her. That wasn't true, not literally. I'd be in jail if I had, would I not? She did die Mrs Linkleader, but it was not by my hand".

"They wouldn't just print something that wasn't true would they?" she more said than asked.

"They can get things wrong, anybody can" he replied, "remember they're in the business of selling papers. Implying I killed someone would sell more copies than saying I loved someone".

"You can't love a nun. That's perverted. Mr Linkleader thinks I'm being silly but I think it's this house. I didn't tell you the last time we talked about it but people have died here before and gone missing, maybe been killed".

"Priests and nuns are just people like we all are" he said, "what happened in my life was before I came here".

"That's what I'm saying" she said, her tone suggesting she was finding his lack of logic surprising, "you came here. It was like the house was calling to you".

Feeling that nothing he could say would change her view Adrian changed tact,

"I'd still like to know more about the history of this cottage, what did happen here?"

"Like I told you, they did that exorcism thing. They wouldn't have done that if they hadn't thought there was evil in this place. I thought it would be ok to come after all these years".

"What was the evil that they thought was here?" he asked.

"The Sinclairs" she replied, "I've told you. There was something wrong with that family. Always was, probably always will be".

"So what do you think is wrong with them?" he asked,

She looked uncertain how to go on.

"Well" she said, "you know. Like not normal. Not like the rest of the people in the village. Oh they looked good alright. That was half the problem. My mother used to say they were like the fairy people that could put a spell on you, bewitch you. All you had to do was look at them and they had you. It didn't matter if you were a boy or girl, man or woman. Ask Old Kennedy, about that boy".

"What boy?" asked Adrian.

"I'm not saying anymore" she replied "it's not my place but he was never the same after it".

"Was there ever another piano teacher who lived here?" he asked.

She looked at him for a moment as though puzzled that he should ask, then replied,

"Another piano teacher? Oh that goes way, way back. It was something my grandmother knew about. He was a Sinclair alright, one of the bad un's I'd say which was the most of 'em. The story is he just disappeared. Went off somewhere. Maybe debts or a woman or with that lot, even a child".

"Did any children ever go missing?"

She looked reluctant to go on then said, "maybe. A lot of children died young in the old days. And sometimes the gypsies came. They'd take children you know. Are we going to have a lesson or not?"

"We are Andrea" he said relaxing back into first name terms, "and I'm glad you came. Thanks for the information about the Sinclairs".

Adrian extended the lesson by about half an hour to make up for the delayed start and because he was feeling a need to keep some of his customer base.

He was, none the less, pleased when it was over. Now for the first time he had the house completely to himself. John had gone off to work saying that he'd start work on clearing the garden when he got back. The highpoint of Adrian's morning had been Gabriel coming down for breakfast immaculately dressed in his school uniform. He still carried the same ethereal quality about him.

As John had previously said Gabriel was plainly not happy about going to school but he did not manifest his reluctance in refusal. He said Monday was the day they had music but he would not sing for them. He would however play the piano. The new music teacher Mrs Jardine, had asked him if he had music lessons. She had said he must have a very good teacher. Gabriel had smiled in the direction of Adrian as he told his father this. John had in turn looked at Adrian and said,

"I'm glad you have a good teacher Gabe. You know your mother always said a good teacher can change you".

Adrian remembered his own comment "and a wonderful pupil can change the teacher".

He had felt a raw protectiveness as the slender figure of his pupil gracefully made his way towards the bus stop, the black ringlets catching the little available light and sending them back as a keepsake. He felt the child's anguish in setting off to be in a place that he did not feel he belonged, that sense of perpetual loneliness made cruel by the presence of others. It was so like his own schooldays, then the seminary and later the priesthood and now, it was in danger of happening again in the village.

Grieg's solitary piano concerto played in his head, its lyrical evocation of a world of belonging eased the agony enough to allow him to carry on. Occasionally he was accused of passivity but he did not feel this captured what he believed was happening. It was to him more a latent pessimism, something akin to a realistic acceptance that nothing he did would change the outcome to something he would experience as better.

It was mid-afternoon, still before Gabriel's much anticipated return from school when Adrian received a call. It was from John Barrowman.

"Adrian" he said earnestly, "you know I asked you to look after Gabriel if I had to go away. It's today, if you wouldn't mind. I know it's short notice and very bad timing but is it still ok for you to do it? I should be back by tomorrow, at the latest Wednesday".

"It's no problem, my pleasure" responded Adrian then asked, "is everything alright John? You don't sound happy. Do you need anything from the house?"

"No, everything will be ok" came the unconvincing reply.

Adrian was impatient for the return of his pupil. He thought he would tell him right away that his father would not be home tonight but that everything was ok. That way they could equally share the anticipation of a meal and an evening of music together. Privacy had always been important to Adrian. Music, even at a concert surrounded by other people, he had always experienced as a private thing, operating intimately at a visceral level. Importantly too it seemed to slow the world's acceleration, stopped it crowding in on him, overwhelming him. With music the outer and inner worlds merged, the rush became controlled by the music's tempo, breathing moved from shallow gasps for survival to a rhythmic inhalation and exhalation that imbued a reassuring sense of being part of something larger that would endure and you would survive with it.

Gabriel's quiet acceptance that his father would not be back for one or possibly two nights was interpreted by Adrian as showing that he was confident that he would be cared for. When he was asked if he normally changed out of his school uniform in the evenings he nodded. He took Adrian aback by asking him what he would like him to wear.

"Whatever's comfortable for you" he replied then added, "your white outfit really suited you".

When Gabriel came back downstairs he was wearing the all white ensemble he had worn the day Adrian had taken the photographs to which he had so often returned, the day Gabriel had also sung 'The Minstrel Boy' to him for the first time. They had smiled at one another. To Adrian it was like a smile of shared understanding.

Before they ate they had played together on the piano. Adrian tried to introduce his pupil to the pleasure of jamming. Gabriel did not need to be told how each note has different feelings locked in the sounds. Even in their earliest attempt when they hadn't yet agreed on a chord pattern they seemed to chime. He could see that Gabriel was the most relaxed he had achieved so far. He had also smiled in a more boyish way when Adrian had used the word noodling. He had at first just liked the sound of the word but then nodded and immediately began to play when Adrian explained the simple enjoyment of what it meant.

That evening was also the first time the two of them had eaten together alone. Adrian had responded with a collusive,

"I won't tell if you don't" as he poured some wine for him when Gabriel had pushed his water glass towards him. It had pleased Adrian when Gabriel ate a little more of his food than he had before. Whether this was due to the wine, the relaxed atmosphere or wanting to please his teacher, Adrian had no way of knowing.

They had completed their evening by returning to play on the piano. Gabriel had again sung for Adrian, this time his rendering of 'A Song for Celia' seemed to have even more poignancy.

When it was time for Gabriel to go up to bed he had once again kissed Adrian on the cheek then held him with a penetrating stare and kissed him a second time. He watched as the graceful white clad form of the boy had moved away from him towards the stairs. For a moment he wanted to call him back. He didn't want this evening to end. His pupil had sent him late a blood red kiss not so much honouring him, as knowing that upon his cheek, it would not wasted be.

Adrian returned to the kitchen and tidied things up being less punctilious than he knew John Barrowman would have been. He paused briefly at the boy's bedroom when he went up but did not hear a sound. He wondered if he should look in on him but decided not to.

Adrian got into bed though he knew it was not going to be easy to sleep, that it would be another giraffe night. He had, once more, left his door a little ajar, so he would be aware of any sound or movement outside.

Having to conjure up music was never good. Perhaps Celia was right about requests but tonight, when he merely waited, all that came to him were the lamenting echoes of 'Tears of the Teacher'. He lay there sometimes approaching sleep and sheltering in that place in all our minds that harbours the forbidden. Throughout his priesthood, doubts had swarmed around him like noisy cicadas roused from their underground slumber by the hot weather and hungry, not for food, but for sex. He tried to think of Siobhan. So often beautiful young women had been his undoing.

Adrian had no idea how long it had taken him to slide towards slumber, his mind still troubled by the flagitious feelings of the other piano teacher who had once apparently played music and preyed on the innocent from this cottage. Certainly he hadn't heard his door open or anyone approaching. Nor did he know what instinct it was that caused him to open his eyes and sleepily sit up. In the partial light he thought he saw the figure of a young girl in a dress of translucent white. He alerted more fully to the sudden violent pumping of his heart. Now she was not there but in her place and within arm's reach stood his beautiful pupil, captivatingly naked and looking pleadingly at him.

"I want to come in" said the boy, "I want to sleep with you". Now the uninvited music in Adrian's head in all its passionate sensuality and fast accelerating energy was Liszt's masterful Mephisto Waltz.

"Gabriel" he said softly, then hesitated, "oh Gabriel" he went on, "we cannot, must not".

"I need to" replied Gabriel, "I have no one. You are my teacher. Who else do I have?"

As he saw the solitary tear that drew an unwanted line on the flawless skin, Adrian moved a little to the right, then threw back the duvet sufficiently to create a space to allow the boy in.

Once in the bed the child turned towards him, smiled then lay back and, with a look of sublime contentment, seemed to close his eyes. He made no attempt to pull the duvet over him. It was Adrian who did this. He thought he detected the faintest smile of gratitude. What, he wondered, beyond their defencelessness, is it that makes the sleeping person seem so vulnerable and with some, like this boy, so innocent. Can it be that there is a special beauty in innocence that draws our attention because it is innocence that is the unnatural state?

He recognized the absurdity and peril of his situation. Here he was alone with his pupil both of them naked in his bed and he musing about the nature of beauty and innocence. The Mephisto Waltz played on. He knew that St Augustine had led a lustful and profligate life as he had openly recounted in his Confessions. Had he not had an affair with a woman who had borne him a son out of wedlock? Was she not sent away because she was unsuitable perhaps because she was an ex slave but did Augustine's lustful need not continue so that he sinned more and more? Did his family not try to find him an acceptable wife and did he not become betrothed to the girl who would have been ten years old so was two years too young but he said he liked her well enough and was content to wait? And what is nakedness but the natural state of man? And did not Benjamin Britten, whose music enriched his life, have a chaste desire for young boys between the ages of nine and fourteen and, was it not the case that without such love, Persian poetry would have had virtually nothing to write about, no prophetic rendering of 'What choices have I, if I should not fall in love with that child? Mother time does not possess a better son'.

As he lay there with his naked muse by his side, it was not just legal peril and moral jeopardy that Adrian feared. His life and any meaning it had was predicated on rarified beauty not hedonism, always more Apollo than Dionysus. Beauty was about sensibility not sex. To Adrian, when something or someone leads to sexual arousal, it became a loathsome thing, a reprehensible and limiting lust. The only thing that could redeem it was to live a life of aesthetic consciousness. When he had once said something like that to Ciara, she had asked with the calm quiet of all her cloistered years,

"How is it that we best deceive ourselves when we are most certain that we do not?"

But now as Ciara's words imbued his thinking with a melancholy, the duvet slid down a little and, with the shortest, sweetest moan, the boy stirred and his left arm swung across Adrian's uncovered chest. He lay there as though the lightness of the touch soothed his fears and electrified every aspect of his being. He looked towards his still sleeping pupil. He wanted the duvet to slide slowly away to reveal them both together in this way. And, as the Mephisto Waltz was approaching a climax, it seemed to Adrian to be like a score to the unwritten story of his life with this moment's struggle at its core. He needed the simplicity of the devil to be made manifest, to bargain with the soul he no longer believed he possessed. What's one more falsehood in a life so rich in them? Yes, he would do a deal with that devil, his soul in exchange for the ability to resist this temptation.

But with the experience of all the ages of the damned, the devil handed him his harp and sang with the sweetness of the boy, 'The Harp you love will not speak again, You must tear its chords asunder'.

As the morning light eased itself warmingly into the room, the boy again stirred and lay once more on his back, his arms by his sides. Adrian thought he saw a look of approaching serenity on his features. For a moment he wanted to gently slide the duvet down so that he would see once more all of the perfect form and proportions but instead got out his side of the bed and positioned the duvet over his pupil then, picking up his clothes left the room. He now knew that the nobility of resisting temptation can come at the price of increasing it and pitted will against nature.

Chapter 23

Sweet Moan

Gabriel made no mention of coming to Adrian's bed when he came down for breakfast, already dressed for school. But then Adrian could not bring himself to do so either. John Barrowman had not been quite right when he had said that Gabriel would be no trouble. His sublime beauty, his astonishing talent, had conspired to torture Adrian. The calm gracefulness, the power of the secret smile, the ambiguous pleadingness of his coming to Adrian's bed, the reminder that happiness is possible but for others. There was in all this also the confirmation of Santayana's dictum that beauty is objectified pleasure, of the inherent loneliness in its need to be appreciated but not involved and yes also in lustful Augustine's view that beauty is composed of integrity, clarity and harmony.

Even before Gabriel had gone to school, Adrian had received a call cancelling his student for that morning and until further notice. Gabriel had seemed to recognize something in his demeanour,

"Your eyes are sad" he said continuing the unchildlike style that Adrian had grown to expect, "I will sing for you tonight".

Adrian had pulled the boy to him and held him for a moment, "thank you" he said, "you, your gifts, your music, your singing, just how you are, will always make me happy".

Gabriel had kissed him on the cheek and left for school. Adrian stood in the doorway watching till his pupil disappeared then wandered into the now dead living room and stood staring at the unoccupied piano stool. He felt alone and palely loitering.

Periodically he had experienced moments like this throughout his life. He had never found that playing cheerful music worked to change his mood. What he needed was to match his mood with sublime music that then moved him forward. He wouldn't spoil the effect by decoding the next diary entry just yet though he knew he needed to do so soon. He looked at his collection, still physical CD's, not downloads for him. He chose Schoenberg's Verklarte Nact. It would not be the first time he had used it in circumstances in which his needs and desires mismatched his world. The theme of acceptance and understanding fitted the moment. The dark but tentative opening mood with its repeated falling phrase, the harmony that comes close to dissonance in the touching repentance revealed through a delightfully elongated viola solo, the build-up to something more serene with the full ensemble. He admired the manner in which it pivoted from the desolated and tortured even anguished early part to the release into the bright fulfillment, the emancipation of the ending, forgiveness and a new beginning.

Though he was able to listen to the work without interruption it failed to have as much effect as he had hoped. None the less he would not deny it had made a difference. What was again troubling him was just how many more of his students would be withdrawn. He would not be able to afford to stay. For the moment John Barrowman paying half the rent was his rescuer together with what remained of his roll.

When lunch time came he slowly prepared something for himself as much out of habit as need. He pushed his food around his plate and merely nibbled, eating only about as much as Gabriel might have. He had hardly finished the half-hearted washing of the few dishes when he heard someone coming in. He looked around. Siobhan was standing there dressed in a simple, unpatterned peasant smock and sandals. She was not wearing any make up.

"All alone?" she asked.

"Aren't we all?" he responded reflexively.

"We could change that by being alone together" she said.

"What have you done to the land of poets and scholars?" he asked.

"Left them alone" she responded.

"Together" he said.

"I try to be" she responded, "and what's more I've finished my piece, saved up my pocket money for the admission fee and zapped it off in the direction of the Pulitzer committee".

"Wrong nationality" he responded.

"Can't be" she retorted, "I'm Irish, that's numerically in America isn't it? Anyway nearly half of all presidents have claimed some Irish ancestry".

"That's a lot of responsibility for one small country. How are the Irish ever going to afford the compensation that's bound to be due one day?" he asked.

"That's easy" she laughed, "we'll sue the English as causing a big lump of the diaspora".

"Or the Catholic church for making the big lumps possible" he added.

"And while on the subject" she said a little more seriousness creeping into her tone, "have there been any repercussions to the tale of the tentacles of guilt that stretch from that organization to hell but not back?"

Adrian began to tell her what had been happening.

"Stop" she said, "there never was a story that wasn't the better for telling over a drink".

"Stereotype" he said.

"Racist calumny" she rejoined, "that's always been the slur the English have so much in their mind that they hear it on our voices which then makes them think we've been drinking. There's a fine of a couple of pints of Antique Ugly due for immediate payment for perpetuating it. Anyway, the sooner the gossips see you out and about the better".

Adrian was unsure that he was ready for this after last night. It didn't feel like prevarication. He remembered his favourite teacher from the seminary telling the group that they must never put off till tomorrow what they can put off till next year. The evolutionary purpose of prevarication, he had said, was to prove that the thing wasn't worth doing anyway.

Early afternoon there weren't many people in the Mitre. None the less Adrian felt all eyes were on him. When he mentioned this to Siobhan she smiled and said "thanks, you know how to flatter a girl".

Over the few weeks since he was first introduced to Antique Ugly he had come more to appreciate the roundedness and variety of its flavour. Even the name was no longer unharmonious to him. When she brought the drinks to the table Gwyneth asked Adrian how he was coping. She told them that when she had discovered that the story had been spread she had ended the arrangement with the theatre group.

"Anyway" she added "who needs to have a watered down version of Dr. Faustus when I see it every night for a pint of this stuff".

Adrian would have dwelt more on the reference to Faustus had he been given a chance by Siobhan whose ability to move effortlessly and lightly from topic to topic swept him along. Musically he thought she was like a cross between Mozart's exuberant overture to the Marriage of Figaro and, since she often seemed to him to be from another planet, Holst, particularly the Jupiter suite. Still, despite the frequent gear changes she was never less than fun to be with and well matched the needs of the moment. Nor was he unaware that being seen with a beautiful woman could confirm to the village that he was a red blooded member of the club, one of them, normal.

Siobhan asked him what time Gabriel got back from school. "So" she said "just over two and a half hours".

"Beautifully calculated" he replied.

"They don't call me Siobhan for nothing".

"I'd no idea Siobhan was to do with mathematics and calculation" he said.

"It isn't" she grinned, "it's my name".

He smiled at her, "that's better" she said, "so the lucky seven letters of my name has worked again".

"I think I'd like to read your article" he said, "I hope you mentioned that Schoenberg feared the number thirteen".

"I hope you don't read it" she said "that'd skew the age demographics of the readership totally. If there was a letters' page there'd also be correspondence outraged at leaving Schoenberg out, the sin of omission, teenage girls are big on sin".

"So I take it you also failed to reference the biblical scholarship on the subject, the unity of the four corners of the earth and the Holy Trinity".

"I'm sorry Father" she said, "for I have sinned and would like to sin more".

"And my child" he responded, "what further sin would you like to commit?"

Siobhan picked up her handbag and got out something that looked like a makeshift clerical collar.

"Fornication Father, I am but a simple and obedient virgin girl. I seek a holy Father for guidance".

For a moment Adrian recoiled. Recently he had been thinking more about Ciara, about everything that had happened and about the deal he would like to do with the devil. How many times in how many parishes? He had never felt guilty. It wasn't that he didn't understand the notion of abuse of power. It was just that he couldn't think of any situations in which there was ever fully informed consent on either part, not without divination, itself a sin.

"You're not happy with this, sorry Adrian" came the voice of Siobhan who picked up the collar and put it back in her handbag.

He looked at her. There was no doubt she was beautiful and, though young, unquestionably an adult.

"No child" he said, "let us go to a private place for your instruction".

Once in the house she immediately fixed the collar to his shirt. It startled him as he caught a glimpse of himself in the hall mirror. There was something in this moment that was a merging of his past and present worlds. He had become Father Adrian Grayling. His penitent was not allowing time for second thoughts. She took his hand and led him upstairs. He hadn't made the bed which looked to him as though two people had slept in it. Perhaps she was so locked into her role as a simple virgin girl that she seemed not to notice.

Adrian had expected this time to mirror exactly the previous one in which he had undressed her, then himself and they had tenderly made love. He was already fully aroused. This time she wanted to resist more, pushing his hands away, feigning confusion and distress, vaguely asking "what are you doing Father?"

He had briefly stopped. "No" said the firm adult voice of Siobhan, "keep going".

Of course he knew about rape fantasies and that women have them as well as men. He just hadn't been part of one before, at least as far as he knew. One never actually knows what another person is thinking during a sexual act. He was still fully aroused but less comfortable with this scenario. He took her by the wrists and put them firmly by her side.

"No" he said, "remember who I am. You are a sinful child who must be punished. You will stand in naked repentance for the evil of your thoughts".

Lifting her smock over her head Adrian saw immediately that she was naked underneath. She must have planned this in her thinking. She managed to look embarrassed, humiliated and contrite.

"Kneel down" he said. She didn't move. He took her firmly by her shoulders and pressed down. She knelt.

"Have you a confession to make?" he asked.

"I do Father. It has been a long time since my last confession. I have lustful thoughts about a boy but do not know what it is for a man to be with a woman".

"It is a very grave sin outside the sacrament of marriage" he said "and there is an exact penance for it".

As he said this he began to take his own clothes off. Trying not to break the magic of the fantasy Siobhan said,

"leave the collar on Father".

He felt foolish standing there naked and fully sexually aroused wearing only the collar.

"Can I be forgiven Father or is my sin too grievous for that?" asked the peasant girl.

"Your sin can be forgiven if you do due penance and act in full obedience to the Holy Church" he said.

"Tell me what I must do Father?" she pleaded.

"Lie on the bed" he said.

She looked worried. He repeated what he had said. She got up and lay face down on the bed.

"Turn over" he said.

She did so. She managed to look fearful as he straddled her and seemed again to try to push him off. He took her wrists and held them either side of her head,

"Remember obedience and your penance" he said.

He forced her legs apart with his and observed the look of apparent anguish as he entered her but soon felt her whole body responding. Repeated thrusts by him were responded to by an energetic arching of her back, accompanied by an effete attempt to free her hands. He experienced the full gamut of allegretto then allegro through vivace till finally as he achieved presto, she gave sweet moan.

Once he had stopped they lay side by side. He hadn't expected to hear the words,

"O almighty and merciful God, I truly thank thee for the forgiveness of my sins: bless me, O Lord and help me always, that I may ever do what is pleasing to thee, and sin no more. Amen".

Siobhan's escape from victimhood to full autonomy was immediate,

"thank you for going along with that" she said, "it's one I've never shared with anyone before but then I haven't slept with a laicized priest before".

"My pleasure" he said, "I had a bit of difficulty for a moment back there with the rape bit. I knew it was a fantasy but just not one I've ever had and you were very convincing".

"So were you" she said, "when you got into it. So what about you. Any fantasies you have yet to fulfil, anything on your bucket list or should I call it a fuck it list".

"That would be telling" he smiled.

"Or rather with you, not telling" she replied, "just so long as you know I'd be willing to enjoy most things with you".

"Oh I know you would Siobhan" he said "you always seem to be away with the fairies".

She propped herself up on one elbow and, looking at him intently, said:

"Come away, O human child!
To the waters and the wild
With a faery, hand in hand,
For the world's more full of weeping than
you can understand".

Siobhan now lay back and went on,

"It's from a poem called 'The Stolen Child'. Yeats was a great one for the fairies too. He never really got over the fact that Maud was Gonne. If the timing's not too crass I think that's what's happened with you and Ciara. You know that after their solitary consummation after years and years of his longing he wrote 'the tragedy of sexual intercourse is the perpetual virginity of the soul'. You should read all of his work".

"There's a better way" said Adrian as he lay savouring what she had just said, "if I sleep with you often enough I'd rather hear it all from you. I do think I get what he means by the perpetual virginity of the soul though".

"Maybe that's why I like my virginity to be reborn" she said, "and it will be again and again. You know Maud Gonne conceived her daughter Iseult in the mausoleum of Iseult's brother trying to reincarnate him. Then at age eleven Iseult was abused and I mean sexually, by her step father and at fifteen she herself proposed to Yeats. The next bit you'll believe because it's about Yeats, when she was twenty-one he proposed to her but she turned him down. So you see Father, I come from a hard to shock race but maybe that's because we think everything's made up, like any Catholic church press release on child abuse".

"I know very little about Yeats, man or poet" said Adrian, ignoring the understandable jibe at the church, "though I'm always worried that people use snippets of biography to narrow their understanding of people. Gabriel will be home soon. I have to get dressed".

"You're very attentive of that boy. He has a dad to look after him you know. I still find him bizarre, maybe a bit creepy, no not creepy, unnatural, asexual".

Adrian got out of bed and began to dress,

"We obviously see him very differently. I think he's a beautiful boy, special, with an astonishing musical gift" he said, "ok so he's a bit traumatized by being abandoned by his mother".

"I have noticed the way you talk about him and even look at him" she said "I hope that's not the fantasy you're not telling me about".

"Oh Siobhan" he said "so much for the 'hard to shock race'. I think better of you than that. You must know there have always been monsters. First it was the adulterers, then the gays, now the paedophiles. In between witches have been burned, communists rooted out, Catholics suppressed. Every society has somewhere at the edge of their map the words 'here be dragons'. Industries grow up around slaying them. Those who challenge the slayers can be accused of being in league with the monsters".

"And are you?" she asked, "in league with the monsters?"

Chapter 24

Objet Trouve

Adrian was pleased that Siobhan had left before Gabriel came in from school. He hadn't seen the sense in what she said about him. How could someone, so sublimely beautiful, be seen as creepy. Now the asexual bit, that was different. She had something there. Her comment about hoping that Gabriel was not the source of a fantasy for Adrian had also troubled him, no not troubled, more upset him. She was an intelligent and sensitive woman who quoted Yeats with such feeling and scattered ideas about her like wild flower seeds, without waiting to see if any took root. Surely she could see it is possible to regard another as exquisite without being physically aroused by them. A gay man could see a woman as very beautiful but not be at all sexually stimulated by her.

The standards by which beauty is defined were to him self-evidently independent of sexual arousal. He thought of Father Curran whom he had met in one of his parishes. Some of the things he had heard him say about thoroughbred race horses would surely, by this distorted way of thinking, have him condemned for bestiality. Adrian knew Siobhan's views on gender equality and on the behaviour of men towards women yet she could act out a rape fantasy. No one should dream of condemning her for that. Common sense by itself should be enough to show that such a fantasy was merely a way of enriching arousal and enjoyment, not a validation of rape. The fantasy would likely be enacted with someone one is attracted to and certainly someone trusted. The creator of the fantasy is in control and can stop or vary it at any time. As so often in life, control is the thing. No, a fantasy isn't a rehearsal for the real thing, nor is it worship of it. It's more like an objet trove.

Adrian had never really liked referring this form of creativity as 'found art'. That seemed too dismissive of what the artist/finder brought to it. Though he had never considered any such piece to achieve greatness, he could see something in the transformation, the way in which the artist's eye has identified that the object can be modified to serve a new purpose without losing the essentials of its original form.

He had made a drink and the smallest of snacks for Gabriel. The idea of his coming home had a rightness to it. Home. Somewhere where he belonged. When he had finally arrived Adrian had found himself conventionally asking how his day had been. School he had reciprocally learned was just school. If there had been any reference to Father Adrian Mann it was not shared. Gabriel had seen Mrs Jardine though it was not a music lesson day. She was covering for another teacher and had again told him how much his playing gave her pleasure and how wonderful it was that he was being taught to read music. Someday, she said, it would be good to meet his wonderful teacher. Gabriel had smiled as he recounted this before going up to the attic to do his homework.

There was, to Adrian, a peculiar and clanging dissonance in the requirement to do mundane homework for such a sublimely gifted and different person as Gabriel. What he now feared was that his own exposed history could come to devalue the boy's talent. Any words he found to reassure himself were about as helpful as telling Pandora she'd probably find an alternative use for the box.

From the attic view of the road Gabriel must have seen his father come back much earlier than expected. Adrian acknowledged his own disappointment at the premature return. There had been a chance that John would be away for two nights. The previous night had been the first time since his mother had left that Gabriel was not with his father but he did not immediately come down to greet him. To Adrian their relationship was detached and distant, even remote, despite nightly sleeping in the same bed. This was more a matter of convenience than intimacy. Didn't Walt Whitman claim that his Calamus poems which included fond reference to sleeping with men in the outdoors, were non sexual and was it not the case that Abraham Lincoln could sleep in the same bed as Joshua Speed for about four years without it seeming unusual in his day. Bygone times, condescendingly dismissed as naïve. Adrian was ill at ease with the labidinized lens through which everyone now tried to view the world. Even expressing this thought would be enough for him to be misunderstood, even pilloried. To him it was both intellectually wrong and socially a danger that things had been allowed to develop so that everything is about sex, in one form or another. No other motives or interpretations are tolerated.

As John entered Adrian could see that something was not quite right.

"Can I talk to you?" he immediately asked Adrian, "if you're not in the middle of something".

They sat in the piano room.

"What is it?" asked Adrian, "John, what's the matter? You don't look at all happy".

As John looked towards him Adrian could see that only an act of will, that could weaken at any moment, was preventing the release of the tears that were accumulating in his eyes.

"It's Celia" he said as though finding saying her name difficult, "she's dead".

Adrian had never tried to keep count of the number of times during his years in the priesthood that someone had brought him news of the dying or the dead. There was a practised routine to the priestly response that had felt to him like the mechanization of mourning. Ritual and routine he could see largely served the purpose of providing a link perhaps even a bridge between the world as it had been and now was, a conduit and contrivance through which things could go on. Times like that would otherwise be a discordant medley of the musical scores of memories, guilt and regrets. Something was needed to determine the order in the hymn sheet at the mass for the dead. And the rituals were also simply something to do.

"What happened?" asked Adrian.

"I've been to identify the body" said John, "we'd never divorced. I'm still her next of kin. I was notified. She was in hospital for a few days. She didn't want anyone sent for. They don't have a cause of death yet. I think they're regarding it as a sudden but not suspicious death. I don't like the idea of her being cut up but there'll be an autopsy".

"Though you weren't together this is still obviously a very tragic time for you" said Adrian, "and for Gabriel. His feelings for his mother. His expectation of being reunited one day".

"Would you tell him?" asked John, "I'd be there but would you do the telling".

"Tell me what?" asked a quiet voice from the doorway".

Adrian went to the doorway and kissed Gabriel on the forehead. He led him to the settee and sat him by his father. John looked at his son and tried to put an arm round his shoulder but somehow this just didn't work.

"I'm sorry Gabe" he said the tears on his voice distorting the sound, "I'm really sorry".

Gabriel looked towards Adrian his eyes doing all the asking, "it's your mother" said Adrian, "Gabriel, your mother has died. Your father has been to identify the body".

As much due to the fact that he needed to continue to talk as because of any feeling that the timing was right Adrian went on, "she had been taken to hospital. We don't know yet why she died. Gabriel it will not feel like it now because you loved your mother deeply but your suffering doesn't have to be a bad thing. Others have been changed by their pain too. You know Tchaikovsky missed his mother terribly when he was sent to boarding school at age ten, nearly the age you were when your mother was not with you anymore and he was very deeply affected when she died when he was about fourteen yet he went on to create some of the greatest music ever written".

Adrian stopped perhaps realizing that, not for the first time, he was substituting musical facts for feelings.

"She needed me. I was not there. I should have sung for her. Now she cannot come" the lamenting voice of the pupil occupied the room, changing everything in it.

He got up and went to the piano. He played the Clara Schumann with as much feeling as Adrian had ever heard it played, than he believed it could be played. Adrian and John Barrowman sat and listened. Neither made any response when, at the end, he stood up and without saying anything left the room.

"You should go to him" said Adrian.

"I don't know what to say. I've never known what to say. Maybe Celia wouldn't have left if I'd ever had anything to say".

"Sometimes being there is all that's needed" said Adrian.

He knew from his own experience that wasn't always the case. What he had most wanted when Ciara had died was to be alone. The voices of the living all around him had provoked him, taunted him, enraged him with the empty pointlessness of their continuity. She was not dead while they were not saying it. He saw again the distinctive habit of her order. He remembered the first time he had seen her in full regalia, her eyes intelligent and alive looking at him with bemused interest from her wimple. He again wondered what was it in him that had recognized the depth of longing in those eyes? And he remembered the magic of the initial moment he first saw her naked.

Then came the struggle with the decision to leave the order, the rape of her beliefs. Now, for a moment of unmeasured time, he saw her body, the face once more serene and restful after her long exertions, a rosary clutched in her hands. At peace, they had said, a peace he knew they had stolen from her with their hypocritical entreaties, relentless hints of possible forgiveness, and poisoned prayers.

John did not spend long with Gabriel, "he wants to be alone, to remember his mother" he said. He looked intently at Adrian and asked, "will he be alright?"

Adrian read the expectation of a preferred answer that comes with such questions,

"He will be changed" he replied, "everyone is. Grief isn't a well that can be drained. It is a path you must follow. Where it leads and whether it ever ends depends on how prepared you are for a voyage without charts. He is a very special boy. If he is lucky he will hear music, if he is very lucky it won't be sirens. John you must think of yourself too".

He recognized that his style and what he was saying was like a priestly whistling in the dark, something that could only tell the monsters where you are.

"I can't just sit and think. I don't know how to. I never have. I must do something. Sometimes when I'm busy things come to me. I won't go far. Just into the garden. To start clearing it. I said I would, so I will".

Adrian was once more left alone. He thought of going up to Gabriel. Instead he was drawn again to the piano stool. He got out the last pages of the diary entries to be decrypted. It wasn't something he was looking forward to. At this moment no one in the continuing occupancy of Magus Cottage was happy.

'I fear Samuel, whose love and friendship I have much cherished these many years will betray and disown me. He again writes that I must stop, that madness lies in seeking the unobtainable, that I must have a thought for her. In truth I have thought of little else. The few of my other pupils have ceased attending. They did not give and I did not seek explanations. Were it not that this house I occupy is of the family I could no longer rest here.

This week my perfect pupil failed to arrive. A surly and unpleasant man looking like a broken pugilist, brought a note that said henceforth she would have a tutor in the manor house, a man who was both eminently qualified and familiar with all the requisites of social decorum. It was in the hand of her guardian, clearly an uncouth man of more means than breeding, who may well plan to advance himself by marrying her to a title when what, in all plainness, she hath need of is love and tenderness.

I have of late taken more of the laudanum which I have often found of great assistance and full able to move my musical compositions to new levels but now makes me wan and listless and no music comes, nor can it while the Philistines have her. I know now with a clear certainty that I cannot wait longer for already sleep has forsaken me and I do not take earthly nourishment. Those few who still see me do say how thinly pale I am become.

Tomorrow must I act to save myself and her. Maiden, soon you will be in the arms of he who will cherish you always.

Adrian looked at the few remaining pages their coded contents hiding the final secret. Should he now complete the task and have done with it? He wished to know what happened to this pupil and her teacher though he feared if the only source was the encrypted entries then the laudanum would speak loudest. None the less he picked up the next entry. As he did so he became aware of someone else present. He looked up. A pale Gabriel was standing there. He was no longer wearing his school uniform but was once more dressed in the white. The music Adrian heard was the slow movement from Dvorak's New World symphony with the wistful, hymn like oboe sitting like an aura surrounding Gabriel.

He put down the notes and got up and went to his pupil. "Gabriel" he said, "come. Sit down".

"Do you think I will ever see her again?"

The suddenness of the question seemed to be trying to stop Adrian breathing. It wasn't an unfamiliar question. He did not want to cause hurt to his pupil, not at this time, not at anytime. But if he could not be honest with this boy he could not be honest with himself. There are things to be said about the timing of the telling of truths and about helping the other understand. He had learned with all the circularity of the obvious that the only things that cannot be avoided are consequences. And when, he wondered, had we started to think of consequences only as negatives. A consequence of practice is better playing. He looked again at his pupil whose question had become a fragile link between them that could be broken.

"No Gabriel" he said "I do not think you will, not in the sense of being reunited with her but she need never leave you. You can choose to see her again and again when you put everything that's in you into your playing and singing. Then you will see her smiling in appreciation".

"Do you see your mother when you play?" he asked.

"No" he replied, "not my mother. There was someone else I loved. Her name was Ciara. Since she died she has never left me, I play for her Gabriel, when I am happy and when I need someone to stop me being too sad. All the time and every time, I play for her".

"Will you play for me when I am gone?" he asked.

"I do not want you ever to be gone" said Adrian, "but I always want to play for you and to hear you playing. Most teachers, most people, do not find one like you in a lifetime. I want you to play for me now so that your mother can be happy and smile at you and so that I can see Ciara".

Gabriel turned towards the piano. Before sitting down he closed the lid that was the seat of the piano stool and, positioning himself he once more, placed his fingers on the keys. After his customary paused he began. He did not sing but for the first time played the tune of the Minstrel Boy. Adrian knew that many scoffed at these traditional airs, though no less a one than Beethoven had said what fine melodies they are and indeed had done an arrangement of a number including The Moreen, the tune upon which the words of The Minstrel Boy was based. Three times he played this through then without turning back to Adrian said, "it is for my mother's funeral".

Adrian went to him and put his hands on his shoulders. The reflection in the piano lid smiled sadly back at him as though from a very great distance. Perhaps it was the tear in the lens of Adrian's eye that distorted things. For a moment he thought he saw another image by Gabriel's, a woman or a young girl, also in white.

Chapter 25

'What can be explained is not poetry'

Gabriel had not gone to school since the news of his mother's death. He had spent any time he was not on the piano sitting quietly in the attic looking, without seeing, towards the road down which his mother would now never come. Adrian hoped it was music that filled the space between where he was and his needs. He remembered afresh something from his days as a seminarian. It was what one of the teaching priests had said when he had confessed early doubts. 'You will find' he had said 'that life is about the avoidance of the overwhelming sense of pointlessness, happiness is when we are unaware of this struggle, religion is the means of preventing this being more widely known. Always remember men need religion more than god, women need god more than religion'. Seminaries, he had learned, could be very subversive places.

Though John Barrowman continued to go to work it was now for a shorter day. When he came back he would almost immediately set about other tasks including the garden. Siobhan had come round a lot. In an unplanned way she had spent time talking to everyone individually. Adrian had been pleased that she had managed to communicate to some degree with Gabriel, hopefully getting to know and like him more. Maybe, he thought, particularly now, the situation requires a woman's touch, something the wider priesthood had still refused to learn, perhaps because it was too godly for them.

Though Gabriel never seemed to volunteer anything, he appeared at least willing to answer Siobhan's questions. When she had first told Adrian about this he had experienced an ignominious feeling he didn't want to call jealousy. This boy was not his. At the moment he was no one's. He was lost. And he was not eating.

Adrian's lessons with his few remaining students had become a struggle, the perfunctory was giving way to the mechanical. He felt like a lone audience member at a cancelled concert. Only one thing was coming to matter and that was Gabriel. But even here his pupil had seemed passively to give up any interest in trying to learn to read music. Nor was he yet ready to sing again. What mattered most to Adrian was that somehow music still penetrated both of them.

It had disappointed Adrian that Gabriel had confided in Siobhan not in him that he would like to see his mother. John had sought Adrian's advice. When asked how Celia had looked John had said,

"Beautiful. To me she still had that look, maybe even more so than when she left".

"Perhaps" said Adrian, "that's because she's no longer yoked to some unachievable search for the mythical".

The look on John's face was more one of respect than understanding,

"Her parents have taken over all arrangements" he said, "at least that means they're paying".

"Do you have any idea why they've not tried to see Gabriel?" asked Adrian.

"I don't know. I'd never have stopped them" said John, "all I can say is they were a funny family and Celia was very special, different".

This wasn't the time for Adrian to learn more. The plan was for father and son to go. It would involve an overnight stay. Adrian hadn't expected to be as touched as he was when John had asked if he would be okay alone.

Siobhan arrived as the little blue Ka set off with its two occupants and very little luggage.

Her smile was as invitingly soft as her one word question, "drink?" was welcome.

"Only with thine eyes" he replied, the wistfulness shared with the disappearing car.

"Good" she said, "mine eyes are on a few pints of Antique Ugly".

This time Adrian avoided saying that he thought people were talking about him as he registered the unaccustomed afternoon busyness of the Mitre. He was feeling about as welcome as Hansel and Gretel must have been when they made their way home. There too it had been the mother who had sought to abandon the children.

"Our seat's taken" said Siobhan "but don't worry there's one over there".

A couple Adrian could not remember having seen before was sitting in the window seat that Siobhan clearly now regarded not as his, but theirs. Unusually for this village the man was wearing a suit. He was probably a few years older than the attractive woman who, despite her casual dress, achieved a sense of style. Adrian had taken to registering the presence of strangers.

The whole bar seemed very different from their alternative seat, bigger somehow and more impersonal, with an area Adrian could not see without turning around. Gwyneth brought two pints of Antique Ugly to the table.

"On the House" she said, "I was hoping to see John to offer condolences. How's that pupil of yours doing?"

"He is too sad" replied Adrian.

"It's like he doesn't believe it and has always known it" added Siobhan, "with John you get what it says on the tin, with Gabriel there's no list of contents and no best-before date, with him 'the ceremony of innocence is drowned'".

"Well don't get too maudlin, at least enjoy your beer" said Gwyneth "and tell John I'm thinking of him".

"Cheers-up" said Siobhan lifting her pint, "to the house. And bring us another two of these when you get a chance and have one yourself. He's paying".

As the afternoon progressed it was clear that Adrian's novitiate to the Order of Antique Ugly was over. He had taken his vows. He savoured each mouthful. Unlike the couple at their usual table there was no drinking in silence when Siobhan was around. Her only tempo seemed to be upbeat. Themes cohabited with other topics and subjects partner swapped with salacious stories. It was, to Adrian, like playing hide and seek in a maze while blindfolded and needing the loo. If, within the impatient equal opportunities swirl of the trivial, the poetic and the tragic, there was a leitmotif, it was Gabriel. So he told her about the first time he had set eyes on his pupil, the impact it had and continued to have.

"Christ" she had responded, "it's like bloody 'Death in Venice' all over again, come to think of it you've even got the same name, Mann, 'cept you're an Adrian not a doubting Thomas. I assume you've seen it".

"The film" he said "yes but I preferred the book. To me Mahler's music mismatched the theme in the asceticism and austerity of Aschenbach. There's Britten's opera too and you probably know the ballet. You know that Mann acknowledged that nothing was invented in the book. I think it's a masterful work but he came to dislike it. He said it was full of half-baked ideas and falsehoods. Too much mystification".

"Too much going off the subject" responded Siobhan, "do you really fancy Gabriel?"

"No" said Adrian, "not in the way Mann found his own thirteen year old son attractive. You know he wrote in his diaries about how handsome he is in his bath and talks about the disquiet of seeing his naked premasculine, gleaming body. I find Gabriel beautiful. That's different".

"Is it?" Siobhan more commented than questioned, "or is that just a noble aspiration masking lust?"

"Ah" smiled Adrian signalling to Gwyneth to bring two more pints, "Mann won the Nobel literature prize, so did Gide who pursued flute playing Arab boys, and didn't Marquez, another winner, propose marriage to a thirteen year old girl when he was18, and Tagore have an arranged marriage with a girl of about ten when he was 21".

"Stop" said Siobhan, "just stop with the parade of the perverts. I'm always suspicious about why someone would choose to know this stuff, to remember it".

"And why shouldn't they" said Adrian calmly, "don't you think everyone should? Knowing things must never be allowed to become a sin. I think no less of Mann because of his attraction to Eissi. Progress is never made by not knowing things".

"If it wasn't that we've slept together and I've got to know the man you are, I think I might be out of here" she said, as further drinks arrived.

Adrian chose not to mention that Byron had attractions to both boys and girls, even his half sister, that sexual appetites are not naturally unitary or even required to be consistent.

All those years in the seminary absorbing how to deal with people's anger with God, and his subsequent time in the parishes becoming aware of the therapeutic power of delusion and hypocrisy, had not been wasted. He now had an understanding there comes a moment in the lives of thoughtful people, a moment at which they become aware that what they had thought about as confessional honesty was merely a mechanism for avoiding guilt. The buying of an indulgence. It was too a transformative moment that crystallized elements of their fears and self-loathing so that they came to be paraded as a virtue. The defeat of the 'Cross' again becoming a symbol of victory. To Adrian, now more than ever, in this imperfect world it was all the more important that some things remain private. He knew this had to be part of how things are, of how everything is destined to fall short of the ideal. Except perhaps beauty.

As though reading his thoughts Siobhan said,

"I'm sorry Adrian. I didn't mean some of that in the way it sounded. In the things I write I can be unorthodox so why shouldn't you. What's sauce for the goose is saucier for the gander. And then there's my fantasies that you've been happy to go along with. That's made the sex special for me".

"It hasn't exactly been a chore for me" he replied, holding his drink just short of his lips, "would it be presumptuous to think you might come back with me this afternoon".

She smiled, "Father" she said, "I am a simple and devout servant girl in need of spiritual guidance. I wish more than all else to give myself to worship, to become a consecrated virgin".

"Child" he again responded, "it is an important decision with your immortal soul at stake. You must be beyond all doubt certain of the path you choose and we must test your commitment and suitability before I perform the sacred Rite of Consecration".

"Father" she said solemnly, "I am in your hands. Any test, any challenge or penance I must face with courage and honour".

They finished their drinks and Adrian settled up with Gwyneth.

"She has corrupted you" she said, "how many pints was that? It used to be a half pint of something boring with a steak. Well done Siobhan. The Mitre needs you".

They walked back to Magus Cottage in silence as befitted the role Siobhan was about to enter. In the bedroom he said that he must first ensure that, at a material and bodily level she was intacto, before moving to the spiritual. There is nothing hidden from God so she must stand naked before him for this.

He enjoyed watching her coyly undress and folding her garments then looking at him steadfastly she announced,

"Father, I am ready".

"You know" he said as soberly as four pints of Antique Ugly would allow, "that your priest is In Personi Christi, in the person of Christ. You have, of your own volition and true believing chosen to be a bride of Christ. For this to be a true marriage it is necessary for consummation to precede consecration".

So it was that they found themselves again naked in bed, the carnal in knowledge surpassing the value of knowing. When they had finished they lay side by side. After some minutes she looked at him and asked,

"Don't you want to know why I want to be a virgin again and again?"

He responded without looking back at her,

"If you would like to tell me that's ok. If it sustains the pleasure more by keeping it to yourself that is fine. We all need some part of us that is forever private".

"Are you talking about Gabriel again?" the asking voice soft and it now seemed to him accepting.

"I am talking about privacy" he responded, "if I'm not making it sound too pompous, to me that is part of what defines our uniqueness, it is the solitude we can carry with us. Siobhan, you are a beautiful woman and seeing you naked arouses me but that makes it about me. Knowing how a magic trick is done destroys it. It's like being told the outcome of a novel before you've had a chance to read it".

She leaned over and kissed him,

"A bit pompous but getting there. Do you think that's what Yeats meant when he said 'what can be explained is not poetry'. That or something close to it".

Chapter 26

The Brooch

To Adrian it was a curious thing that he and a beautiful woman were naked together in bed, a woman to whom, not long before, he had made love and who now slept contentedly by his side and yet he was feeling a sense of the absence of another. Siobhan was fond of quoting Yeats to him but it was the words of Alexander Pope that came to him now, 'Know then thyself; presume not God to scan. The proper study of mankind is man'.

Mostly the music in Adrian's head was simply there. Occasionally he thought about it and wondered why a particular piece had come to him. There was no need to agonize as to why now the music that orchestrated his present feelings was Mozart's Don Giovanni.

Adrian knew that the only people in the cottage were he and Siobhan yet, when he thought he heard a sound, his thoughts turned immediately not to John Barrowman but to Gabriel. More tellingly, when the sleeping Siobhan's arm had come across his chest, his smile, the sensation of pleasure and the sense of another's presence were of that boy. He felt the severity of the child's pain at the loss of his mother, even though she had abandoned him. Perhaps, he thought, it was the redeeming umbilical of the money for music lessons that prevented him from condemning her more.

To Adrian the thing that made death so powerful is not that it is the end but that it is unending. The experience of loss must be universal. Could it be that this monumental David and Goliath struggle had to be constructed to end in favour of hope, the sting taken from the eternal by welcoming it?

Siobhan opened her eyes and looked up at him, as though for reassurance that he was still there. Once again he found himself wondering if the real hypocrisy and superficiality of his life resided in his thinking and intellectualizing. Out of the eater came forth meat and out of the strong came forth sweetness.

"What are you thinking about?" asked Siobhan.

"You" he replied.

She smiled. At that moment it didn't matter if he just said it to please her. It had worked.

"I dreamt about Gabriel last night" she said.

"What happened in your dream?" he asked trying not to sound too curious.

"I don't know" she answered "I only know that he was in my dream, not just in it, the dream was about him".

"Was it a good dream?" he asked.

"I'm not sure. I think I cried" she responded, then went on, "there's something else Adrian, something I want to tell you".

He looked at her like a priest through the grill of a confession booth, "so what is it?" he asked.

"I wasn't completely honest with you when we first met. I mean about this house, not about us".

"What about this house?" he asked his interest immediately aroused.

"You know I wanted to write a work of fiction that might have been about this house and I asked you about the cellar. There was a bit more to it than that. I told you I've been coming to this village for years. What you don't know is that my grandmother from Ireland was in service. She used to work in this house. She was some sort of housekeeper or something, I never quite knew what. She was very reluctant to say anything about it. That used to make me suspicious in itself because she was a talker. The last time I was home she'd been moved to St. Anthony's because of dementia. I went to see her. She was raving a bit. Talking about 'bad goings-on' and 'not looking at them'. She kept telling Sister Mary that a cellar was 'a place of evil'. One of the other funny things about her was that she never liked to hear music though her sister had told me years ago that she had the most lovely singing voice in all of Ireland. It became so bad that she couldn't bear to be in the room with a piano".

"And Beckie" he asked, "where does she fit in? Was that part true?"

"That part was all true. I did meet Beckie at Uni. It was a coincidence that this was where her family came from. My grandmother went very quiet when she heard I was visiting here.

I could tell she wasn't happy about it but not why. Over the years I've been trying to do bits of research about the place. Then when I met you there was a chance to see round. After that things just developed. I wanted to spend time with you, not because I wanted to get into this house". She then looked at him coyly and asked "are you hurt that I lied to you?"

"You didn't lie to me" he said "you just didn't tell me everything. As for being hurt, in my experience more people are hurt by knowing the truth than being lied to".

"Confessions must have been an interesting time when you were a priest" she said leaning over and kissing him "but then you have a deal with the devil to protect your soul from damnation by sinning. That part should stay in my story".

"Siobhan" said Adrian, "when we get up I'm going to show you the diary entries I told you about, the ones I have deciphered, about the piano teacher who I think lived here and fell in love with a girl pupil. He seems to have become infatuated, totally obsessed with her. Bruckner was a bit like that too. Apart from his fascination with death and dead bodies, he wanted to be certain of marrying a virgin. He believed the only way to be sure of that was to marry a young girl. There are long lists of those he fancied. His cantata, 'Entsagen' was written after one of his rejections. No one can deny that he did write some great music. You've only to listen to his seventh symphony from the power and passion of the first movement to the sorrowing poignancy of the slow movement. When he was accused of behaving improperly with a teenage girl student he decided to teach only boys but he kept proposing to young teenage girls into his seventies. Some say he died a virgin".

"Bruckner" responded Siobhan, "that must have been a long time ago. If it was nowadays I could have been a virgin for him as often as he liked, well maybe not in his seventies. And thinking that teaching boys could not lead to accusations, now that really dates it. Who was it you said liked girls and boys but preferred girls because if he tires of a girl she can play the boy for him".

"Goethe" responded Adrian, "be careful Siobhan or people might wonder how you know these things".

They got up and breakfasted. Though it had only been a matter of days that Gabriel had lived here Adrian missed him disproportionately. Siobhan showed no sign of leaving.

"When is he coming back?" she asked suddenly.

He immediately spotted the 'he' rather than 'they' but ignored it,

"John and Gabriel" he said, "I assume this afternoon or early evening. I don't know the arrangements for the viewing and I don't know if Celia's parents will be there".

"Perhaps when we've finished breakfast you could show me the diary entries you decoded" she said.

"While you're reading I could have a go at the next one. I really think I need to finish them. There's not much more to do".

In just a matter of minutes they were sitting in the piano room. Though the next dated entry was not long, Adrian frequently distracted himself by glancing at Siobhan to see her reaction to what she was reading. Even if he had been able to be more disciplined Siobhan's voicing of the occasional 'Christ', 'oh my God' and even 'fuck' would have achieved the same effect.

"Do you think this is for real?" she asked.

"Don't you?" he retorted, "it was encoded, the language is archaic, and given the hints about this place and what you know from your grandmother, I'm persuaded there's something in it. Let me just finish this one and I'll read it to you".

After some time he sat back with his notes in his hand and said, "ready". She nodded.

'Mine eyes hath until that day ravished the world of longing and possibility but it hath been not till the gods directed me to bring her to this door that I have fully been able to possess such chaste perfection.

I shall not with ease forget the look of delight and surprise on her face when I found her alone in the garden of her guardian's vulgar house with a pose of flowers, including the red roses of love. Fate had taken a hand to provide a symbol. She seemed most troubled and apprehensive of being caught as I led her from there with many fearful glances back at the foreboding structure that had been her prison till this, the day of her liberation. I told her she would soon have the fullest of explanations and her safety and future be finally secured.

I had stationed nearby a borrowed carriage and we made all speed fearing at any time a mighty hubbub and pursuit.

We went to the dwelling place of a friend who was visiting the land of Ireland so that here we might have sanctuary for some days lest any search be made of the few places she had been permitted to visit. She showed much lasting fearfulness of being found with the resultant cruelty of the guardian that, in her confusion, she experienced a need to resist. My supply of laudanum served well here. I knew from the great writers of the world that the burden of facing freedom and love after such a prolonged period of privation can be too much for the natural delicacy of a well-bred maiden to bear. Seldom does she take nourishment or even sufficient liquid to sustain her fragile frame.

I hear from Samuel who as yet knows nothing of this enterprise that there has been much hue and cry about my former student. He commiserates with me about the loss. Some gypsies have been known to have been in the woods near where she dwelt and are being pursued with all vigour. I will this day seek out that place and leave there to be found the brooch she wears always, though, in her confusion, she made much protest when I took it from her breast. In time, my protecting gods being willing, we can return to the home of my birth and we may be left in peace in the private place I have there made ready. So great is her desire for the coming of that time that, when not at ease with the laudanum, she exhausts herself with tears'.

He stopped and looked up. "Fuck" said Siobhan again, "there was something in the story. He did take her. Poor girl. I wonder what became of her. Adrian you must do the last bit. And now I think I might understand something else. I once gave my grandmother a brooch as a present and she lost it, not the brooch, control. She threw it. I didn't know that she hated all brooches. There may be a connection".

Adrian glanced at the clock on the mantelpiece. He was about to start on the last pages when he heard someone open the front door. John Barrowman and his beloved had returned.

Chapter 27

Admission

The sound of the front door opening was followed by a heavy stillness. Siobhan looked at Adrian who got up. In the hallway was a strained and tired looking John Barrowman with his son just visible behind him rather as on the day of their first meeting. He nodded at Adrian without speaking then turned to Gabriel. Once more Adrian was able to see the same exquisite loveliness but now there was an additional fragility and the eyes that had once penetrated him were more inward looking.

"If you want to go upstairs I will bring you something" John's voice had a different timbre even a tenderness to it. Gabriel acquiesced and moved gracefully along the hallway.

John did not sit down when they went into the piano room. He explained that they were able to see Celia as soon as they arrived. It appeared Gabriel had spent a long time just looking at the carefully laid out body of his mother then, to the horror of his grandparents, had kissed her lips. From John's account Gabriel had not cried but had somehow changed in that moment.

"He just said, 'I am cold too' nothing else. It was strange, like the world and the people around weren't there for him anymore".

It appeared that John's usual verbosity had deserted him. "Gabe just started to hum or sing something. You'd know the word for it. I don't think he meant for anyone but his mother to be listening. He's not eaten or drunk since that moment. It wasn't that he seemed unhappy but whatever he was feeling just wasn't meant for the rest of us".

Adrian and Siobhan listened as John explained how icily critical Celia's parents had been of Gabriel being brought there. They had not seen their only grandson for years but did not offer either greeting or affection. It was, said John, more colourfully than Adrian had ever heard him speak before, as though there were three dead bodies in the room with Gabriel trapped between the two worlds unsure which way to go. However, he immediately reassumed his more usual self-blaming stance and said he didn't know if he'd done the right thing by bringing Gabe there.

"Let me make us some lunch" said Siobhan "and Adrian you could bring something to Gabriel".

As no one either agreed or disagreed, she set about the task.

Adrian brought a drink and a sandwich up to Gabriel who did not acknowledge him as he entered the attic. He put the simple lunch on the table to the left of the chair in which the upright form of his pupil was more positioned than seated and he himself sat on the other seat.

"Gabriel" he said "if you wish to be alone, I will go. If you want to play the piano alone or with us, that is also fine. It you would like to talk to me about your mother or anything else I will always find time for you".

Now the beautiful face turned towards him, an almost smile struggling to linger, in acknowledgment of the offer.

Adrian stayed by him for a while, then stood up. If it had been possible he would gladly have taken all the sorrowing of the child and stored it in the place where his own lay waiting. He leant over and kissed the boy on his forehead and, touching his hair, as though in a benediction, left the attic room.

Downstairs, John had eaten his lunch because it was there. He seemed not to want to talk. In the presence of anyone else there might have been silence in the kitchen but silence and Siobhan Walsh appeared incompatible. While Adrian's head could be richly suffused with melody, Siobhan's was more like a self-activated conversational silo, launching battery after battery of missiles into the consciousness of others.

"I've come to rescue you from Siobhan" said Adrian, "if you want some peace".

"How was Gabe?" asked John.

"It's very early days" replied Adrian as though he had been infected with the language of a thousand hospital visits he had made, "his mother still exercised great pull for him. It might have been easier for him if she had died rather than leaving. Not knowing why she had gone, how she was, whether it was his fault. That can't have been easy for him. Even if he hadn't been aware of them, those little niggling questions would have been there, land mining any peace he might have found. There was a teacher at the seminary. He used to say that the real crisis you're having is nothing to the one you don't know you're in".

"It was the same with me" said John, "I don't mean a crisis, I mean thinking it was my fault she went. I still think that. But at least all this brought him to you. You are important to him Adrian. Music might be his saviour. I hope it is. For me I just have to get on with things. I must have something to do. I've the garden to finish clearing. That'll do for a start".

"I'll give you a hand if you like" said Siobhan.

"Thanks" he said, "if you do we could finish it today"

"Then later we could plant something in memory of Celia" said Siobhan, "a tree or something that Gabriel could tend".

Adrian did not say anything. He had a powerful sense that nothing would be the same again but the improbable thought that Gabriel would be around in his life long enough for a tree to grow held an irrational appeal for him.

As Siobhan and John set about their task in the garden Adrian went back up to the attic room. He stood in the doorway for some time. Gabriel was sitting exactly as he had been, his sandwich and drink untouched. He heard him say,

"I know you're there".

Adrian was about to step forward when Gabriel went on,

"I've always known it. But I don't know why you left me. I was very lonely Mum. I'm still lonely except when I play music. Then I sing for you".

Sadness is a scalpel that carves its name into your heart. His pupil's words occupied the space between them, connecting them by a bridge of sorrow. He went to him and knelt by him and, taking his hands in his, kissed them.

"Gabriel" he said searching in himself for something that would help but the only words that came were, "remember that you are loved, you have your father and know that I love you". Adrian wondered what the boy was seeing when he looked into his eyes but at least for a moment he seemed more content as he said,

"you are my teacher".

The opportunity for the conversation to develop was lost as he heard Siobhan's voice calling him. He felt a momentary resentment. He once more kissed Gabriel's head and went downstairs.

"Adrian" said Siobhan, "the garden. Come, see what we've found".

In all his years at Magus Cottage he had really spent very little time in the garden. Now, having lost its overgrown look, it seemed bigger, more boring, with less of a story to tell. If his assumption that Siobhan had merely found something trivial in the old shed was right, he knew he would have to control his anger. She had called him from his pupil, the freshness of whose grief was in danger of merging with his own more ancient pain. It seemed to him as if somehow he had always known that loss unbreakably connects people as if they had all drunk from the same cup of eternity.

What Siobhan had to show him was not trivial and might even prove to be significant. When John had removed some of the ivy from the back wall there was the clear outline of a bricked-up door.

"The cellar" said Siobhan, "I'm sure it's the cellar. Maybe in some of these very old cottages the cellar entrance is from the outside".

John tapped the stonework, "it feels solid enough to me" he said, "but it's the right size and shape to be a door. What do you want me to do? I could remake the opening if you like".

Adrian hesitated. For an irrational moment he was fearful of what they might find.

"I'd have to run it past the landlord. There may be a good reason why he bricked it up in the first place".

"That could take forever" said Siobhan "and he might say no. There is a mystery about this cottage. I need to know what it is. We can always brick it up again".

John looked at Adrian, "it's your call" he said.

"Do it" said Adrian, his own words seeming to take him by surprise.

"I'll have to go down to work to borrow a chisel and jackhammer" said John "and I can let them know I'll be back tomorrow".

As Adrian turned to go back in, his eye was drawn to the bedroom window above where Gabriel stood looking down at him. He wasn't sorry he'd said he loved him but wished he'd had a little longer to talk through with him what he meant.

Chapter 28

Manfred

John was away for longer than Adrian thought he might be. Siobhan commented that Adrian had gone up to check on Gabriel twice in half an hour.

"He's just lying on his bed. He's not asleep" said Adrian, "he's very unhappy".

"His mother's just died Adrian. What do you expect?"

"He's complex" said Adrian "different. His talent guarantees that. Ciara sometimes got like that before the end. There are too many things happening at once for me".

"Does that include me?" asked Siobhan.

"No I don't mean it like that" he said, "you are my forever virgin. I'm losing too many students and it'll be difficult to replace the income".

"I can help out a bit" said Siobhan, "let's take your mind of this Adrian, let's finish the diaries. You were about to when John and Gabriel came back".

They returned to the piano stool and Adrian picked up the few remaining pages as Siobhan once more read through his earlier transcriptions. There had been little opportunity for progress when Gabriel quietly entered the room. He did not acknowledge them, indeed was apparently oblivious to their presence. He closed the lid of the piano stool, sat down, then, after his customary pause, began to play. Siobhan looked at Adrian whose gaze was fixed on his pupil.

There was a maturity to the performance yet to Adrian something was not quite right. Siobhan moved closer to Adrian and almost whispered,

"What is it, what's he playing?"

"It's Schumann" he said, "not his usual Clara but Robert. It's the Manfred Overture, an arrangement for piano. I've never heard him play it before".

Gabriel had probably got halfway through the piece when he abruptly stopped, stood up and said,

"I do not understand".

As Adrian went to him, his pupil again sat down.

"What is it?" asked Adrian.

"My mother played that to me often. She would not tell me what it is. She said I would find a teacher one day who would dare to tell me. You are my teacher".

Adrian felt a fresh tenderness towards the boy, "now I see what the problem you're having in playing it is" he said, "no one can play music they do not understand, not with sensitivity. You must know where it is coming from. I've told you I hear music in my head, not just at a concert, anytime, whatever I am doing. It's like a companion. Robert Schumann came to hear voices. Schumann wrote that piece when he was tormented by them. He loved literature almost as much as music".

Adrian could see that, though his face remained expressionless, Gabriel was listening with intensity, even were it possible with passion. He went on

"There's a long poem by Byron. It's a wonderful poem. It's called Manfred too. It is about the torment of forbidden love. In it Manfred asks seven spirits to help him forget what he has done. The thing is Gabriel, you can't forget having loved. It's who you are".

As he said this Adrian remembered the heroic defiance at the end of the poem. Great music seems to go with outlawed passion. Still struggling to allow for the age of his pupil he went on,

"You must listen to Tchaikovsky's Pathetique, Gabriel. That's the same. He dedicated it to his nephew. Few knew of his forbidden love for him. He said the importance of this nephew in his life increased all the time, just to see him, hear him, feel him close. It was the paramount condition for his happiness. And he also wrote a Manfred Symphony. Now that requires a big orchestra".

Without a word Gabriel began to play again. As the opening bar of three thrusting chords sprang defiantly from the piano, Adrian returned to the settee and sat by Siobhan who took his hand and squeezed it.

Now Gabriel played with both ease and passion. There was a sense of liberation even exultation. He had understood something that had changed how he saw his world. Adrian knew that Clara Schumann had written in her diary that Robert had been stirred to an extraordinary degree by the Manfred poem. The resulting overture was masterful.

When Gabriel finished he stood up, made a slight bow then left the room.

"Even I could tell the difference" said Siobhan, "Adrian you are a good, no, a great teacher".

"There are no great teachers, only great pupils" he said.

"That's not true Adrian" said Siobhan "maybe great teachers and great pupils bring out the best in each other. You understand that boy. He listened to you. Was changed. You were patient, gave him your time. Didn't someone once say 'time is a great teacher' or something like that".

"Berlioz did" said Adrian looking towards the door through which Gabriel had disappeared, "but he also said, 'unfortunately it kills all its pupils'. Mind you he was a doctor's son so perhaps you could substitute patients for pupils".

"That boy means a lot to you" said Siobhan, ignoring Adrian's attempted diversion into Berlioz's ancestry.

"You're right" replied Adrian, "he does, more than any other pupil throughout my life".

The fear that Siobhan harboured but did not want to express was that one could substitute person for pupil in what he said. Now she diverted herself,

"Let's finish the decoding" she said.

Adrian had only got a couple of minutes into this when John Barrowman returned with the tools he needed. Though he glanced towards the stairs he made no reference to Gabriel.

"I don't want to interrupt" he said "I'll crack on and make a start".

Siobhan appeared to have given up rereading the earlier page and simply sat watching Adrian as he decoded the next section. Though this unsettled him he said nothing. He had not quite finished when John came back in and asked him if he had a torch.

"Does that mean you've broken through" asked Siobhan, now on her feet and looking like a screenshot of someone moving forward.

"Yes" replied John "bit of a fusty smell and very dark in there".

Once again interrupted, Adrian put down his pad and all three went out. John had not removed all the bricks but had created an opening wide enough to fit through. He chose to go first, followed by Siobhan. As Adrian entered he caught sight of the face of Gabriel at the window of the garden bedroom. He appeared to be closely watching. It was unclear if he was smiling. Taking a step into the darkness it pleased Adrian to think that it was so.

Inside the light from the opening extended only far enough to see a set of stone steps leading downwards. Even without the metastasizing of Siobhan's sense of dread that something evil might have happened in this cellar, the darkness and oppressive airlessness would have admonished them to move with caution.

With primeval vigilance they slowly descended, the arc of John Barrowman's torch tracing each tread as they safely reached it and rising along the walls to the vaulted ceiling then back to the steps. The end of the first movement of Prokofiev's second piano concerto accompanied Adrian's unspoken question. How long had it been since the cold certainty of this stone descent had known human footfall? The unknowability of some things appealed to him. A faltering in the echo from their steps alerted them that something was changing. They stopped. The spear of light from the torch bounced off a door that blocked their way. It had the robustness of oak about it.

"Thirteen steps" said Siobhan, who had obviously been counting, "ominous".

"I made it fourteen" said John, whose anchoring to reality must have served many situations well.

"You're counting the bit where the steps turned round like a landing" said Siobhan, half defensively.

Each of them may have had a different sense of what was likely to be behind the door, the outline of which John again traced with the light of his torch. There was a circular handle which resisted even the muscularity of John's arm. Adrian held the torch for him so that he could use both hands. The reluctant handle turned. After the sort of pause that was characteristic of Gabriel before he began to play, John pushed the door. The heavy hinges creaked a limited dissent then the door was sufficiently open to allow them to go in. Their combined dread and curiosity in that moment seemed to burden them with dark meaning.

The area beyond the arched doorway was blacker still. John reached out for the torch which Adrian surrendered to him. He shone it around the perimeter. The ceiling was higher than any of them would have been likely to have expected had it ever occurred to them to wonder about such a thing. On the left hand side was a wooden travel trunk of the sort that once might have seen long sea voyages. On the curved lid was perched some books.

In the centre of the room there was what looked like an old bed that finished in a wooden piece about nine inches high and at the other end a carved headboard with star-shaped brass studs that formed part of the decoration picked up by sweep of the torch. Lying on the bed was what could be the figure of a person. They moved forward, as though controlled by a hesitant puppeteer. John shone the torch along the length of the shape, starting with the feet. Each gave an involuntary exclamation. What was clear was that what lay on the bed was a desiccated body, its hands crossed on its chest. It was wearing the remnants of a white dress.

They stood transfixed, struggling to take in what they were seeing, to assimilate it, each in a manner unique to themselves as they sought to engineer some manageable sense from it, a reframing of reality that would be as limited by their knowledge and experience as by their imaginations. Then something else seemed to hijack their attention. A guttering light struggling in some subterranean draught in the darkness behind them. They turned. Standing there was a silent figure holding a candle that rested on an antique candlestick. It may have been some subconscious reawakening of an ancient archetype that made them shiver in that moment. The light was flickering on a pale face and on the black of the hair on the head that appeared to belong to the surrounding dark and be struggling to emerge from it. It evoked a sense that the figure could be sucked back in at any moment. It was Gabriel Barrowman.

"Is it the pupil?" he asked.

Chapter 29

The Four Last Things

Back up in the piano room, the door of the cellar having once again been firmly shut, they sat for a while in silence, then Siobhan asked,

"What are we going to do Adrian? We have to tell someone".

As she asked this Gabriel, who had again positioned himself at the piano, hit a single key that reverberated around the room like the report of an antique pistol. A warning shot.

Adrian looked across at him, "it's true" he said "we must report this but the question is when? If it's who we think it is then she's been in there for a very long time. A little while longer isn't going to make much difference and we didn't touch anything. If we report it now and hand over the notes, for all we know, the whole house might become some sort of crime scene. We might have to move out. And when the story is out none of the villagers will want to come to this cottage again. We should give ourselves time to think, time to get Celia's funeral over. Time for Gabriel to grieve".

"I could always brick the entrance up again" said John, "no one need be any the wiser. If there was a crime there'll be no one alive to punish for it".

"I'll go with your suggestion Adrian" said Siobhan, "we should wait for a little while. I can finish my research on this place. We can make plans. John and Gabriel can mourn for as long as they need. With a coroner's report and police investigation I should be able to get a book published, you know either based on or inspired by a true story. There's a lot of history here. And we can take time to sort out where to live"

Gabriel began again to play 'Tears of the Teacher', pianissimo. No one present, apart from Gabriel and his teacher, would have heard the message. Music is always a coded transaction between the composer, performer and listener and sometimes it has to be secret.

It was again a suggestion from Siobhan that led to the decision to eat at the Mitre that evening. John had asked about Gabriel. "It's ok" said Siobhan, "he's nearly fourteen, won't be having alcohol, be with you and eating, so he has the trinity of protections as Adrian would never say".

"That's four things" said John.

"So it is" grinned Siobhan.

"His mother used to go on about the Four Last Things" said John, "she never did say what they are"

"Death, Judgement, Heaven and Hell" said Adrian.

"Sounds like the worst ever restaurant review" said Siobhan, "still I'll take the risk. I'll give Gwyneth a ring".

Gabriel went back upstairs while John returned to the garden to make a temporary closure to the cellar opening. Adrian looked at the unfinished decoding. He picked it up, sat down and quietly began completing it.

'*It is a thing of great puzzlement to me how my beloved can pine for me and resist me at the same time. It is like music played out of time. I have made plain she is now safe for they have apprehended the wandering gypsy musicians and tinkers who had passed this way. To save himself from the noose one hath pointed at another. They have it that my beloved be dead at their hands and this was made assured when they came upon the brooch as they searched for the place where she might have been buried. It was of no great difficulty for the magistrates to know that they are the evil ones who took her, being as they were, unchristian and profane in their ways, much taken with mead and other such.*

Still my beloved is not at true ease. Till I find a way to settle in another place she cannot be seen for some might know her and flee thinking a ghost had come among them. Only when we are free of this place do I have it she will be able to give herself fully to me. Daily do I play for her but when another comes to be taught she must rest in the place I have prepared. She will not eat. She pines for the full love of the time when we can truly come to be together. She fades and grows to an anatomie. It is a truly terrible thing to see the harm her cruel guardian and his wanton

mistress have done to her. Surely Satan in his hell must smile,
awaiting such persons'.

Adrian was horrified by what he had just deciphered, a horror
directed as much at the self-delusion of the writer as at the fate
of the young pupil. He picked up and looked at the brief final
page. He knew the outcome could not be good yet he also knew
what he must do.

He again set about the task. When he had finished this he read
it:

'So it has come to this. My beloved had lost all hope of truly
being with me. In her final moment she smiled and reached for
me. I shall treasure the painful bliss of knowing that, in the end,
she desired me. I cannot now put her remains from this place.
She found love and final peace here. This house must remain with
my family till I can find a way to join her. Then our two souls will
forever be entwined like Dido and Aeneas would have been had
it not been for the evil intentions of others '.

In his head Adrian now heard Dido's plaintive lament from
Purcell's opera. That music still surrounded him as he showed
the final pages to Siobhan. He watched as she read them. Then
she looked at him, her emptying eyes rich in some other private
grief as well as the story she had read. Through the coming tears
she said:

'Though nurtured like the sailing moon
In beauty's murderous brood,
She walked awhile and blushed awhile
And on my pathway stood
Until I thought her body bore
A heart of flesh and blood
But since I laid a hand thereon
And found a heart of stone ...

She stopped. Though he had not heard it before he knew there
would be more to the poem, "Yeats?" he said.

"Yes" she smiled sadly at him, "Adrian this is a terrible story that deserves to be told. I'm not sure how my grandmother fits into this but that's not important. Whatever else happens I am going to tell this story. I'm glad we're going out. I could do with a few drinks".

Adrian had never before been in the Mitre apart from by himself or with Siobhan. Everyone in the place turned and watched as the group of four made their way to the table in the window. He had no means of deciding if it was his new and unsought notoriety, Siobhan's short dress or the pale beauty of the boy with them.

The first round of drinks prepared the way for the lightening effect of the second. Gwyneth had offered condolences to John. She had touched Gabriel's cheek lightly and smiled at him. Adrian couldn't be entirely sure if this was in recognition of the extraordinary beauty of her young client or sympathy for the loss of his mother. She looked back at him as she returned to the bar.

It was also as though Gwyneth offering her condolences had allowed Celia to join the table. When her name was mentioned Adrian had looked towards Gabriel. His reaction seemed more to be one of curiosity about what was said rather than pain or even involvement.

"You've only to look at Gabe and you've seen her" replied John to a question from Siobhan, "she was beautiful all right. The thing I never understood was what she saw in me. I don't know anything about music and I've no interesting things to say. Sometimes when I'd say that to her she'd say, 'for a man with nothing to say you certainly take your time about it. You might not be Bergson but I'm here for the duration' then she'd kiss me. She could do harm with a kiss that lassie". John finished his drink then looking at Gabriel went on, "she obviously didn't mean that about being here for the duration. She hadn't wanted a baby you know but when Gabe arrived that was it. At every stage of his life she wanted him to stay like it. She said she'd always been admired a lot as a child but hated it. The other thing is she said she always knew she'd die young".

It had been as if John had wanted to say these things, to get them out of the way, and perhaps then give them time to take it in.

When the food arrived Siobhan ate like a competitor closely followed by John. When Adrian had teased Siobhan about this she'd replied, "it's alright for you, you didn't have to live with the famine. Just because you've not eaten much doesn't give you the moral high ground. If it did Gabriel's had nothing, he'd take the prize for that".

Everyone reflexively glanced at Gabriel's plate. No one immediately said anything though Adrian could see the anxiety on John's face. Adrian was about to encourage Gabriel to have something but Siobhan received a call at that moment. When she had finished she said,

"It was Beckie. She sounds upset. Something has happened. She wants to talk to me and she says she's got more information on Magus Cottage. Sorry Adrian I won't be staying tonight. She's always been there for me".

John Barrowman insisted on paying for the meal. When he came back from the bar he said, "they're all talking about someone called Old Kennedy. He's died".

Chapter 30

The Disciples of Moloch

The days that followed the discovery of the body in the cellar appeared to Adrian, to make empty but tiring haste. Gabriel sat playing very quietly at the piano even more often than he had before. He, who had eaten little, now seemed to eat less. Siobhan felt he should be taken to a doctor but Gabriel passively resisted and his father equivocated. The unaddressed issue from the cellar seemed, succubus like, to be slowly bleeding from Magus Cottage any pleasure or joy that had been there. The cottage itself became more the subject of discussion in the village. Old Kennedy had died. No one seemed to have contact details for his granddaughter. It had been Beckie who discovered the body. She had found a letter to his granddaughter Augusta which he had handwritten but not addressed. Beckie showed it to Siobhan who had photographed it on her phone.

'My dearest Augusta', it read, 'I do not think I will ever see you again for you are a good and kindly soul and I must face the flames of unforgiveness. Out of everyone you have always had a special place in my heart and you were the only one in the family who kept contact. Though I know you will say you need no thanks, I do thank you for it. Perhaps by tomorrow I will have relief. Everything that I have left is yours apart from the photograph I place on the table before me as I write. That I will take literally to my grave.

I know people have wondered who that child is. I have given various accounts. Now I tell you who he was. He is the Sinclair boy. Full fair of face he was and soft of skin, with hair midnight black and eyes of such inviting innocence that no betrayal would be too great just for the chance to look upon. And look upon him I did. Cursed be that moment. From then till I put down my pen this night to seek final rest he has been with me. Whenever I found beauty he was there smiling a pitying reminder that sometimes cruel cupid fires a poisoned arrow and all those pierced by it are sentenced to a lifetime tormented by the unobtainable and unrequitable. Some of us are destined to live with the second death of the valley of Gehinnon where mighty Moloch asks his disciples always for one more sacrifice.

Now forever Augusta, I take my leave of you. Please do not seek out any Sinclair. No good can come of it. And never look at the beautiful ones among them or you are irretrievably lost.

Your grandfather

Adam Kennedy

Siobhan sat by Adrian as he read the letter on her phone. When he finished he looked at her. "So" she said, "what do you think and who the hell is Moloch?"

"And I will set my face against that man, and will cut him off from among his people, because he had given of his seed unto Moloch, to defile my sanctuary and to profane my holy name. Leviticus 20 v 3. Moloch was an ancient God, Siobhan" said Adrian, "one to whom child sacrifices were made. I used to preach sermons that, in the new ways we treated children, we were again sacrificing them to Moloch".

"I won't say anything about the new ways the church treated children" said Siobhan.

"Sadly they were not new ways" said Adrian.

"What you haven't seen is the photo" said Siobhan, "scroll down Adrian. That's the photo Old Kennedy or perhaps I should now say Adam had, the one that he wants to take to his grave".

"You have looked upon it, sinful child" smiled Adrian as he scrolled down. He was going to say more but, with the abruptness of an arrow piercing him, he felt the blood going from his face, as though sacrificially drained from it. The image staring out at him was like a young Gabriel.

He looked across at the boy who suddenly hit a too loud note in the Clara Schumann he was playing then got up and quietly left the room.

Adrian turned towards Siobhan who said, "I know. It's uncanny, creepy".

"What's going to happen to the letter and the photo?" asked Adrian.

"There has to be an inquest. They'll come out. Bound to one way or another. You can just imagine the impact round here" replied Siobhan, "and the rumours about them will be worse".

"And people have seen Gabriel" added Adrian, "there'll be repercussions as if things weren't bad enough for him. He doesn't cry but he's inconsolable, wretched. I think he's despairing Siobhan and then today John got a letter to say her parents will only have traditional hymns at the funeral. He wanted The Minstrel Boy. They wouldn't hear of it".

"So has the funeral been arranged?" asked Siobhan.

"Yes" replied Adrian, "John has asked me to go with him and Gabriel".

"Will you?" asked Siobhan knowing how he felt now about religions.

"Yes" he replied, "I will go for Gabriel".

"I would like to come" said Siobhan.

Chapter 31

Aura

John had gone in to work for part days. When not there he found a surprising number of things that needed to be done around the house. He had even ventured back into the garden. He had also spent some time preparing the short eulogy he felt obliged to give. On the Friday of the funeral everyone was up early and ready. Only Gabriel had not eaten anything. John had swapped cars for the day with his boss so that they would have something bigger and more comfortable than his Ka.

The church of St. Jude was much more packed than John had expected. It included some former friends from his St Andrew's days. All expressed disbelief that Celia was dead and amazement that she had a son. All knew that if she ever had a child it would be beautiful but Gabriel seemed to transcend all this. Despite his father's encouragement to wear his school uniform he had come down in white and could not be persuaded to change.

The music in Adrian's head from early in the morning but reaching a climax at the church was the German Requiem which he considered one of Brahms' master works. It seemed to him to be especially appropriate today since Brahms had composed it while grieving for the death of his own mother. There was another reason for linking it with Gabriel. Brahms had been close to Clara Schumann and had performed with her. It also greatly appealed to Adrian that Dvorak had found it difficult to accept that a piece of such richness and depth of feeling was composed by a non believer.

When the time came for the eulogy both John and Gabriel went up to the front. Siobhan moved closer to Adrian.

"My name is John Barrowman" he began, "and as some of you here know I married Celia. This is our son Gabriel. Celia and I met at St. Andrews where she was a beautiful philosophy student and I was a humble maintenance worker. As all who knew her were aware she was a most stunning and yes, different person. I do not mean this unkindly and I hope her family will not take offence but I would go so far as to say she was a strange one and one of the strangest things she ever did was to marry me. I do not know why she married me or why she left me. I only know that I loved her and that she loved our boy.

She read books faster than I could make book shelves for them but above all else Celia needed music. She heard it everywhere, in the woods and on the seashore, on the mountains and in the passing traffic, in the wind and in the rain. It was in the sunshine that warmed her skin and in the cold that made her shiver. Yes, she felt it in all these places but she lived it in her head. It was always with her. I do not know what that must be like. She was a seeker after beauty with a belief that there was a teacher somewhere who could set her free. I hope she found the teacher that I could never be. I stand here with our son able to say only that we loved her. Today is the day we say goodbye to Celia Sinclair".

John stopped. He put his arm around Gabriel's shoulder and gently squeezed it. They stood in that moment in the spotlight that is the concentrated gaze of the eyes of others which was made brighter still by the silence. Then Gabriel stepped forward, the stillness that Adrian knew to be his pupil's aura illuminating him so that none could look away. In a voice, pure beyond possibility, rich beyond wealth and with the haunting beauty of eternity, he rendered 'The Minstrel Boy' in tones of such chaste innocence that, whether or not any had heard it before or liked it, none would ever forget. Adrian wondered if many had noticed that he had changed the words so that it was 'the minstrel girl to the war had gone, in the ranks of death you will find her, her father's sword she had girded on, and her wild harp slung behind her'. And it became 'the harp she loved ne'er spoke again for she tore its strings asunder'.

They did not return to their seats in the pew but paused as they got to it. Gabriel smiled at his teacher. As they all left it was, to Adrian, as though the sea of people had parted to make safe passage for them. Going at this time had a rightness to it that few in the church would have understood.

Chapter 32

Requiem

Everyone apart from Gabriel had changed out of the more formal things they were wearing when they got back from the funeral. They all sat in the room caught in the net of the unsaid. Adrian knew that loss is made of unsaid things, of uncompleted penance that becomes unending, of quiet laughter now only heard in the minds of those left, of remorseful regrets and, with the greatest cruelty, of all the tomorrows that might have been.

Everyone noticed that Gabriel did not go to the piano. He sat by his father on the settee. Siobhan had suggested that they all drank to Celia. It was she who sorted out the drinks.

"To Celia" said Adrian, "though I have never met you I have met your son. He is your gift to the world"

Everyone drank to Celia, but, though Gabriel raised his glass to his lips, he did not take a sip, whether already drunk on his memories of her or drowning in them no one would ever know. After a period he got up and left the room.

"He's so like his mother" said John, "he needs to be alone".

It was again Siobhan who responded, "John" she said, "he isn't drinking or eating. Hasn't for days. Don't wait too long to do something".

"I will take him somewhere" replied John, who was then silent before saying, "I didn't know Gabe was going to sing, I had no idea. That song, it's still in my head, going over and over. His mother used to say he was her heart and her harp".

"We knew he wanted that tune at her funeral. It was her father who didn't" said Adrian, "some people are more the slaves of tradition than its guardian".

"There's something else I want to let you know" said John, "the Bishop, her father gave me a letter. I have inherited money from a trust fund that Celia had. She got it at twenty-one. She's never mentioned any trust fund. It's quite big. I'd be more than in a position to help out financially. The most important thing is

Adrian, if you're willing, you can be like a tutor to Gabe. Bit of a coincidence but last night he said he's had the twenty-first lesson. I didn't even know he'd been counting".

"Thank you" said Adrian, "we should talk to Gabriel about it, to see if that's what he wants".

"The other thing we have to decide" said Siobhan "is what we're going to do about the cellar. There's the girl's body still down there. We can't go on ignoring that".

"Well" said John, "while you're deciding that I'll go and check on Gabriel and ask him about what he wants".

"Before you go up" said Adrian, "I want to clarify one other thing. In your eulogy you said you married Celia Sinclair".

"Yes" said John, "some years ago she took her mother's maiden name. I don't know why. I never knew why with that one".

"And she came from here?" said Adrian.

"That's what she said"

Adrian and Siobhan exchanged glances then Siobhan filled everyone's glass.

"I'll have mine when I come down" said John.

When they were alone Siobhan put down her own glass and, going to Adrian, kissed him.

"Let's make this a fresh start for us too Adrian. I want to be a virgin again. I want to work on the book about this place and you can be with Gabriel. Everyone can get what they want".

Before Adrian could reply John came with unusual urgency for him,

"Come quick Adrian, I think there's something wrong with Gabriel" he said.

They all made their way to the bedroom. Gabriel was lying naked on the bed staring at the ceiling. The look, for too long one of remote sadness on Gabriel's face had transformed into a smile of quiet acceptance, even perhaps serenity. Adrian went and knelt by him. He put his hand on his forehead and then picked up his limp wrist. He turned round and, tears in his eyes, said, "phone for an ambulance Siobhan. Tell them it's urgent. Tell them a priest is giving the last rites to a child".

No one should blame an ambulance crew in a rural area. In any case there is no arrival in time when the patient has no will to live. When they finally got there Adrian was still kneeling by the bed, Siobhan with her arm round him. John Barrowman knelt at the opposite side repeating, "she tore his strings asunder" and shaking his head. It was Siobhan who heard them arrive and showed them up.

The tenderer strains of Faure's requiem eased Adrian's mind as he thought how it is always the way of things that those who of us of flesh and blood, the loyal devotees, must still bay at the heavens where Ganymede now abides.

The End.

About the Author

Billy Conn was born, brought up and educated in Ireland. What he saw and experienced in the unusual world of his childhood spawned his interest in psychology. He regards himself as weaned on the wireless and the few available books then liberated by the library. Important too was a small number of good teachers who, like all of their kind, have the potential to change lives. There is something special about using a series of well-crafted questions to lead youthful dogmatists to see the absurdity that would follow from their assertions.

He read psychology at university then trained in that profession in Ireland before moving to the British mainland to practice. There he worked as a psychologist specializing in cases of severe abuse and neglect of children, routinely providing assessments and expert testimony to the courts.

For some 40 years he worked with the children, their families and the abusers. The children and young persons generated him an enormous respect for their courage and resilience.

Upon retirement he returned to an earlier aspiration to write. He has to date written seven novels under his own name and two thrillers under the pen name Kingsley Cross with another coming out soon in this series. Details of all these books as well as opportunities to buy either the print or ebook versions can be found on his website, billy-conn.net.

He has often said that he enjoys writing which he has likened to a conversation with a possibility but then he has also said both that it is hard work and not like work at all. Everyone has to make up their own minds about the weight to be put on what is said by people who spend most of their time making up things.

Billy currently splits his time between London and his West Cork home in Ireland.

Visit the author's website at:

billy-conn.net

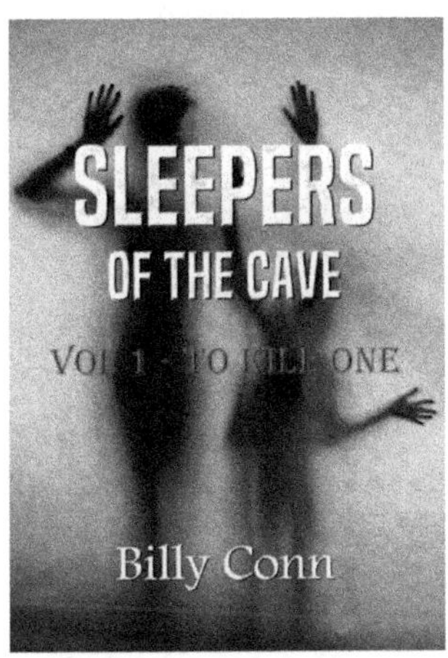

Sleepers of the Cave: Vol. 1 – To Kill One
By Billy Conn

A dead child – sadistically murdered – his twin missing. A ring procuring children for the rich and powerful. A sinister organisation led by a shadowy figure known only as 'The Stoatmaster' whose cold tentacles seemingly stretch unendingly so that no place and no one is safe – not even the police.

A Muslim detective, himself a twin, whose background renders others suspicious of him. His ruthless intelligence and tenacity converge to an obsession with finding the missing child and her brother's killer.

His problem - he wants to leave the police.

One last case can be a case too far when a child's face relentlessly haunts you - pulling you further into the abyss and your own family is in danger of disintegration.

When depravity is licenced by money and everything, even a child, has a price, the only word left is 'evil'.

Sleepers of the Cave: Vol. 2 – By the Waters of Tasnim
By Billy Conn

Rahman Khan cannot leave the police. At least not yet.

He has a new team, a new supervising officer and an old obsession - to finish what he had hoped would be his one last case - if it will let him.

Driven to find a virtual foe known only as the Stoatmaster – behind the procurement of children for wealthy and powerful paedophiles, he must first solve the riddle of the Purples.

The abyss of the dark web looms and hypnotically beckons.

Another fugitive they cannot find – this time of flesh and bones - the killer of a colleague, the sadistic terrorizer of children – an enemy who is to them incarnate evil, indivisible, inescapable, evil – and seemingly as elusive as the Stoatmaster.

They cannot find this creature – but it can find them.

Sleepers of the Cave: Vol. 3 – The Zaqqum Tree
By Billy Conn

Someone is killing children. Inspector Rahman Khan does not know who, where or how many intended victims there are. He knows only that they will die unless he gets to them first. Is something thwarting efforts to find the Stoatmaster or is he just not up to the task?

A religious sect called the Farm led by the enigmatic Sister Cade beckons mysteriously. Is pressure to infiltrate a London Mosque suspected of links to trafficked children a lead or a diversion?

A whistle blower in the Five Eyes Network leaks information that warns the Stoatmaster how close they are and puts a price in Bitcoins on the head of Rahman Khan.

When there is no one left to rely on how do you know you can trust yourself? A secret so deadly that anyone who knows it dies. And now Rahman Khan knows that secret.

And Nothing But The Night by Kingsley Cross

An Inquiry into torture on British soil. The judge's daughter missing. The time for orthodoxy passed. Enter Marc Logadon – ex mathematician and ex security services. The Judge is advised at the highest level to consult him. From the start they neither like nor trust one another.

A case with no clues is bad enough, but one with too many, including a machine called a synchrotron that crops up time and time again! Then an old foe regarded as one of the most dangerous men on the international espionage network re-emerges. What is the basis of the enmity between these two men and will it get in the way of finding the missing girl?

The maverick Marc Logadon trusts no one apart from his own oddball team of a one armed female bomb disposal expert, an ex heavyweight boxer, an almost invisible undercover worker, and a gifted transgender hacker known as the Arachnophile. As they close in and the body count mounts, time runs out for the judge's daughter.

At the Counting of the Dead by Kingsley Cross

A plot hatched in a small town in the West of Ireland

An improbable alliance

A risk to all of London

And Crucible now has a new case

No one said it was going to be easy

No one could be sure it was even possible

But if Marc Logadon and CJ didn't succeed thousands would not be saying anything at all

To prevent the slaughter they must first solve the riddle of The Fari Dolls

But the Countdown to Armageddon has already begun.

***The Owned* by Billy Conn**

An Irish woman and her children sold into Caribbean slavery by Cromwell's regime.

A historian, working on a TV series on slavery, finds her story compellingly conveyed to him through the randomness of the night. He learns how easily reason is held to ransom by the dark.

He ignores the apparent parallels in their lives till they accelerate to a collision point on the Island of Barbados.

"We can all have irrational thoughts or behave irrationally at times. But so long as you know you're being irrational you are not yet insane".

His colleague's advice works well in the daylight, he thought, but not when, uninvited, his visitor's narrative again infiltrates in the privacy of the dark.

The Garden of Lost Remembering by Billy Conn

Memories are tricky. You can't really trust them. Things only get worse as you get older. What if the memory is of something that happened more than ninety years ago? When does a memory that won't leave you alone become a haunting? Who is the tearfully pleading child whose voice she hears time and time again?

The young volunteer on a reminiscence project is slowly drawn into the ever changing and uncertain world of the woman he visits. At first he is fascinated by the quirky and quixotic view of the previous century seen through the eyes of this former journalist. Slowly her concern with what she thought she saw becomes his obsession, gradually submerging him in her world till neither of them is any longer sure if he is from her past or present, is a fiction or an aspect of a psychosis.

The synopsis of a dream is another dream, of a scream another scream. You can't turn off memories as you can a life support machine. She once wrote 'Death makes everything else too late except justice'. It's just that some days, she can't quite remember writing that.

The Murder Club by Billy Conn

Frank Doyle is dead. If he wasn't the postmortem would have seen to it. The classic MG he was working on had fallen on him. An accident? Routine police work had Detective Sergeant Powell not discovered the Murder Club. That changed everything.

Kaleisha Powell had often thought of writing a detective story. Would there ever be a better time than when faced by the combined forces of Holmes, Poirot, Morse, Jessica Fletcher, Miss Marple, Maigret and Vera? Did one of them kill Frank Doyle?

Challenged by the Murder Club, Kaleisha begins to write. A girl and her dog disappear from a village and no one sees anything. It's not easy to keep the worlds of fiction and real investigation separate. She was finding the writer was less in charge than she had thought.

Then there is the fact that Sergeant Kaleisha Powell herself may not be all that she seems.

www.ingramcontent.com/pod-product-compliance
Lightning Source LLC
Chambersburg PA
CBHW061244120726
48001CB00001B/128